9.9.91.

The tenth in the
series — just hatched!
With love to Yvonne.

Anthea Cohen.

Recording angel

Agnes Carmichael, alone in the world but the surprised and delighted recipient of a grateful patient's substantial fortune, is purring through the manicured landscape of wintry Leicestershire in her silver Porsche.

She has been sent by the Nursing Co-op on her first private assignment to Nettlestone Manor. An experienced nurse, she is nevertheless nervous.

But in the next few weeks as she tends the injured Lady Bellamy – by reputation tipsy and irascible – her emotions are to face the severest test. For beneath the luxurious 'upstairs/downstairs' elegance of the big house, undercurrents of a dangerous and frightening nature bubble and boil.

A question of paternity and a gruesome car accident force Carmichael into the role of both judge and liberator.

Anthea Cohen's crime novels featuring Sister Carmichael – 'one of the most original chiller series around' (Felicia Lamb, *Mail on Sunday*) – have been likened to the work of Patricia Highsmith and have become extremely popular with crime fiction enthusiasts.

'Oh, never mind, Gran. I'll take it to the garage and get it looked over properly. They'll probably be able to fix it.'

'I might have a go,' said Nigel, but Alison grinned at him and shook her head.

'You're not all that good at cars, Nigel,' she said.

'Get the garage to have a look at it and if they think you need another one . . . well, you shall have one, and let them take that one in part exchange.' Lady Bellamy motioned to Agnes as Maud appeared to say that dinner was served. Carmichael helped her up and they made their slow way into the dining-room.

Agnes Carmichael had learned a lot from the kitchen staff while waiting for meals and trays to be taken up to Lady Bellamy. She would much rather not have listened to the servants, but it was almost impossible not to do so. Nigel, she learned, acted as Sir Edmund's secretary and bailiff and helped him run the estate. According to them he did most of the work.

The estate consisted of nearly a thousand acres of woodland and farmland and boasted seven farms and a trout stream. Maud had informed Agnes with some disapproval that owing to, as she maintained, Sir Edmund's extravagance and, according to her, laziness, land down near the village had been sold with planning permission for a building development.

'Thousands it's fetched, Sister – thousands,' she had said, pouring water on to Lady Bellamy's early morning tea at the time. 'Thousands, and all for those awful bungalows.'

Hetty, giggling, had confided later to Agnes that Maud's one aim in life was to get out of her thatched cottage in the village and into one of the new bungalows. To Carmichael in her present state of mind, this did not surprise her in the least – what people said and what people thought were often two utterly different things.

This evening dinner progressed with rather more conversation than Agnes had expected, bearing in mind the four nights she had already dined there when Lady Bellamy had not been present.

Nigel interested her more than the others. While Sir Edmund became more bellicose the more wine he drank and Alison chatted about cars, horses and the fact that Penny Stratton Lane was going to be closed for new drainage pipes to be laid – things of little interest to her – Nigel became (presumably because of

Lady Bellamy's presence) more charming and amusing. Darker clothes suited him. His pallor, which looked rather unhealthy in daylight, in the soft light of the dining-room became interesting. He looked foreign – Italian or Spanish perhaps, Agnes thought as she watched him wield his knife and fork with his long, slender, white fingers – he had rather girlish hands. His mother, she had learned from Maud, had been Italian. Occasionally a look passed between him and Alison – a long look – which also interested Agnes. Could there be a relationship between them, she wondered? She was beginning to revise her first impression and think that perhaps there might be.

The arrival of tomorrow's guests was also discussed and what they could do to entertain them. Sir Edmund's brother was fairly crippled with arthritis by the sound of it, but his wife would no doubt like to go into Leicester to look at clothes shops.

After coffee in the sitting-room Lady Bellamy signalled to Carmichael that she had had enough and was tired, and they started the long, slow climb up the staircase.

'Do you think this does any good?' Gladys Bellamy had finished cleaning her face with the cleansing cream and was now twisting the top off a night cream that Carmichael herself used, and she asked the question again as Agnes helped her into bed.

'I don't know, Lady Bellamy. I buy it, use it sometimes, then often forget to use it at all for nights at a time.'

Lady Bellamy looked at her shrewdly. 'Why do you bother nursing an old woman like me? You don't need to, financially I mean, do you?'

From Lady Bellamy the question did not somehow seem impertinent.

Carmichael shook her head. 'No, I don't need to financially, but there are other reasons why one occupies oneself doing something one likes.'

'True.' Gladys Bellamy left it at that and then sank back thankfully on to her pillow.

'Television?' Agnes asked.

She shook her head. 'No, thank you, Agnes. There's nothing I want to see. My hip hurts me.'

Carmichael gave her two painkillers and the glass of water needed to take them.

'Stay and talk, will you?' The blue eyes looked into Agnes' as

46

RECORDING ANGEL

Anthea Cohen

Constable · London

First published in Great Britain 1991
by Constable & Company Ltd
3 The Lanchesters, 162 Fulham Palace Road
London W6 9ER
Copyright © 1991 by Anthea Cohen
The right of Anthea Cohen to be
identified as the author of this Work
has been asserted by her in accordance
with the Copyright, Designs and Patents Act 1988.
ISBN 0 09 470510 0
Set in Linotron 10pt Palatino by
CentraCet, Cambridge
Printed in Great Britain by
Redwood Press Limited, Melksham, Wiltshire

A CIP catalogue record for this book
is available from the British Library

Prologue

Nurse Hillman looked away – let her eyes roam from her patient's white face. She looked round the small side ward – its green walls. She hated green. There was so much of it in this hospital: shining, green paint. She looked at the door that was painted white and was slightly ajar. She saw a nurse flit by and wished she was out there. She didn't like being shut in with a patient, particularly with a policeman outside the door.

She felt tired and she was bored. This woman she was specialing had been shot answering her front door. She could have been killed; only the fact that the man, the mugger or whatever he was, had used a small-calibre revolver and had aimed badly had saved her. He had shot her through the lung and the arm, not the heart – this had saved her life. They had been able to remove the bullet – both bullets, one from the fleshy part of the patient's forearm, the other from the lung.

Agnes Carmichael felt she was rising to the surface of a green, turgid lake. Her body felt buoyant. She opened her eyes.

'Oh! Decided to wake up, have we?' The disembodied voice seemed unnecessarily loud, cheerful, intrusive. 'It's all over. You're back in your own bed now.'

A nurse – Agnes recognized the words, the phrasing, the tone of voice. She had used similar words herself so often to patients coming round from anaesthetics. Usually they answered by asking another question, 'Have I had the operation, nurse? Is it over?' or something like that. She was about to ask the same question automatically, foolishly, when memory hit her.

The explosion of the gun went off again; it seemed close to her. She winced and tried to cover her ears, but only one hand would move towards her face, the other was tethered and

5

painful. The outline of the nurse came more into focus; still fuzzy but she could see her – pretty, young, silky blond hair smoothed back tightly. Agnes Carmichael approved the neatness but disapproved the two small red and gold studs in the girl's ears.

'Ear-rings, I never allowed those,' she said, not realizing how thick her voice was. Then she turned her head away as she thought how stupid her remark must sound if the nurse had heard it, or understood what she had said.

The nurse made no reply. Then: 'How do you feel, Miss Carmichael?'

Agnes rolled her head gently from side to side on the pillow.

'Have I been to the theatre?' she asked.

The green water was subsiding, the white bed, the nurse, the small room too, were coming into focus. She must be ill . . . She tried to remember. A vision floated in front of her face – an opening door, a bang, this time not heard but remembered – the night outside, the rustling leaves. Except for those leaves the silence . . . No, there had been water, the sound of water, then the . . .

At that moment the door of the room opened and a man's voice asked, 'Is she round yet?'

The nurse moved away and in her place loomed a bearded man – white coat, stethoscope. 'I'll get Sir James to tell her. Then the police will want a word, but only when she is good and ready, nurse.' He placed his fingers on Agnes' wrist and looked down at her. She felt she was drifting away again, but she made a great effort.

'What did they do in the theatre? What did they do to me?'

He bent down to hear her better. Agnes could smell his aftershave; nice, like Brian's, she thought. Then the swirling green water seemed to engulf her again. She just heard his reply.

'We removed a bullet from your lung and another from your upper arm. You're a nurse, I hear.'

'A Sister,' Carmichael heard herself say – what did it matter now? She was going to be married to Brian; it didn't matter now whether they called her Sister or Nurse or Mrs Beresford.

She felt herself drifting almost pleasantly away from them again and she didn't hear the bearded man say softly, 'She doesn't know yet, does she? You haven't told her?'

6

'No, she's only just surfaced. She'll know soon enough that he's dead. Why did Mr Beresford have to go chasing after a man he knew had a gun?'

The doctor shook his head and shrugged his shoulders.

'I hope they get him,' she said.

The doctor grunted. 'Bastard,' he said. 'He could have finished the old lady off as well when she came back, but I suppose he'd gone by then. Lovely house, though, down by the river. The police say he had a car parked on the main road.' He peered down at Carmichael. 'Fancy her and Brian Beresford! He'd be quite a catch. She's no chicken – not a looker either.'

'Perhaps he was in love with her,' the nurse said softly and rather reproachfully; then 'Shut up, she might hear you.'

'No, she's out like a light again.' He took his stethoscope from round his neck, folded it and thrust it into the pocket of his white coat.

Carmichael stirred again and spoke, 'I'll look after Hannah, don't worry, Lavinia,' she said.

'I told you, she's gone off again. No wonder, she was pretty heavily anaesthetized; a couple of ribs gone, you know, to get at that slug. She'll be sore when she really comes to. Is she written up for anything?'

'Yes, she is, thanks.'

'Cheerio, then.' The young doctor was about to close the door of the room when the Ward Sister stopped him and walked in. She gazed at the patient.

'All right, Nurse. Everything all right?' She walked nearer to Carmichael. 'Has she come round yet?'

'Yes, Sister. She has spoken a few words, but she seems to have drifted off again.'

The Sister looked at the monitor, nodded, then looked at her watch. 'Poor woman,' she said. Then briskly, 'I'll see you're relieved in another half-hour, Nurse Hillman.'

'Thank you, Sister.' Nurse Hillman sat down again and she, too, watched the monitor that clicked steadily with each of Carmichael's heartbeats.

Sister left and there was silence in the room for a few minutes, then a loud tap on the door. Nurse Hillman got up, went to the door, opened it slightly, looked back at the patient and then opened the door a little wider.

7

'Detective Inspector Warwick.' He sounded almost apologetic. 'How is she?' he asked.

'Satisfactory, but not round yet.'

The detective peered over the nurse's shoulder. 'Who'll tell her?' he said. 'They've taken the old lady to a nursing home; she's not fit to . . .' The detective shook his head. 'Nasty business. Nothing taken. Just another bloody killer, I guess. We'll get him, Nurse. It's raining,' he added, then half smiled at the banality of his remark.

'Is it?' The nurse closed the door and came back to the bedside, checking the dressing on the side of Carmichael's chest and the bandage on her arm. She sighed a long sigh and sat herself on the hard chair again. She put one elbow on the bedside near Carmichael and rested her chin on her hand. She had known Mr Beresford, General Surgeon. She'd nursed patients for him; taken a case once in theatre. Well, not taken it, just acted as a runner. He was retiring and this – this woman . . . She wondered if they were going to marry. If he had been in love with her. Well, he was dead now. Shot by the very man who tried to kill her patient. She turned and looked at Carmichael's face again. At that moment it was expressionless. She wondered how she would take the news of Mr Beresford's death. How close had they been? Had they been lovers? Well, time would tell; but, as the Inspector had said, it was a nasty business.

Three days later Carmichael knew it all – she had been told, sympathetically, quietly, by the surgeon who had operated on her. At first the shock had been so great she couldn't believe it – couldn't take it in. Brian! At first she grieved for him, then for herself, her last chance of happiness gone? Her lovely house – she could never go back there, only to pack it up when she was well enough and rid herself of all of it. She tried to shut her memory like a door – it was the only way she could cope.

If only Brian had not tried to stop Derek, had left him to run and disappear. If only . . . but bravely, she supposed, he'd tried . . .

Would she ever see Derek again? She prayed not. She also prayed he would never be caught. He knew a lot about her –

too much, perhaps. She hoped that now he had really murdered someone he would go away for ever – far away, where he and she would have nothing to fear from one another, and would never, never meet again.

1

Agnes Carmichael switched off the headlights of her new Porsche as the dawn streaked the sky with a rather sinister grey and pinkish light.

'No flowers, no sun, no hope, November,' she thought, then shook her head to banish the depression that overcame her all too easily. She was on her way to a new county – at least new to her – Leicestershire, to her first private case, a lady with a fractured hip.

As the dawn light became daylight and London gave way to suburbia so the streets became cleaner, less littered with hand-crushed tins, crisp packets, greasy chip pokes; grass verges appeared; there was more variety in roof contours. She passed a small park where a man was walking a Dalmatian. A watery shaft of sunlight lit up the man and his dog, making the scene sharp and colourful. The brief glimpse lightened Agnes' mood and made her feel hungry and thirsty. She had only had a cup of tea at the nurses' hostel before she had set out that morning. At last she entered the motorway and the wheels of the Porsche ate up the black tarmac miles. Carmichael loved driving the car – loved the way it leapt forward at the touch of her foot, answering her like an unleashed animal. She watched out for a Little Chef or some roadside café where she could get refreshments. There was no hurry to get to her destination – she'd been careful not to specify her time of arrival. At last she saw the familiar sign ahead and drove into the large gravel car-park. Even though it was still quite early there was a line of cars and people leaving and entering through the automatic doors. Inside the noisy hangar-like structure beige formica tables stretched away in the distance, their lines broken by showcases of toys, children's games, stockings – anything that might tempt bored travellers.

Agnes took her place in a queue of about ten people, all slowly pushing their plastic trays along the silver chromium rack. She helped herself to a paper plate, a saucer and two plastic-wrapped ham sandwiches, a plastic spoon and a little envelope containing brown sugar. She stopped, and without looking at her the large black woman behind the counter hissed coffee into a cup and pushed it towards Agnes. She passed another expressionless woman and paid her.

Seated at a table she broke open the small tub of cream and poured it into her coffee, added sugar and stirred it abstractedly.

At the table in front of her were two fat white-haired women, one older than the other. Agnes watched without interest as the older one wrestled with the small cream tub with arthritic fingers. Her companion watched her then took it from her and, a trace irritably, opened it deftly.

'It's just a knack, dear,' she said, passing the container back.

'Well, I haven't got the knack,' the older woman answered, pouring the white stream into her cup. She tore open the pack of sugar easily, then felt round her saucer. 'I've no spoon, Alice,' she said.

The younger woman rose to her feet and as she passed Agnes' table she raised her eyes heavenwards, then waddled back to the counter.

Agnes sat without speaking. Perhaps because it was so early in the morning there was little noise, only the clatter from the counter. Most people she noticed as she glanced round looked sleepy and bad-tempered, sipping their coffee or eating their sandwiches as they gazed straight ahead.

When she had finished she went to the ladies' room, powdering her nose and looking at herself critically. She felt refreshed by the meal. She proceeded through the café again – the two women had gone – and made for the doors.

She saw that the inhabitants of the next table were making their way down the outside steps to the car-park. The younger was helping the older, who was taking the steps awkwardly, crab-wise; she was also using a stick.

'Arthritis of hip. She should lose weight.' The diagnosis and medical advice sprang to Agnes' lips readily. She proceeded down the steps. The doors closed behind her.

Then they opened again and she half turned. A youth, slim, blue-jeaned, red-anoraked, was standing on the top step fastening the chin strap of his helmet. He was still for a second. Agnes turned away and went on down the steps. The two women were by this time making their way towards their car. Then, sudden movement. The boy leapt down the steps, brushing against Agnes as he did so, stopped by the two women and grabbed the white handbag slung from the older woman's arm. She lurched, tried to keep her balance, then fell heavily to the ground. Her companion screeched and people came running.

Agnes walked on. She didn't want to get involved and there were enough people round the woman. She saw the boy, lithe and cat-like, tearing across the car-park towards a red and white moped parked beside her Porsche.

'Stop,' she yelled at him. His helmeted head turned towards her. He grabbed the handlebars of his bike and slewed it round her car. There was a sickening sound as the moped hit the wing of the Porsche. Agnes heard it and felt it as if it were a wound. The moped, kicked into life, sped out into the road.

Agnes reached her car, running. She put her hand where the bike had hit the wing and smoothed it. The scratch was long, six or eight inches, not deep – but the paint, the beautiful silver paint . . . She got into her car; she felt very cold. He must pay for what he had done. She drove fast – no one seemed to be following him. Her teeth were clenched so that her jaw ached. Every other thought had left her head. She would not catch him, she would follow him.

In a lay-by two miles from the restaurant Kenneth Martin thought he had lost the Porsche. He stopped, straddled the moped and proceeded to examine the contents of the white handbag. Credit cards? None. Smelling salts – poor old tit. He tossed the bottle on to the ground; the glass splintered and a strong smell of ammonia came up to him. A make-up bag, lipstick, compact – silly old fool, what would she want with those? Paracetamol. He opened the purse: nine ten-pound notes, two fivers, a few coins. Not bad, enough for a fix and a bit more. He stuffed the notes into his pocket, took out the coins, rattled them in his hand for a moment and popped them in his pocket. Then he threw the white bag and its contents over

13

the shrubs at the side of the lay-by. As he did so the silver Porsche drew in behind him. He turned his helmeted head and looked. 'What does she want?' he said aloud. The big car looked menacing, but the door didn't open and the woman – he could see it was a woman, he'd seen that back at the restaurant – didn't get out or anything. He reacted, started the machine; it sounded sluggish.

'Christ, why didn't I nick something fast, not this heap.' He drew out again, opened the throttle, but he knew he had no chance against the great German car, no chance. What was she playing at, just driving up behind him? He must take a side road, then a lesser side road. She was probably going somewhere up north. She'd soon give up.

He took a fork left, then another. Still the silver car followed him – not closely, quite some distance away, going too slowly, he knew, for the kind of car it was. Do a hundred and twenty, he thought, easily if she wanted to. What's on? What gives? What does she want?

His engine began to splutter, then stopped. Petrol. He leapt from the bike. He was outside a pair of wrought iron gates – beautifully tooled, even he could see that, picked out here and there with gold; expensive gates. He tried them. They were locked. The Porsche moved gently round the bend and came into his view.

He'd got to get away from her, this bloody woman – he'd got to get away. He almost threw the moped against the wall beside the gate, took a leap on to the saddle, then leapt again, grabbed the top of the grey stone wall, almost slipped but managed to grip. He pulled himself up to the top – a gigantic effort – then rolled over and dropped down the other side. He let out a cry of pain as he landed, his ankle twisting under him. No time to think of that. He stumbled away, but in the stillness he heard the car door open on the other side of the wall. Well, what now? What was she going to do now? He stumbled on through the shrubs, following a path, trying to see over them. The path might lead to the house, he thought, and surely somewhere there would be a back entrance, even a front entrance, he couldn't be sure. But he wanted to get back, back on to the road again, hitch a lift, get away from her, get away from that beastly car. He looked back, just once, he had to look back – and he saw the woman standing at the gate, watching him.

14

'What the hell do you want?' he yelled at her, but she didn't answer. She just stood there, watching him.

Agnes watched the youth limping away. When he yelled at her she didn't answer. She had no idea what she wanted or what she would do. She waited, waited for something to occur to her. She didn't feel that ringing the police would . . . After all, supposing the man did appear in court, he would deny everything. Nobody could prove anything. She had not seen his face – but there he was now. She waited and heard him stumbling away.

A minute went by, only a minute, and a man approached down the road. He had two Rottweiler dogs on leashes. He wore a rough tweed coat and hat, breeches and leggings. He touched his hat to her. 'Want something, miss?' Then he looked at the car. 'A friend of his Lordship's?'

'No, no. I just stopped for a moment – lovely gates, aren't they?'

He nodded, took out some keys from his pocket and unlocked the gates. Agnes moved towards her car; both dogs stiffened, their white teeth bared, their low growls ominous.

'Come on, lads, no need for that.' The man looked curiously at Agnes, but said nothing more and locked the gates behind him, then bent down to unleash the dogs.

Agnes watched his brown, rather gnarled hand taking off the clips from their thick leather collars. She could have said something, but she didn't. The two dogs bounded away from him.

Agnes Carmichael stood, watched, listened, waited. Two minutes passed or two seconds, she had no idea, but then she heard what she expected to hear – a frenzied barking, growling, snarling, a terrified screaming. She turned away; she had heard enough.

She touched the injured wing of her car as she made her way round to the driver's seat. Once in the car she backed it out carefully and rejoined the motorway. When she had the opportunity she moved over into the fast lane; the Porsche was more comfortable there. She switched on her radio. The music swelled around her and she, too, like her car, felt more comfortable. This morning's incident had made her feel part of the world in

15

which she lived, not just a lonely spinster going to a private case, but a dispenser of justice and someone to be reckoned with.

As the music swelled around her the noise of it isolated her strangely. She saw in her head the thin, insect-like figure of the boy, the shining helmet, the dark visor; his eyes must have peered through that seeing her directly. 'What do you want?' he had yelled at her. What had she wanted? To revenge the old woman who had fallen with that hard, hurting thud to the gravel? To compensate for the rifled handbag? Or to make him pay for the long, ugly scratch on her silver car? She acknowledged it was the car she had wanted him to pay for – even with his life. Not right, of course – she acknowledged that, too – but that was how she was.

She leaned over and switched off the music; normality had returned. She glanced at the speedometer: sixty, low for the Porsche. She put her foot down a little harder. 'Sorry,' she said to the car.

2

Agnes Carmichael almost missed the turning to Penny Stratton; she backed her Porsche and turned off the main road. After about half a mile the houses of the village began to appear. Some were thatched, pretty white cottages with bulging walls and small windows. Near them and scattered amongst them, there were copycat cottages pretending to be old, with the same thatched roofs but giving away their later date of birth by their larger windows and pristine, shining, almost golden thatch.

The gardens, though, looked smaller. In November all cottage gardens look the same – shrubs, brown leaves, frost-bitten, a few dead chrysanthemums and even geraniums giving glimpses of tatty colour. Carmichael glanced from side to side. 'Turn right at the church': these were the instructions given by the Nursing Co-op she had joined in London.

This was the first private case she had been sent to and she was nervous at the thought of a patient without the supporting hospital surroundings and personnel; she wasn't sure how it

16

would be. She was glad enough to get to this part of the world – Leicestershire, also new to her. She liked what she saw, the flat fields, the hedges, the generally well-kept appearance – hunting country.

As she approached the village of Penny Stratton it became even prettier, unspoiled. She enjoyed driving through it – that and the smell of her new car; the interior leather and spotless carpeting gave her pleasure. She felt almost guilty now if anything gave her pleasure. So much had happened, so much that was tragic. Brian. Lavinia, her friend; now she was dead. But still she did feel pleasure. That's what she must expect from herself, that's how humans were, she thought wryly. In time they forget; they are not constant.

The church was as charming as the rest of the village. The old gravestones were weathered, some leaning a little sideways, some flat on the ground; the newer ones were upright, fingers of winter grass growing round them.

Agnes turned right; second house to the left she had been told – Nettlestone Manor. She reached the two red pillars that supported the wrought iron gates, which were open. 'Nettlestone Manor' on the gate was so weathered that it was hardly readable.

She drove in through neat, clipped hedges to a circular drive. Her wheels crunched on the gravel. The small country house of grey stone, looking attractive in the winter sunlight, hardly merited the title 'Manor'. She drew the car up in front of the three steps which led to the oak door, on which shone a large, brass door knocker. She got out of the car, wondering briefly about her suitcase, then decided to leave it in the car for the moment. She mounted the steps, then turned and looked back over the garden surrounding the drive. It was well kept, the lawn still green, the shrubs too – some evergreen. The two stone vases on each side of the steps she had just ascended contained almost dead geraniums and a fringe of brown, lacy, dead lobelia, long shrivelled in the autumn sun and the winds.

She turned and lifted the big, solid door knocker. Almost at once the door was opened by a neatly clad maid: black dress, pretty cap and pretty apron (an unusual sight in these days), black stockings and shoes. Agnes appreciated the uniform; she admired the tidiness, the badge of efficiency it indicated. She remembered her nurses. She had been pleased to see them tidy

17

– an untidy nurse was a bad nurse, that's what she always said. It wasn't always true, but nevertheless she had kept on saying it.

The girl looked out of the door and saw the silvery grey Porsche.

'Oh! Could you please put your car to the side; Sir Edmund will be back soon and he doesn't like . . . Miss Carmichael, isn't it?'

Carmichael, slightly surprised at the request, answered, 'Of course. My suitcase is in it. Perhaps someone could fetch it, it's rather heavy.'

'Yes, of course, I'll get Basil to. Please come in.'

The girl crossed the hall and made for the stairs. She started going up. 'I'll just let Lady Bellamy know.' Her pace quickened and she disappeared up the stairs.

Carmichael went out to move the car. When she entered the house again there was no sign of the maid or anyone. She stood for a moment, then closed the front door behind her and looked around.

The hall was as attractive as the outside of the house, panelled in a light wood. The polished parquet floor was strewn with rugs with fringed ends and predominating colours of red and blue – Indian perhaps, Agnes thought. A flower arrangement on a corner table lent colour to the hall. Carmichael walked over to it. Plastic? No, the pink carnations had a lovely perfume. She touched them. A grandfather clock ticked gently, its gold face reflecting the light from the window. There were three doors leading from the hall, all shut. Carmichael guessed the door to the kitchen and other offices was to the left and partly hidden by the graceful staircase.

She waited, wondering what to do next. Presumably the maid would return. The hall felt pleasantly warm. She made her way to a polished Tudor-style chair and sat down. Suddenly, one of the three doors opened and she had a glimpse of a log fire. A young man leaned for a moment against the door lintel and surveyed Agnes.

'Can I do anything for you?' He stood looking at her and put up one hand and ran it through his rather long, dark, curly hair. The curls immediately fell back again on his forehead. He straightened up and came forward into the hall and Agnes was able to see him more clearly.

18

'No, thank you. I'm just waiting for the maid to show me my room.'

The young man did not appear to be interested. His dark shirt and jeans accentuated his tall, slim figure. One hand was raised to his shoulder and a coat or jacket hooked on to his fingers hung down his back rather like a cloak. He put up his hand once more to brush his hair away. Both sleeves of his shirt were rolled up above his elbows. The pallor of his face was more evident, too, as he walked up to Carmichael and passed her as he went towards the door.

'Right then,' he said. His eyes shone as he went by. A good-looking young man.

'Will you come this way, Miss Carmichael?' The maid had returned. 'I'll get your suitcase taken up to your room for you.'

'I'd better unlock my car then,' said Carmichael.

The girl did not answer Agnes, so she went out of the door again, down the steps, unlocked the boot of the car and lifted out the case. She locked the boot, carried the heavy case up the steps and put it down in the hall. She felt slightly irritated. There was a feeling of indifference in the house as if nobody had expected her. Surely someone must have seen her car arrive? Her case would be brought up to her room, so the maid had said, but how would it have been got from the car if she hadn't fetched it? Who was this Basil the maid had mentioned?

Almost curtly she said to the girl, 'Very well, then, I'll leave it there if someone will bring it up.'

The maid nodded, sensing her irritation. Her pretty, rather vacant face flushed.

'Yes, Miss – er – Carmichael. I'm sorry to have kept you waiting, but Madam, Lady Bellamy . . .'

'That's all right. Let's just go up to my room if we may.'

They were just mounting the stairs when the front door opened again. A man came in – presumably Basil.

'Take your shoes off, Basil,' the maid said, stopping on the stairs and turning round.

'All right, for God's sake, you know I always do. Anyway, I haven't been working in mud. I've just been round by the horses.'

'Well, that's just as bad,' said the girl pertly, and then looked at Carmichael, shrugging her shoulders slightly as if to say 'These men.'

The man, Basil, took his shoes off at the door, picked up Carmichael's case as if it were a matchstick and followed them upstairs. He was a short, stocky man, with close-cut, greying, curly hair.

'This is your room, Miss – er – Carmichael.' The maid seemed to be having difficulty with Agnes' name. She opened the door and the man barged past them rather rudely.

'There you are then.' He plonked the case down with a bang, turned and ran down the stairs in his stockinged feet. As they stood there Carmichael heard the front door bang.

'Sorry, Basil hates to be – hates to be interrupted when – '

'Never mind, he's brought the case up and that's the main thing. Where shall I put the car? Shall I leave it where it is?' They were still outside the room Carmichael was to occupy.

The maid hesitated. 'Oh no, miss, that will go round the back. There are garages by the stables. I wouldn't let Basil do it, though. I don't think he's a very good driver and it's a posh car, isn't it? He's all right with the Rolls, it's old-fashioned, but he's not used to these modern fast cars. That's what Miss Alison says, anyway.'

That remark pleased Carmichael – 'a posh car'. Yes, it was, she was proud of the Porsche.

'All right. When I've unpacked I'll go out and drive the car round to the back and put it away.'

The maid picked up the case that Basil had plonked down, carried it across the room and placed it on the suitcase stand at the bottom of the bed. It was rather like a hotel, Carmichael thought, but a very pleasant room.

'That's all then, miss? Dinner is – well you'll hear the gong.'

'Gong?' asked Carmichael, somewhat surprised.

The maid smiled suddenly. 'Yes, we still have a gong. Sir Edmund doesn't like it, but Lady Bellamy does, so we have it.' She kept her eyes down as if she did not want to see Carmichael's reaction to this remark.

'Right then,' she said, in exactly the same way as the dark boy had said it in the hall, and Carmichael replied, feeling less irritated and more in humour with the situation, 'Yes, all right then.' The maid withdrew, shutting the door perhaps a little too firmly behind her, but – Agnes felt – rather through carelessness than anger or intention.

3

Carmichael felt her nervousness returning. Should she go in search of her patient and introduce herself, or should she unpack and wait until they met at the dinner table? – providing, of course, that Lady Bellamy came down to dinner. She had, according to the information given to her by the Nursing Co-op, been back from hospital for only ten days, having had her broken hip pinned, and during this ten days they had sent her two nurses neither of whom had, according to Lady Bellamy, been suitable. Indeed, the second one had walked out after, according to the Co-op, a heated argument with Sir Edmund Bellamy, the patient's husband.

Agnes decided to unpack. She hung in the wardrobe the dresses, blouses and skirts she had brought. Beside them, on hangers, she put the three white coats she intended to wear as uniform. The rest of her things she placed in the neatly white paper-lined drawers, all of which were empty. She put her leather-bound luminous bedside clock on the table, with the silver-framed picture of the blind white cat, Fluffy, beside it.

She hesitated before putting her various cosmetic items on the dressing table. They were all expensive and anyone seeing them would perhaps wonder. Then she shrugged her shoulders; let them wonder, she thought. If they came to the conclusion that she was not doing the task for money they would be quite right – but what business was that of anyone but her? That she could not bear to be any more at leisure to think of the past was also no business of anyone but herself.

She aligned the Elizabeth Arden pots almost defiantly against the mirror on the dressing table, touched lipstick to her lips, combed her hair and went across the room and opened the door that led to a small, beautifully appointed bathroom. She washed her hands and dried them on the monogrammed linen towel hanging on the heated towel rail. It was almost a shame, she thought, to crease it. Carmichael was getting to love beautiful linen. She looked round her room and the bathroom appreciatively. It was better, much better, she thought, than the hostel she was living in at the moment, which was owned and rented by the Nursing Co-op. Nothing, though, would ever resemble the lovely house she had had to leave. She would find a flat, a house, utterly unlike Cat's Cradle – nothing to remind her: no garden, no river, no lovely sound of lapping water.

Her sad thoughts were interrupted by a light tap on the door.

'Come in.'

The door opened and a girl stood on the threshold. Her dark hair was bundled into a comb on the top of her head; tendrils of hair fell at the sides of her face and along her forehead to her long eyelashes. These tendrils moved as she blinked her eyes, but appeared not to feel them. She came forward into the room, looking round, noticing, Carmichael felt sure, the Elizabeth Arden cosmetics because of the 'Hallo-o' that seemed to point to the fact that she was surprised.

'I can smell Joy perfume; that's not a nursy scent.'

Agnes smiled. 'Maybe not, but it's my favourite,' she said.

'Mm.' The girl sat down on the bed. 'Agnes Carmichael, Miss, isn't it?' she asked.

Carmichael assented.

'Agnes – pretty awful. About as bad as mine – Alison. Ghastly, isn't it! Parents have a lot to answer for.'

Carmichael smiled again. 'Yes. I don't like Alison much – it's almost as bad as Agnes,' she said. For some reason the girl's attitude, chummy and familiar, was putting her more at ease.

'You're going to find Gran a handful. She likes her bevvy. Perhaps that's why she fell down the stairs and broke her hip – just one too many. Poor old dear. She only has a couple when she feels depressed.'

'Really?' Carmichael made no other response and showed no surprise.

'Yes. Nigel says Grandpa probably pushed her; he's longing to get rid of her. But that I can't believe. He's pretty diabolical, Grandpa, but not that bad – at least I don't think so.' Her long, white hands with their purple-painted nails played with the twine which laced up the front of her tight-fitting scarlet jacket.

'Nigel,' said Carmichael. 'Is that the young man I met when I arrived, crossing the hall?'

Alison looked vague. 'Yes, that would be Nigel, I expect.' She crossed her jean-clad legs. 'He'll be at dinner, and Grandpa.

22

You needn't change, though, nobody does. Only if Grandma comes, then we do, but she won't come down tonight.'

Carmichael at that moment did not look forward to the dinner, although she was hungry.

'Perhaps Lady Bellamy would rather I had the meal with her in her room?' she suggested.

'No, she's not keen on nurses. She may give you a hard time. Come on, you'd better meet her.' She got up and stretched her arms above her head in a long, almost feline stretch.

Agnes followed the girl out of the room and waited with some trepidation as she put her head round the door of her grandmother's room.

'Are you decent, Gran?' she asked.

'Of course. Am I ever anything else?' This reply rather added to Carmichael's reassurance. At least her patient had a sense of humour.

Alison pushed open the door further and in they went.

'So you're Sister Carmichael?' The eyes that met Carmichael's were blue and young in the ravaged face. White hair, beautifully and recently coiffured with obvious care and expertise, made one wonder if the hairdresser had only just left.

The room was, to Agnes, unbearably hot. The large double bed, the pink satin bedspread matching the dressing-table petticoat and the peignoir that Lady Bellamy was wearing, the elegance, the heat and the all-pervading perfume reminded Agnes of a stage set rather than a patient's bedroom. On the whole, she liked the look of her first private patient. However, she missed the atmosphere of the private hospital rooms that she had been used to and the rows of beds in the ordinary hospital wards. It was hard to imagine that this woman in that bed was her patient.

'How is your hip, Lady Bellamy?' she asked.

'Broken and pinned with some dreadful apparatus that hurts.' Lady Bellamy reached for a cigarette and motioned to Agnes to light it for her. She drew the smoke down into her lungs with enjoyment and then turned again to Carmichael.

'You know, you are the third attempt by your very efficient Nursing Co-op to find a nurse who suits me,' she said, coughing a little as the smoke billowed round her head, hardly moving in the draughtless room.

23

'Yes, Lady Bellamy, it was reported to me that you found two of my colleagues unsuitable.'

'Unsuitable! Let us say they didn't fit into the household very well. My granddaughter will tell you we are not a very easy family.'

'I see, Lady Bellamy.' Agnes Carmichael's reply drew a quick smile from Lady Bellamy and the silence that followed was broken by the sound of a gong.

'We have a gong in this house. It's old-fashioned and you won't hear one anywhere else I'm sure, but I prefer it. My husband, Edmund, does not like it, but I still prefer it.'

Agnes felt there was no answer to that, so she ignored the remark.

'Would you care for me to dine with you here, or would you rather I – '

'No, not this evening. You'd better dine with the family. You can help me to bed after dinner. Switch the television on, Alison, and pass me the control, and my glasses.'

Carmichael regarded this as a dismissal and left the room, followed by Alison. As they went down the stairs Alison looked at Carmichael with appreciation.

'I think you'll be OK with Gran,' she said.

'What makes you think that?' asked Carmichael.

'Well, you don't mind what she says, do you? You're not sort of bothered; you're a bit remote – unmoved by it all.' Agnes smiled but did not reply and Alison went on: 'I hope you can deal with us lot,' as they walked into the room that Agnes had glimpsed through the open door when she had first arrived. Again a tiny flash of apprehension attacked her when she confronted the two men standing by the fire. How did one behave? Accept a pre-prandial drink if offered, or refuse? After all, she was in this house as an employee, not a guest.

'Gin and tonic, Sister Carmichael?' the elderly, bearded man asked her, looking at her from under bushy eyebrows. His eyes were small and he had a mean little mouth, surrounded by a bushy pepper and salt-coloured moustache and beard. She decided 'Yes'.

'Oh, sorry. This is my grandfather, Sir Edmund Bellamy, and Nigel – Nigel Calvi.'

Agnes took the glass Sir Edmund proffered and sat down. The room was crackling with tension. She wondered if there

24

had been an argument, a row, going on between the two men before she arrived. There was a rather long silence, which gave Carmichael time to look round the room.

There were six large over-stuffed chairs and a settee with pretty cretonne covers; flowers arranged in one corner of the room; various small, expensive-looking antique occasional tables. The furniture reminded Agnes a little of Lavinia and the house she had left, but she pushed that thought away from her quickly and turned her gaze back to Sir Edmund.

He had the same, almost studied elegance which she had noticed in Lady Bellamy. He was tall. His grey suit, beautifully cut, flattered his slim, upright, rather military figure. He poured himself a stiff whisky, Agnes Carmichael noticed, and came and sat down beside her.

'How well the young dress these days, Sister Carmichael, always a collar and tie,' he said, gazing with some distaste at Nigel. Both he and Alison were wearing jeans – his, the same dark ones that he was wearing when Carmichael first encountered him, and Alison's of faded blue. Nigel had changed his black shirt for a clean white one. Alison displayed a slim, tanned midriff between her jacket and the top of her jeans.

'Oh, come off it, Grandpa. What's there to dress up for anyway, here?' she said. Sir Edmund appeared unruffled by this remark.

Carmichael sat rather stiffly, sipping her gin and tonic. She felt she had landed herself into rather a warring family. Still, there was little she could do about it in the way of making peace, and anyway she assumed she would spend most of her time with Lady Bellamy. She was pretty sure she would like her, as she had, through the years, liked all her patients.

'That your Porsche?' Her thoughts were interrupted by Sir Edmund's abrupt remark.

She looked up. 'Yes, Sir Edmund.'

'Rather a flash car for a nurse, isn't it?'

'It really depends on what kind of car you think a nurse should have, Sir Edmund.' Carmichael's voice was low and calm.

'Humph.' Sir Edmund got up and went and freshened his whisky. When he sat down beside her again he did not look at her. She was not sure whether her remark had offended him – neither did she care.

'I think it's an absolutely super job. I wish you'd let me drive it one day.' Nigel looked across at her, his eyes wide open, bold, in his handsome face. 'Nasty scratch on your wing though.'

'I know,' said Carmichael, and left it at that.

'He drives fast, does Nigel,' said Alison, almost proudly.

At that moment the door of the sitting-room was pushed fully open and a fat, white-haired woman, clad in a spotless apron, announced that dinner was served. They all got up and, allowing Agnes Carmichael to walk out of the room first, the family followed her across into the dining-room.

The dining-room was as splendidly furnished as the rest of the house. An elegant carving table stood at one end, where Sir Edmund officiated, carving the joint of lamb with an electric carving knife. The immaculately polished dining table was big enough to seat eight; four of them seated round it looked rather isolated and far apart.

The meal was good; the conversation limited. Nigel and Alison occasionally exchanged remarks, but, as had been apparent in the sitting-room, the two young people were not comfortable with Sir Edmund – who, when he did speak, usually managed to make some sarcastic remark about work-shy young, terrible modern music, awful clothes and hairstyles. It was only during the sweet course, when the unfortunate Sir Edmund managed to get a raspberry pip lodged under his dentures and was seen obviously trying to dislodge it, that Alison and Nigel cheered up and glances of hidden mirth passed between them – this, to Agnes, amounting to real malice. She wondered whether it was his constant disparaging remarks about the young that antagonised them – or was it something far deeper?

As they all left the dining-room to go back to have coffee in the sitting-room Agnes slipped upstairs to see if Lady Bellamy wanted her. She didn't. The television screen flickered in front of her and the room was very dimly lit.

Lady Bellamy had placed the dinner tray which had contained her meal on the floor beside her couch, and when Carmichael went to pick it up she said, 'Leave it – that's Hetty's job. I don't want you yet, Sister Carmichael. I'll ring.' She waved Agnes away and did not once take her eyes off the screen.

As Carmichael was leaving the room she felt slightly resentful, but Lady Bellamy banished the feeling by saying, 'I'm so sorry.

26

I don't mean to be so abrupt, but they had discovered who the thief was.' She smiled and Carmichael smiled back.

As she made her way down the stairs her mood changed. She realized that the resentment that had flooded over her and the tension passing from one person to the other in this house had made her, for the moment, forget the deaths of Brian and Lavinia and the loss of her newly found and pleasant lifestyle. The emotions in this house had pushed her sorrows away from her mind, and that was good, she thought.

The fact that a large amount of money now belonged entirely to her made her free to do as she wished. She could stay or go, and for the moment she felt that staying was better for her.

'Money is just another word for freedom,' she said in a whisper to herself as she crossed the hall. She then entered the sitting-room with all her apprehensions and rebellious feelings towards Lady Bellamy gone and found herself looking with academic interest at the three people drinking coffee.

Alison and the boy Nigel were sitting wide apart on the sofa and were not looking at each other. Alison was gazing into the fire and Sir Edmund was having some kind of argument on the telephone.

Lady Bellamy had appeared to be fond of Alison; but as to the rest – well, it would be interesting to find out.

Carmichael's entrance roused Alison, who got up and brought her a cup of coffee. Agnes sat down on the pretty Sheraton chair between the large settee which flanked one side of the fire and the two armchairs on the other side, one of which was occupied by Sir Edmund.

'Do you prefer to sit there?' Alison enquired of Carmichael as she took the coffee from her.

'Yes, thank you, and anyway Lady Bellamy says she may be ringing at any moment. I mustn't get too comfortably ensconced.'

She sipped her coffee, and the argument between Sir Edmund Bellamy and whoever it was on the other end of the cordless telephone went on. This had started whilst Carmichael was out of the room; it was obviously about money for Sir Edmund ended the conversation with: 'You've had enough out of me. Find yourself a job.'

He pushed the rod of the cordless phone down and placed it on the arm of the chair, then got up, went towards the fire,

27

seized the long, brass poker gleaming against the fire dogs and jabbed viciously at the logs.

'We can't get over your car, Agnes.' Alison cut across the silence. She did not appear ashamed or embarrassed by her grandfather's remark – indeed, it was as if she hadn't heard it. She spoke as if she was merely bored and wanted to forget any of the conversation that had gone on at dinner or now.

'Yes, I had an unexpected legacy and I've always wanted a Porsche. I'm very pleased with the car. I've only had it a short time.' Anges thought the half-truth was enough.

The scene round the fire was, she thought, rather like a play. The whole thing had a curious dreamlike quality, an old-fashioned air, like something written by Agatha Christie. Sir Edmund, having flung down the poker into the hearth, went back to his seat and, in spite of his age and height, almost flung himself into the chair. The phone clattered to the floor and no one made any attempt to pick it up.

Carmichael felt that if she didn't break the spell they would all suddenly freeze into a still photograph. Fortunately a log, probably unbalanced by Sir Edmund's attack on it, fell forward with a clatter and a shower of sparks. It was Nigel who got up this time and kicked the log back with the toe of his shoe. The energy with which he jumped almost toppled the small table beside him. He saved it gracefully with one hand and then grinned at Alison. There seemed to be an understanding between these two, although they spoke so little. Then, with a husky 'I'm going to my room,' he left.

Agnes got up more slowly. She heard Sir Edmund make a remark to Alison in quite a different tone from that which he had used on the telephone.

'I want to hear the news,' he said.

'OK. I don't mind.' Again Alison said this with a smile and Sir Edmund crossed over and switched on the large television set.

Carmichael broke in. 'Good-night. I must go and see if Lady Bellamy is ready to go to bed.'

The blare of the television programme before the news drowned whatever Alison or Sir Edmund said. Carmichael grimaced to herself. It might have been 'Good-night' from Sir Edmund or 'Good riddance', she thought. She had seen Alison's warm smile as she picked up a magazine, perhaps rather pointedly, to make it known that she was not interested in the news. Well, that was their affair. Carmichael closed the door quietly behind her and made her way up the stairs.

This time she was pleasantly greeted by her patient, who had switched off the television and was ready to be helped to prepare for the night and go to bed.

On the whole it was a fairly easy task to help Lady Bellamy with undressing, her bath and getting her into her nightdress. During the process she spoke little; she was obviously tired and her hip painful. Carmichael, once she had put her between the sheets, gave her two sleeping pills and handed her a glass of water with which to take them.

'You're better than the other two. You don't keep on being cheerful and saying funny things,' Lady Bellamy said, looking up at her with those piercing blue eyes surrounded by wrinkles.

'Well, I'm glad that I'm more suitable,' Carmichael said with some of her old primness, now slightly spiked with irony. To her surprise Lady Bellamy grinned rather widely.

'More suitable! The others were cack-handed, rough,' she said, handing Carmichael back the small glass that had contained the water.

'Well, I suppose we're all different and have different ways of doing things – even nursing,' Carmichael said, rather airily. She, too, was feeling tired and rattled by her first introduction to nursing in a private house.

'We are indeed,' said Lady Bellamy. 'The thing about you is that you don't really care whether you have this job or not, do you? Alison told me you came in a beautiful car and she admires your perfume. Perhaps you do this just for . . . ?' Her voice lifted at the end of the phrase so that Carmichael would know she was questioning her.

'I love nursing more than anything else and I prefer doing it to being idle,' Carmichael said.

'You mean you do it for love and not for money? Don't let Edmund hear you say that or he won't pay you.' The smile on Lady Bellamy's face was quite roguish as she settled herself more comfortably against the pillows. 'You can put the light out. I think I shall sleep well tonight, I feel more – secure. Perhaps it's because you're here.'

Carmichael then smiled too and pulled the sheets up a little further over her patient's chest. She waited for her to go on, waited to see if Lady Bellamy wanted to add anything else. She didn't.

'Very well. Shall I say good-night then?' Carmichael stood again. She had that rather uncertain feeling she had had when she first arrived at the house. There were, she realized, night calls to think of.

Lady Bellamy replied, 'Oh yes, give me my bell. I'll try not to call you, though. I don't seem to need much in the night – it's just if the hip gets particularly painful or I need to go to the bathroom.' Lady Bellamy accepted the small silver bell that Carmichael handed to her and placed it on her bedside table.

'I hope you'll hear it. I hope you're a light sleeper.' Lady Bellamy again said this smiling.

'I shall hear you,' said Carmichael. 'I'm a very light sleeper.'

Lady Bellamy nodded, still looking at Carmichael, almost searchingly. She tinkled the bell suddenly and Carmichael looked at her. The brown spots on the backs of the old lady's hands – she was old, perhaps older than Sir Edmund? It was hard to say, but as if she had followed the direction of Carmichael's eyes, Lady Bellamy said, 'If there was a doctor who could banish these spots from the hands of the aged he would make a fortune.'

'I'm sorry. I wasn't particularly looking at your hands or noticing the spots.'

'Yes, you were. Well, perhaps not particularly, but people do notice them. I hate them. I said, if you were listening, that if there was a doctor who could find a cure for these spots on people's hands when they get old he could make a fortune. I'm sure actresses must be bedevilled by them, but of course their hands can be covered with make-up.'

'Do they worry you?' Carmichael asked curiously and looked down at her own white hands.

'Of course they worry me. I think they're disgusting. I'm quite vain, you know, in spite of the way I look.' The eyes of the two women met and lingered for a moment; Carmichael felt that she was beginning to size up Lady Bellamy and Lady Bellamy was doing the same with her, and that somehow the feeling they had – or at least Carmichael had – was one of friendship, a mutual liking.

She stepped back from the bed. 'Good-night, Lady Bellamy. Have a good night and if you ring I will be in straight away.'

'Thank you.' Her hand went up and switched off the bedside light, leaving Carmichael to negotiate the rather large bedroom and go through the door into the lighted hall.

'Don't close the door, nor your own,' Lady Bellamy called.

Carmichael looked back in+o the darkened room. She could just see the outline of the old lady's head on the pillow.

'I won't. Good-night again, Lady Bellamy,' she said and she pulled the door to behind her, leaving it open about two inches.

As she went along the short distance to her own room she heard the front door downstairs slam noisily. Someone coming in, or someone going out? She had no idea. She looked at her watch – eleven o'clock. The evening had, on the whole, gone quickly. She was glad.

Oh well, the household business would go on around her and she would concentrate entirely on Lady Bellamy. She wondered, though, as she started to get undressed, how she was going to deal with her days. Perhaps Lady Bellamy was more active than she had been led to believe. Well, she would see. Maybe she would be able to see something of the country-side – she didn't know the Midlands very well. She believed she could take off two hours a day, or something like that. She would negotiate with Lady Bellamy tomorrow.

She got into bed and then realized she hadn't opened a window. She got out again and went over and pulled back the curtains slightly. It was moonlight. Her room was situated at the front of the house, next to Lady Bellamy's. She looked down and saw a slight figure. It wasn't Alison, she thought; perhaps it was Nigel; she couldn't be sure. The moon was not that bright and at that moment a cloud drifted across it.

She saw the figure walking round to the back of the house where Basil – handyman, she presumed he was, or chauffeur – had taken her car. Oh well, it was nothing to do with her. She opened the window, closed the curtains again and got back into bed. She lay there for some time, watching the curtains billow out softly in the breeze. Although it was November it was not cold and the moon made a square of light through the curtains. In spite of her strange surroundings and the strange bed, she soon fell asleep.

4

In the kitchen the large, pale fawn Aga made the air warm and cosy.

'For this coffee I'd go anywhere.' Mrs May, the Bellamys' cleaning lady, three hours daily at £2.50 an hour, sipped from her mug with noisy relish. 'It's nectar after the Johnsons'. Theirs looks like mud and tastes like mud.'

'It's the title that does it,' said the maid, Hetty, sarcastically. She was leaning against the sink, her red hands cupped round the mug. 'The aristocracy, you know; they always have everything better than anyone else.'

'Aristocracy my bum. They're not aristocrats, Hetty – not this lot.' Mrs May was contemptuous.

'Well, he's a Sir and she's a Lady – can't get away from that, Mrs May.' The maid looked at Maud, the fat cook, with round, grey eyes, her nose slightly reddened by the steam from the cup.

'A Lady – she's no such thing – nor is he a Sir. I mean, well, he is Sir, but not a proper one. Not like the Bowdens; they were real ones, that was a real title, you know, came down father to son, Baronet. This is just – well he's been knighted, that's all,' agreed Maud.

'Why do you get made Sir anyway?' asked Mrs May, holding out her mug for a second filling.

'Don't know, really. "Services to the community", that's what they usually say. But that was before I came. I don't know what it was for. There isn't any more coffee.'

Mrs May got up, disappointed. 'Best do the bathroom then, shall I?'

The white-haired cook nodded and turned irritably. 'Shut that door, for God's sake.' She turned right round as the kitchen door opened, letting in a draught of cold air from the entry outside.

'OK. Let's get in then.'

'Take your wellies off, Basil. I've done this floor.' Mrs May cast a rather flirtatious eye to the man, who did not respond or

look at her, but he did put one toe against the heel of the other foot and prise off his muddy boot. A small cascade of grassy earth fell off the back of the heel as he did so, then he bent down to take off the other welly. He continued to ignore Mrs May and nodded to Maud, then he padded over and sat down at the kitchen table.

Basil Kent was a short bull-necked man – he looked about fifty. He was short of leg and short of temper; his wavy, black hair was close cut and greying; his face was weather-beaten – red. His expression, habitually surly, did not soften now as Maud Spencer put before him a mug of tea and a generous slice of madeira cake.

'Ta,' he said. 'Hope I'm not going to be asked to clean that bloody Porsche,' he went on, through a mouthful of cake.

'Porsche?' Hetty, the maid, came forward to the table. 'Is that what it's called? That's the new nurse's, that is.'

'Yes, I know that. Lovely job.'

'Here you are, Harold.' This was from Mrs Spencer to a lanky young man who was still struggling with his wellingtons at the kitchen door. He approached somewhat diffidently, sat down and attacked the smaller piece of cake and mug of tea that were placed on the table for him. Having demolished the cake, he put up a dirty hand and stroked back the lank fair hair that almost reached his shoulders. He glanced towards the trim figure of Hetty.

'Doing anything tonight, Het?' he said.

Her face coloured and she glanced hastily and guiltily towards the cook, Maud.

'That'll do, Harold. You're not here to make dates.' The cook turned from him to the girl. 'On your way. Go and polish the dining-room table – and do it properly. Give it a good polish. She may be down tonight to dinner. That nurse, I reckon she's one of them who will get her moving, her Ladyship. I can tell.'

'What's she like, the nurse – pretty?' Harold asked. Then, 'Is there any more cake?'

'No, she's not pretty and no, there's no more cake.'

As the door closed behind the reluctant Hetty, Basil looked at Harold. 'Can't see what she sees in you. With that hair you look like a girl.'

Harold grinned. 'She knows I'm not a girl, Bas.' He looked at

Mrs May and winked. Maud sounded cross with him, but he did not retract.

'I don't want that kind of talk in my kitchen. Out you go, you've had your tea, both of you.' She gathered up their mugs and plates.

Harold got up with another wink at Mrs May, minced across the kitchen wagging his bottom and tossing back his hair. 'Come on, Basil darling,' he said.

'Any more of that and you'll get a kick up the arse,' grumbled Basil and with muttered thanks he followed the young man out.

Mrs May looked curiously at Maud. 'What does he mean about Hetty? I know she likes him, but he wouldn't try it on with her, would he? I mean . . .'

'He'd try it on with anyone, but I don't want to hear that chap Harold talking about her like that.' Maud banged the percolator back on the stove and Mrs May watched her, hopefully.

'Let's have another cup. He's upset you, hasn't he?' she said.

The suggestion was agreed to and Mrs May sank back on the chair again.

At that moment the kitchen door opened and Agnes Carmichael walked in. In her white coat and navy silver-buckled belt she looked trim and efficient. She regarded the two women curiously. The atmosphere in the kitchen was comfortable, she thought, but they looked as if they'd been interrupted in some wrongdoing.

'May I have coffee and biscuits for Lady Bellamy, please?'

'Of course, Nurse. It's ready now.'

Maud took the percolator off the stove and fetched a tray, cup and saucer and small plate. She put biscuits on the plate then poured the coffee into a silver coffee pot and set it on the tray, adding a small jug of cream.

'There you are, Nurse.' She handed the tray to Agnes.

'Sister, not Nurse,' said Carmichael, with a touch of her old air of authority.

'Sorry, I'm sure,' said the fat, white-haired woman and went to open the door for Agnes, at the same time glancing towards Mrs May. She shot her eyebrows up as high as they would go and put on an expression of long suffering.

As the door closed behind Agnes Carmichael she said, 'Hoity toity. They're always like that, nurses.'

Mrs May got up from her chair at the table. 'That's our coffee

34

gone, then,' she said and, taking the household holdall with cleaning fluids and cloths in it, she left the kitchen, banging the door behind her.

It was on her way to the kitchen again to fetch another cup for herself, as her patient had suggested, that Carmichael first encountered Madge Hillier. As she walked through the hall there was a long peel on the front door bell and a bang on the knocker. A loud voice called out, 'Hallo, Basil, me old reprobate. Still polishing the Rolls then?'

Agnes, as she was now passing the front door, opened it – to be confronted by a large woman with a tweed hat, suit and cloak. The hat was perched precariously on top of a mop of bright brown hair which curled out from under the brim; her fat face beamed with health, amiability and vigour. In one arm she held a bunch of chrysanthemums, the large, ball-shaped heads resting on her ample shoulder – pink, yellow and bronze flowers. In the other hand she held a large, bulging, leather handbag, and hooked round her fingers was a dog lead. Beside her well-polished brogues sat a black and white spaniel, tongue hanging out. The woman smiled and the dog smiled. She entered the hall, with the dog frisking round her heels.

'Are you the new nurse then?' she asked, in much the same bellow she had used to Basil, who was now retreating in the background, moving round to the back of the house. She did not wait for an answer, but put the chrysanthemums down on the polished hall table. A few petals fell to the floor.

'Freda!' she yelled at the dog, who took not the slightest notice of her and bounded up the stairs. 'Blasted dog,' she said. She held out a free hand to Carmichael. 'Madge Hillier. Next-door neighbour. Mile and a half down the road.'

Agnes shook the proffered hand. It was a good, firm hand-shake and before she could say anything the woman forestalled her again in that same deep voice. 'Maud, Hetty, where the hell is everyone?'

Hetty emerged from the kitchen in her morning garb – light blue dress and apron.

'Put these flowers in water and bring them up, and some coffee too.' She looked at Agnes, trim in her white overall and navy silver-buckled belt. 'Wish I had your figure. Name?'

'Sister Carmichael,' Agnes answered and as she did so the

dog pelted down the stairs and rushed across the hall towards the kitchen, sliding on the mat nearest the kitchen door.

Carmichael and the visitor mounted the stairs together.

'How is the old buzzard?' asked Madge Hillier. 'I haven't seen her for a week – more. Been away. Do you ride?'

'No, I'm afraid not.'

'Play bridge?'

Carmichael shook her head again.

'Well, you'll have a thin time here, then.'

She breezed into Lady Bellamy's like a galleon in full sail and threw her cape on the bed. 'Got you up then, has she, Gladys?' She bent down and kissed Lady Bellamy's cheek. Carmichael's patient's face lit up.

'Madge, you're back. Had a good time?'

'Of course, never go anywhere unless I'm going to have a good time. Bernard was a bore though; wanted to come home all the time; hated France; and was worried about what would happen to the pheasants while he was away.' She sat down with a bump.

'This is – ' Lady Bellamy was about to introduce Carmichael but didn't get that far.

'We met in the hall. Saw Basil, too. That man looks more like Bill Sykes every day. Ordered coffee – hope you don't mind.' She leaned back in the armchair she had plumped down into, fat legs apart, the lace edge of white directoire knickers showing on one fat thigh.

'Good to be back, though. Not too keen on the Frogs myself.' She turned her face in Carmichael's direction. 'My daughter's married to one – stupid girl. He's a doctor – all hand-kissing and heel-clicking. Still, she's happy; at least I think she was at first.'

Hetty came in with a large tray of coffee and three cups. She put the tray down on the table near Lady Bellamy, who seemed to be surrounded by coffee cups. Without ceremony Madge took the larger coffee pot. 'I'll be mother,' she said, and looked at Agnes. 'Black or white?'

Carmichael, who was somewhat breathless with the kind and matey manner of the woman, answered, 'Black, please.'

'Knew you'd say that.' Madge turned to Lady Bellamy. 'Nice figure your new nurse has got. What happened to the other one?'

'She and Edmund didn't get on; nor did he with the second one. This is the third, and Sister Carmichael is quite a different personality. I couldn't stand them either.'

Both women laughed, rather to Carmichael's annoyance. Then Madge looked shrewdly at Carmichael.

'Well, it'll take more than Sir Edmund, won't it, Nurse – Sister – to worry you, I feel sure.'

For once Carmichael didn't mind whether this woman called her Nurse or Sister.

'I'll take that time off you suggested, Lady Bellamy, while your friend is here,' she said, after she had finished her coffee.

Lady Bellamy nodded.

'Goodbye. Nice to have met you, Mrs Hillier.' She opened the door and was passed by the spaniel, who rushed by her and greeted the two women with joyous barks.

'Expect that fool Maud has fed her something,' said Madge. 'I'm always telling her not to, but it makes not a damn bit of difference.'

Just as Agnes was softly closing the door she heard the visitor remark, 'Nice-looking woman, that, Gladys. And that perfume – no cheap rubbish. Joy, same as Alison wears. I gave her some at Christmas, remember?'

Agnes did not hear her patient's reply, but she smiled to herself. Madge Hillier was like meeting spring in the middle of winter, she thought.

Carmichael left her white coat in her room, put on a warm coat and gloves and made her way downstairs. It was only when she was going round the end of the house to find her car that she remembered seeing that solitary figure leave the house last night, going in the direction she was following now, and she wondered again who it had been.

As she walked round the end of the house the low November sun dazzled her and she held up her hand – palm outwards – to shield her eyes. Then she could see that opposite the back of the house was the stabling – or at least what had once been stabling. There was a row of six divisions which used to house horses. They had been partially converted into two large garages, leaving four stables with their double doors at the end. The 'up-and-over' white-painted doors of the garages spoiled the attractive yard. As she stood there Agnes could picture it as it might have been when all six were stables and horses moved about inside all of them, maybe thrusting their heads out of the half-doors looking for lumps of sugar and apples. Only four such stables were left and two held horses. One, a grey, did poke his head out and look at her with mild, brown eyes.

On the centre roof of the row of buildings was a clock tower facing the house, its white, useless face possessing one hand only, which pointed to the V of the Roman numerals. One garage door was closed, the other open, and two cars stood outside: her own and the old-fashioned Rolls. Side by side they looked incongruous, the modern and the fairly ancient. The Rolls was shining, its maroon body and black top high and elegant. Her rakish car beside it looked like something from another world.

Agnes planned to go for a drive to the village or further. She unlocked the door of her car and got in. There was not a sound in the courtyard, but as she shut the door of her car with its soft expensive thud a pair of white doves or pigeons, Agnes was not sure which, flew up into the air, their wings flapping strongly. At that moment the man, Basil, emerged from the open garage in front of the Rolls, carrying a yellow plastic bucket.

'Good morning.' Agnes was determined to be polite in spite of the man's surly expression. She touched the window control of her car and spoke through the aperture. 'It's a beautiful car, that Rolls Royce, and so well kept.'

The man nodded, not quite so brusquely. He was about to walk away then seemed to change his mind about how to treat her and came over to her car.

'Nice car, this – no garage for it, though. Miss Alison's is in there.' He motioned towards the closed garage door beside the open one.

'It doesn't matter. It won't hurt being outside for a little while.' Agnes patted the steering wheel of her car gently, as if she was talking about something alive.

'Yeah. Well better under cover, that car,' he said. 'I'll see what I can do.' He touched his forehead and walked away, then turned. 'I'll get that scratch fixed for you in Leicester if you like?'

Agnes felt vaguely surprised by his amiability, which was at odds with his demeanour. She thanked him and backed the car, carefully avoiding the Rolls, and drove round the side of the house, along the drive and out into the road.

As the car purred along, Carmichael was conscious of her

own self-induced complacency. She had determined to clear her mind of the past, the horrors, what she had lost, and concentrate purely on here and now. Concentrating on the present was, she felt, the only way she could survive – and it was working. It was as if she had sponged clean a slate on which had been written 'Memories, both bitter and sweet', and now the entire slate was wiped off and blank. She had fought depression which had several times almost overcome her – that she knew. Depression was her enemy. The blank on the slate was now making her receptive to the characters, the personalities, of the people who were entering her life.

The landlady at the Cornish guest-house where she had convalesced after her operation; the woman who ran the Nursing Co-op she had joined; the other nurses in the hostel in London that was run by the Co-op. She was now capable of regarding them and listening to them, with interest sometimes, but without involvement. She did not feel anything now, and it was pleasant and restful. Whether this feeling would go on she was not sure; that was in the future and she did not want to think about it.

She wondered if this was why the characters she was now meeting and who were flooding her consciousness seemed rather like characters in a play. She was amongst them, but not of them. Perhaps it was because they knew nothing of her past? Well, they were not going to learn – not from her.

Lady Bellamy was giving her no trouble. She had helped her bath and dress this morning and walked her round the room without too many protestations. Lady Bellamy did not want to walk, but Carmichael knew that if she didn't try now she might become couch-ridden. Already she felt warmth towards the old lady, who seemed so peculiarly isolated in that room. Only the girl, Alison, seemed really to care about her.

Sir Edmund Bellamy: she'd not made up her mind about him. The fact that he never asked about his wife, or had not done so up to now, interested her.

Alison and Nigel – were they lovers? She was inclined to think not. Alison appeared to be a quite normal vivacious girl. She liked her in a disinterested way. Nigel, she didn't know.

Basil, the servants, were all interesting. She smiled to herself. She would watch them all – feeling quite absorbed in their antics, but not involved. It was probably, she thought, the perfect way to live.

It was fondness, affection, love, attachment; they were the feelings to avoid – they trapped you and then they hurt. 'Stay cool,' she had heard her young nurses say more than once, and she remembered the words; they constituted good advice.

As Agnes came to a straight stretch of road she put her foot down on the accelerator and the power of her car surged under her feet. The fields and the hedgerows rushed by. 'Stay cool,' she said aloud and she smiled and looked around at the flat countryside. It was not pretty, exactly, but after Cornwall and its rocky shore it was utterly different. But, there again, she didn't particularly mind where she was as long as she was comfortable, and in this present post she was certainly that.

The Bellamys, the family, they were enough; that small canvas was enough for her at the moment. She would watch them all with her new objective eye. There were undercurrents there, she felt sure, and she would be amused to see where they led – if she stayed that long.

After going about ten miles she stopped the car in a lay-by and sat musing. She saw several horses cantering across the field, their riders well dressed. Well, this was Leicestershire. Then she turned the Porsche round and headed back to her patient.

She was pleased with her short drive, the flat fields and neat hedges. No barbed wire, somebody had told her; that, of course, would be because of the horses and it being hunting country.

As she drove back into the stable yard she noticed that a rather battered Metro was parked in the corner and the second garage was open and empty.

Basil came towards her. 'Miss Alison says to put your car in there, miss,' he said.

Carmichael stopped. 'Oh, I don't want to turn her out of her garage,' she said.

'Won't hurt that old banger, miss, to be out,' he said.

Carmichael felt a few spots of rain and rather thankfully eased the Porsche into the garage. She must thank Alison, she thought.

5

Lady Bellamy lay in her bath. Only her face, neck, forearms and hands were visible above the copious sweet-smelling bath bubbles. Her blue eyes were fixed on Carmichael and she was chatting.

Agnes had been at Nettlestone Manor for four days now and this was the first time she had been allowed to stay in the bathroom while Gladys Bellamy was actually in her bath. To be helped in and helped out was all she had permitted for the first two or three mornings. Agnes thought that this concession might be a sign of her patient's growing confidence in her nurse; that, or Lady Bellamy felt it was useless trying to hide the scraggy figure she had become. The livid scar across her hip added to the disfigurement and Carmichael sympathized with her feelings.

'X-rays tomorrow. Damn nuisance.' Lady Bellamy covered her face with the face flannel from the hot water.

'Never mind.' Agnes Carmichael, seated on the pretty white-cretonned chair, spoke loudly. 'It will make a change for you to get out.' She had discovered that Lady Bellamy was a little deaf and often answered 'Yes' when actually she had not heard a word said to her.

'Madge is a nice woman: genuine. It's her dog – well, both of them – they're out of control mostly.' Lady Bellamy emerged from the face flannel. 'How do you get on with Alison?' she asked, abruptly.

'Very well, I think,' Carmichael answered.

During her two hours off duty yesterday, she and Alison had driven into Leicester to buy a dark green blouse Alison had wanted to go with her new slacks. Although Alison had a car of her own, she seemed to prefer to go with Carmichael and had driven part of the way home, loving the way the Porsche handled.

'She's a dear girl. The only one in my family who cares a damn about me. Came to the hospital every day when I was there. Edmund came once. Families! God gave us relations, but thank God we can . . . and all the rest of it.' She looked at Carmichael with her bright blue eyes. 'How do you get on with your relatives?'

'I haven't any.' Agnes left it at that, but Gladys Bellamy continued to look at her shrewdly.

'None at all? Well, that takes some working out. What happened to them all?'

'I don't know – I was brought up in an orphanage.' Carmichael found herself saying the word almost proudly.

Gladys Bellamy continued to look at her, but made no further comment.

'Are you ready to get out now?' Agnes asked.

Gladys Bellamy shook her blue bath-capped head. 'Not yet. Water makes my hip less painful. Put some more hot in, please.'

Agnes ran the hot tap, then sat down again. Before she did so she picked up the big, fluffy bath towel that had dropped off the heated rail on to the floor and replaced it.

'My husband, Edmund, killed my daughter and son-in-law. Did you know that? Did Alison tell you?'

'She certainly did not,' said Carmichael, looking surprised.

'Well, she might have done. She needs someone to talk to, that girl. Someone like you, I mean, someone who isn't . . .'

Carmichael almost shook her head in disbelief.

'Oh, it's true. I'll tell you about it some day.' She remained silent for a while.

'I think it's time you got out of the bath now,' said Agnes, firmly.

'All right.' Lady Bellamy looked at Carmichael and smiled broadly. 'You think what I said is the ramblings of a senile old lady, don't you? Well, I assure you it's not. It's absolutely true.'

'I wasn't thinking about it,' said Carmichael, rather lamely and untruthfully.

'I bet. Come and help me out, then.'

When her ancient, scarred body was wrapped in the big bath towel Agnes helped her through to the bedroom. Gladys Bellamy sat down on a stool in front of her dressing-table mirror, took off her bath cap and gazed at herself, shook her white hair and ran her fingers through it.

'Good God,' she said. 'Look at me. Do you know, I was in *The Tatler* once at the races at Ascot. Pretty I was then, lovely legs I had and golden hair. Age is a . . .' She unscrewed the top of a pot of foundation cream, touched her finger on the top and put a little on her face. 'Agnes, old age is tough.'

'You had *The Tatler*, though – and the prettiness and the races,' answered Agnes. 'Some people have nothing – no good memories at all.'

Lady Bellamy grimaced. 'Oh, quite the little philosopher, eh?' she said, but she said it kindly and without rancour.

Later, when she was dressed and again looking at herself in the mirror, she suddenly turned to Agnes. 'You know, I think I'll go down to dinner tonight. I can manage those stairs with help, can't I?'

'Of course you can, with me and your tripod.' Carmichael talked to her patient in the mirror, smiling at her.

'You know, Agnes, you're good for me. I can talk to you. I can't talk to many people. Don't wear that beastly white coat at dinner, though, then I shall feel you're a guest, a friend, not my nurse.'

Agnes assented and felt pleased. The whole conversation confirmed that Gladys Bellamy was feeling better, and Carmichael was always pleased when she saw any improvement in someone she was nursing.

'Tell them at lunch. I want them to know that I'll be there at dinner.' Gladys Bellamy sounded as if she was quite looking forward to it.

However, when Carmichael informed them at lunch, their reactions were different. Lunch in the Bellamy household was rather a light, scrappy meal. Sir Edmund was eating a salad and looked up and grunted through a mouthful of lettuce, but did not meet Agnes' eye. Nigel smiled, if a trifle wryly, and said, 'Oh, dress clothes will be worn. Good-oh.'

Only Alison seemed really pleased. 'That's good, Agnes. I hope it won't be too painful for her, getting down the stairs, but you'll know how to help her, won't you?'

Carmichael appreciated the remark and the warm smile that went with it. She had learned that Alison was not as scatter-brained as she had at first appeared.

'Grandma has to go to Leicester Hospital for an X-ray tomorrow, hasn't she?' Alison continued.

'When?' Sir Edmund looked up.

'Eleven o'clock,' answered Agnes.

'Hmm. Doris and Herbert are coming for the weekend.'

'Oh Lord, I'd forgotten that.' Alison turned to Agnes to explain. 'That's Grandpa's brother and his wife. I'd better go and see that the room is ready. I'm sure Maud will have remembered, even if I haven't.' She got up hastily and left the room.

'Don't know why they're coming. Extraordinary visit. I suppose they think they ought to look over Gladys; see how she is.' Edmund pushed his plate away.

Carmichael hardly knew what to say, but ventured, 'Do you see much of your brother, Sir Edmund?'

He looked up. 'Not if I can help it,' he said.

Nigel looked across the table at Carmichael and screwed his eyes up in an expression that Carmichael couldn't quite fathom. Then he smiled and gave a little tiny wink; Carmichael came to the conclusion that it was just a joke and that probably Sir Edmund would be quite pleased to see his brother.

The presence of Lady Bellamy that evening made a difference to the behaviour of her family – in dress particularly. Sir Edmund had put on a well-cut dark suit, and his white shirt and dark tie were immaculate. Nigel looked particularly handsome in an equally well-cut Italian suit. His hair shone; it had a deep wave in the front and Carmichael wondered if he had pressed the wave in place with his long white hands when he looked in the mirror before he came downstairs.

Alison arrived later than the others. She kissed her grandmother and gave her a little hug. Her long Indian cotton dress swished round her legs as she went to the trolley to pour herself a drink.

'Sorry I'm late, Gran dear. The car broke down again. Luckily old Cartwright from Upper Farm tinkered about with the engine and it started again. I'm afraid it's getting past it, it's always breaking down.'

'Surely you don't expect a new one – that car is only six or seven years old,' Sir Edmund said, gruffly.

'Eight and a half actually, Grandpa,' corrected Alison.

Sir Edmund did not answer that, but poured out his third stiff whisky and returned to his seat.

Gladys Bellamy looked up sharply. 'Anyway, that's for me to say, Edmund. If this estate is being run properly it should make enough money to keep us all, and if Alison needs a new car she should be able to have one.'

she bent over the bed. 'I don't feel like going to sleep, it's too early.'

'Of course.' Agnes drew up a comfortable chair to the bedside and sat down.

'I like that dress, green suits you. You've got good taste, Agnes.'

'Thank you.' Carmichael settled more comfortably into the chair. She felt relaxed up here in the bedroom with her patient – more relaxed than downstairs in the sitting-room with Lady Bellamy's family.

As if she had sensed her thoughts, Lady Bellamy's next remark surprised Agnes.

'Do you think Alison is getting attached to Nigel, or he to her?'

'Alison?' The question had caught Agnes Carmichael off her guard. She had noticed their long looks; she had also noticed their hands touching when it was not absolutely necessary. Once, when Nigel had passed behind the settee on which Alison was sitting, she had seen him lightly touch a curl of the dark hair that reached her shoulders. However, she gave a cautious, non-committal answer.

'I think they like each other.'

Lady Bellamy moved rather restlessly on her pillows. 'Don't prevaricate. You're observant; you're trained to be observant; your profession makes you that.'

'Well, yes. I would say they were attracted to each other, but I'm not really sure, Lady Bellamy.'

Lady Bellamy sighed a long sigh. 'Yes, I think you're right – and it's got to be stopped. It's got to be stopped soon.'

She slipped off the diamond ring she had left on her finger even when she was creaming her face and put it beside her on the table – then thought better of it, picked it up and handed it to Carmichael.

'I forgot I'd got this one. I don't often wear it. Put it on the dressing table for me, Agnes,' she said.

Carmichael got up and did so, then sat down again. 'His prospects – Nigel's prospects – are they not good?' she asked. 'I thought you had told me, or someone had told me, that he'd been to agricultural college and done quite well and was employed on the estate to help your husband.' She stopped.

Lady Bellamy put up her hand again as if to stop the

47

conversation. 'No, I didn't mean that. It's nothing to do with that – nothing at all.' She played for a moment with the coverlet on her bed, pulling it straight, then crinkling it up and pulling it straight again. 'No, it's just that they're related. Alison is Nigel's half-sister. It's a long story and in a way I'd like to tell it to you. I've never told anyone, not the whole thing, parts perhaps, but not all of it.' She looked directly at Agnes and then away again. 'It's so dreadful – the consequences – and once a thing starts up it gets like a roller-coaster, you can't stop it. Well, I couldn't stop this and I can't stop it even now. That's why I'd like to tell you about it.'

Carmichael sat up a little straighter in her chair. 'Are you sure you want to? I mean, maybe you'll regret telling me afterwards.'

'I don't think so – I don't think that at all. It's just that I'd like to piece it together, tell you all of it and I'd feel better about it, I think. I started to tell Madge once, but before I got very far I could see she was not interested. Oh, she's a sympathetic person, Madge, but she lives very much in the present and perhaps I live too much in the past.' She looked at Carmichael speculatively. 'Will you bear with me? Somehow I know I can trust you,' she said and she folded her hands together on the sheet in front of her and looked down at them, then up at Carmichael, as if for an answer.

'Of course I will bear with you, Lady Bellamy, of course I will.' Carmichael felt really interested, just as she would in any story that was not her own. She settled herself more comfortably and prepared to listen.

6

Lady Bellamy, too, settled herself on her pillows and gazed, not at Carmichael, but across the room as if into the long-distant past.

'It was about twenty years ago,' she said. 'It was a snowy, cold, rather disagreeable Christmas Eve.' She paused for a long time, then suddenly became more alert and looked more directly at Carmichael. 'I won't bother you too much with what went before. Suffice it to say that when I married Edmund he was a handsome young man, but he had problems which my family saw while I, of course, was too much in love, too stupid to think they would matter. He was actually a braggart, a gambler and a womanizer even then, but when you're in love, Agnes, you don't see these things, or if you do you thrust them to the back of your mind to be dealt with at another time when love isn't so strong, sex isn't so urgent. I'll just say that my family heartily disagreed with the marriage, but went along with it. I was pleased and flattered that Edmund wanted me.'

She gave a wry laugh. 'Wanted me! He didn't want me – he wanted Nettlestone Manor and my money. We got the Manor sooner than we thought; my father died suddenly, my mother moved into the Lodge and we moved in.

'A young couple, you would have thought, with everything before us. Well, we can skip all that. Soon I became pregnant and Edmund seemed inordinately pleased and wanted a boy. He was obsessed by his wanting a boy. I don't know why – something to do with his name being carried on, though God knows why. Bellamy! My name was something – no, that sounds snobbish, I mustn't talk like that.

'Anyway, the baby was born and turned out to be babies – twins, a girl and a boy, Sheila and Paul. Edmund scarcely looked at Sheila – I don't think he even liked her, I could never see quite why. Anyway, Sheila lived and became a bright, vivacious, attractive girl and Paul died when he was two. Perhaps I should say Edmund never got over that. He thought we'd have another child, so did I; but we didn't, so there was just Sheila. I must skip a bit here or you'll be bored.'

Carmichael shook her head. 'So far it has not been boring at all – moving, but not boring,' and she meant what she said.

Lady Bellamy went on. 'I didn't tell you, by the way,' she smiled to herself, 'a Freudian slip, no doubt – I was forty-one when the children were born, Paul and Sheila, so really there wasn't a lot of hope of my having another. Oh, there was some, but it didn't happen. Edmund watched me like a hawk, certain that he could create another son, but he didn't. His obsession was strange. Then, as time went on he was knighted – he was very civic-minded at that time, did a lot for the village and the surroundings. He seemed to throw himself into that to try and forget Paul's death. Anyway, he was here at a royal visit – Mayor of Leicester, no less – and he got a knighthood. That

49

pleased him. I thought it would make up for the fact that he hadn't a son. It didn't.

'Don't think I didn't suffer over the death of Paul – I did. It's terrible to give birth at that late time of your life, then have the joy of two, only to lose one. It was dreadful.

'Maybe I was to blame for what happened next. I concentrated everything on Sheila. I adored her and the closer I got to the child the further Edmund got from both of us. We got a nice fat nanny from the village who worshipped the little girl as much as I did. Sheila grew up into a rather spoiled, pretty and affectionate girl.

'Then, it seemed, history repeated itself and she married someone I didn't approve of. I don't think Edmund minded one way or the other – I think he would even have been glad to see her unhappy. That sounds horrible, but I really feel that.

'The man she married was well off; he owned a large firm of building contractors. I never trusted Sheila's husband, Bob. Bob was the wrong name for him. Bob is a nice, solid, comfortable name, but he was not a nice, solid, comfortable man. He was thin, anxious-looking, ready to take offence if you said the wrong thing. Sheila didn't seem to notice it – she was such a happy-go-lucky girl, and she was pregnant.

'They came quite a lot to Nettlestone Manor. Sheila loved coming, and Bob didn't seem to mind. Sheila was so happy pregnant – nothing seemed to worry her, nothing at all.

'We had a maid at the time. She was Italian, Maria – very religious, must be got to church to Mass every Sunday. Edmund used to drive her there.

'Bob and Sheila came often to the Manor during her pregnancy. They came for Christmas. I've got to it at last. The snowy Christmas Eve sounds like the beginning of a thriller, doesn't it?'

Lady Bellamy took a sip of water from the glass by her bed. Carmichael sat quietly. She felt the old detachment. She was listening to a story that was not her own, and that was better than thinking of Brian and what might have been.

'They came on Wednesday. Christmas Day was on Sunday. I'd asked them to come early because the weather forecast was not good – snow. I decided that once they got here it didn't matter about them getting back, they could go back when the snow cleared. Bob always seemed to be able to manage his business from here on the telephone – I had no worries about that.

'Sheila looked radiant. It was so lovely to have her here for such a . . . well, a fairly long time. They weren't going back until the New Year, which was as well, I thought at the time, because on the Wednesday night it began to snow really heavily and got colder. Nettlestone Manor seemed warm and safe.

'On Christmas Eve we went to bed early and I woke up, something woke me, at about half-past one. I looked over at Edmund's bed, it was empty. He was with Maria, I knew. I didn't often wake up, there hadn't been any intimacy between us for years. I was just disgusted.

'I fell asleep again – I suppose it was only minutes later. I hadn't realized that Edmund had only just got up, just crept off, up the servants' staircase. And what did he find there? If it hadn't been for Sheila it would have amused me! Edmund had found Bob in bed with Maria – French farce almost, isn't it?'

Carmichael shook her head. 'It must have been awful for you,' she said.

'Yes, but it was worse for my daughter. I thought the two men would come to blows. Bob certainly wasn't a physical type, but Edmund – when they got downstairs after they'd left the shrieking maid – Edmund knocked Bob down! Oh, it was a very pretty scene, believe me! I was worried, not about myself, but I hurt for Sheila – young, pregnant, vulnerable. She stood there in her nightdress. At first she couldn't understand what had happened. Then Edmund told her, shouted at her, and told them to get out of the house. Get out of the house! The snow was a foot deep on the lawn outside. It was freezing and still snowing – quite a blizzard. For the first time in my life I begged Edmund for something. I begged him to let them stay, but it was no use. The two men were like two stags locking antlers about the busty little Italian girl upstairs. Above all the fracas we could still hear her cries and sobs.'

Carmichael stood up suddenly. 'Don't you think you should stop now and tell me the rest tomorrow?' she said.

Lady Bellamy looked at her quizzically. 'No, I don't, not unless you want me to. It's done me good to tell you this. I've never been able to talk about Sheila before, not like this. If you can bear it I'd like to go on – let's have another gin.'

She suddenly looked rather roguish and Carmichael felt the

51

story was not tiring her patient as much as she feared. She poured out two more gins and tonics, handed one to Lady Bellamy and sat down, preparing herself to listen to what she thought was the end of the story.

'Well, in the end there was nothing I could do. I often wonder if I had been stronger – barred the door, locked it and taken away the key so that they couldn't get out – what would have happened; but I feel Edmund would have got them out somehow. They packed and left. I can hear now the scrunching noise the car made on the ice as it went round the house. I prayed that it wouldn't go, that something would stop it, the snow perhaps. But no! They went.'

Lady Bellamy took a sip of her drink. 'They skidded and ran into a tree, right in Leicester – they had got that far. Bob was killed instantly. Sheila was alive, but went into labour. The baby was born and Sheila died. It was Christmas Day when they rang us, still dark. The baby was saved, they said.

'I don't want to tell you any more about my reactions – enough to say that when the child was well enough, Alison, she came to us. Where else would she go? She was my grandchild and Edmund's, too. I think he felt it was another daughter, and again he never liked her, never loved her.'

'Is that the end of the story? How terrible,' said Carmichael.

'Oh no! It's not the end of the story. After a few months, during which time Alison thrived, the very fact that she was here, a baby, and my child, saved my sanity, I know that. But during that time we found that Maria was pregnant – a charming situation, particularly when the maid confessed she was not sure whose baby it was as she'd been sleeping with both men. Bob had visited her sometimes when he was here and Edmund a great many times, so she wasn't sure which was the father.'

At that moment the bedroom door was pushed open and Alison poked her head round. 'Hallo, you two, still yacking – and boozing,' she said, with a wide smile. She came over and kissed her grandmother. 'I'm going to bed, I'm worn out,' she said, laughing.

'Good-night, darling.' Her grandmother put her arms round her and hugged her.

'Nice to hear you two chatting away,' Alison said, smiling at Carmichael and she touched her shoulder affectionately as she passed by her chair. 'Don't sit up too late,' she said in rather a motherly way, which made her grandmother and Carmichael smile. She went out and closed the door behind her.

'Well, that's nearly the end of it, but not quite. Maria was bundled back to her family in Italy. She was a Catholic, so of course she couldn't have an abortion. Soon afterwards she married an Italian. Of course Nigel thought he was his real father. When he was seventeen they were both killed in the big Naples earthquake – so he was an orphan.' She picked up her glass and sipped a little more of the gin and tonic.

'Edmund kept in touch with her. It was a son, you see – he'd made a son and he wanted him back. Oh, I held out for a long time, but what did it really matter? I felt that as long as I would never see the woman again it would be, well, tolerable – and I had Alison.

'When he was orphaned Nigel came back. He was a little younger than Alison, but it made a companion for her. Edmund put him through agricultural college and then took him on as a sort of steward here, a bailiff.

'Now you know it all. Now you know why there can be nothing between Alison and Nigel, because he's either her half-brother or they have the same grandfather. So you see it would hardly be wise, would it? And anyway, I want something better for Alison. I want her to get out of this polluted atmosphere that is our family; get out into the world. She's been to university, but she never seems to have met anyone she likes. She's brought several young men home and I was very hopeful – but no. She and Nigel are – Oh, I knew they were very close and I suppose I should have thought – but you can't think of every problem can you? You can't think of every hazard.'

Carmichael shook her head. 'Indeed you can't. You never know how the past is going to catch up with you,' she said.

Lady Bellamy looked at her. 'That was said with feeling, Agnes,' she said.

Carmichael smiled and waved her hand dismissively. She went up to the bed and took away what was left of Lady Bellamy's drink. 'I'm a bad nurse for letting you drink, and so no sleeping tablets – you'd better not,' she said.

Lady Bellamy laughed. 'Don't worry, I think I shall sleep tonight; I feel relaxed. Telling that story hasn't brought back hateful memories, but rather discharged them on to you. How selfish we are, aren't we, all of us? A trouble shared is a trouble halved; that means the other half has gone on to the other person.'

Agnes settled her patient's pillow, then threw back the bed covers and they walked together to the bathroom. She helped Lady Bellamy back into bed and she could see that her patient was more relaxed and didn't complain about her hip at all. Carmichael saw that she was comfortable, switched out the bedside light and, as she was leaving, Gladys Bellamy spoke.

'Thank you, Agnes,' she said, 'for listening.'

Carmichael didn't answer that, but said, 'X-ray tomorrow.'

'Leave the door ajar – and yours – won't you?'

'I will,' Carmichael said. She pulled the door to within two inches behind her and went into her own room.

7

When she awoke the next morning Agnes Carmichael was conscious of the difference in the light coming through her bedroom window. She had felt cold in the night, but nevertheless was surprised to see the lawns and shrubs dusted with snow and to see the flakes falling softly by her window. She shivered and closed the window before she bathed and dressed.

The white covering outside brought to her mind Lady Bellamy's story. She had thought about it for some time before she fell asleep last night: particularly she had thought about the two men, one of whom was Nigel's father – but which? She could not help smiling a little as she put on her lipstick. 'It's a wise child who knows its own father,' she murmured.

After breakfast the Rolls was ready at the door. Carmichael helped Lady Bellamy down the snowy steps and into the car's capacious interior, settled her comfortably with a cushion at her back and a rug over her knees before she herself got in and sat beside her.

Basil drove the car smoothly out into the road. He seemed very pleased to see Lady Bellamy; he looked different in his chauffeur's cap and smart coat.

As they travelled through the snowy landscape Lady Bellamy seemed to be enjoying the change of scene. She pointed out several farms which, she said, belonged to the estate. One farmhouse flanked the road, another stood back two fields away, another was down a side road, nearer Leicester.

A mile or so along the road stood a pretty stone house, slightly smaller than Nettlestone Manor, which Lady Bellamy said was Madge's. Agnes was interested to see it and she asked: 'Has Mrs Hillier any sons?'

Lady Bellamy shook her head. 'No, only the one daughter. She has a nephew, a nice boy. Well, man, rather – sadly I think too old for Alison; he would make a good husband. However, he doesn't seem to bother with girls – pity.'

A little further along she pointed to a less attractive, modern house. Just visible on the corner of its driveway was a large, white-painted gate separating it from the grass verge and path.

'I've bought that house. It's occupied at the moment by a temporary tenant on leave from Nairobi. I intend leaving it to Edmund. I didn't tell him that until after my accident.'

Agnes said nothing; indeed she felt so surprised that there was little to say and Gladys continued: 'When I die everything will go to Alison, but I can't very well leave my husband without accommodation – that will do very well for him.' She turned and looked sharply at Carmichael. 'You're an expert at the "No comment", Agnes,' she said.

Agnes smiled; she had noticed a slight stiffening of Basil's shoulders and the brief glance he had taken in the mirror. He had then put up his hand to alter the angle slightly.

'When I told Edmund that it was to be his home when I die I thought maybe it would make him want me to live longer; he likes living in the Manor even though he does so little about the upkeep of the estate and the problems of the tenants.' Gladys Bellamy laughed, but without much mirth.

Again Agnes was silent; again she could not think of anything to say in answer to these remarks. She asked her patient if she was comfortable.

'Yes, thanks. You know a great deal more about the Bellamys than I do about the Carmichaels.' Lady Bellamy seemed to be trying to lighten the conversation.

'There are no Carmichaels, only me,' answered Agnes, and she was flooded with a feeling of utter, utter loneliness. She added, 'I'm not part of a family, I am a fictional character – made up by other people, even my name.' As she said this to her surprise she felt tears come into her eyes. She turned her head away and tried to blink the moisture away. If Lady Bellamy noticed this, and Agnes thought she had, she did not mention it.

The Rolls drew up outside the hospital. 'Leicester Royal Infirmary' – she read the gold letters arched over the door. She helped her patient from the car, Basil holding the door open for them.

The moment she entered the hospital and smelled the familiar hospital smell her eyes dried and her feeling of loneliness vanished.

The receptionist, a blonde, motherly woman, left her desk, maybe inspired by Lady Bellamy's title, and fetched a wheel-chair. She was even ready to take the patient down the long corridor above which hung a large sign with the words 'X-ray Department' and an arrow pointing the way, but Carmichael explained who she was and she and Lady Bellamy started the journey indicated by the large arrow on the sign.

On the way they passed wards to the right and to the left. To the left was Emerson Ward and almost unconsciously Agnes Carmichael slowed down and peered in, her heart quickening as she saw the lighted ward, for the morning was now dull and overcast. Only the ends of the beds were visible. She could see plainly the familiar arrangement of the polished tables down the centre of the ward, with their vases of flowers. A doctor in a dark suit, followed by three or four white-coated students, stood at the end of one bed, then they were past the ward.

Another ward to the right showed a similar scene, only this time the beds had high steel supports and hanging weights – the Orthopaedic ward. No doctor was visible here, just nurses and a flower lady wheeling in a trolley of freshly arranged flowers. It was all so familiar to Agnes, yet it seemed so long since she had been part of it.

As the wards fell behind them she was aware of a nostalgic feeling, rather like homesickness, and she longed to be part of this world again with its little wars, its excitements, its boredom, the tiredness and the wonderful feeling of being in charge – full of the knowledge of what must be done, what signs and symptoms must be noticed and which could safely be ignored. She sighed softly as she pushed open the heavy swing doors and manoeuvred her patient's wheelchair under the black and white sign which read 'X-ray Department. Please enter.'

She wheeled the chair up to the receptionist's desk, behind which was a dark-haired girl who greeted them and took the form Lady Bellamy handed her.

'Would you please wheel Lady Bellamy over there.' She pointed to a row of dark blue plastic chairs against a white wall at one end of the department. 'You won't have to wait long.'

One woman and a small girl of about three were already sitting there. The child was wriggling, her small fat legs struggling to get to the floor. 'Sit still, Mary.' The woman sounded irritated and she thrust a teddy bear into the child's arms. The little girl threw it across the floor and managed to get away from, presumably, her mother's restraining hand. She ran after the toy and fell headlong. The woman got up, gave the child a sharp slap on the back of the leg and the little girl opened her eyes wide and started to scream.

Lady Bellamy's eyes met Agnes' and she raised them to heaven.

A man emerged through the two wooden doors labelled 'X-ray in progress. No entry' and joined the woman. He was carrying a large brown envelope.

'The pictures are in here,' he said. 'We've got to go back to the clinic.' The three of them made their way out, the child still wailing but less loudly now. The door closed behind them.

A woman, white-coated, emerged from under the 'No entry' sign and looked towards the wheelchair. She then went to the receptionist, collected Lady Bellamy's form, read it and made her way towards them.

'Lady Bellamy. It's your hip, isn't it?'

Agnes Carmichael rose, intending to push the chair forward, but the girl shook her head, clasped the handles of the chair firmly and steered it expertly through the two big doors, shutting them firmly behind her.

During the next half-hour two people came into the department: a porter in a grey coat and white theatre shoes, and a nurse in a grey and white striped uniform with a white belt tight around her tiny waist, her cap perched precariously on the top of dark, frizzy hair.

'You're not very busy this morning,' Carmichael said to the receptionist. The girl was about to reply when the telephone rang; she picked up the instrument and started to talk into it with her head down.

Agnes Carmichael began to lose the feeling of security and familiarity that the hospital had given her when she had first arrived. The atmosphere here in the X-ray department, the girl behind the desk, the porter, the radiographer, the screaming child and its mother – long long ago, it seemed to Carmichael, this would have been a situation in which she would have had a part to play; her role now was only that of an onlooker. She hated the feeling. As Sister Carmichael she had been looked up to, listened to, respected – now she was responsible for one old lady, who really only needed her as a sort of lady's maid. She suddenly hated Lady Bellamy and the position in which she found herself. 'If you don't ride or play bridge you'll have a thin time here.' She remembered Madge Hillier's words. Who wants to play bridge or ride? she thought. Certainly not me. I suppose this is what is known as loss of identity, and what do I do to regain it?

The girl behind the reception desk put the phone down and looked up at Carmichael, but Agnes turned away. She did not feel now that she wanted to repeat her remark.

At that moment the doors opened and Lady Bellamy emerged, talking animatedly to the radiographer. The girl pushed the chair over to Carmichael and handed her the brown envelope.

'Lady Bellamy's X-rays. She tells me you are seeing Mr Picard at twelve.' She looked at the watch pinned on her white coat. 'If you go along to Out-patients now he'll probably be ready to see you. His clinic does sometimes overrun, but I haven't had anyone from the department to X-ray for the last hour or so, so probably you won't have to wait.'

Agnes took the X-rays and pushed the chair towards the exit doors.

'Anyone else for me?' the radiographer called out. They did not hear the receptionist's reply as the door swung to behind them.

The Out-patients department was practically empty and the nurse ushered them in to see Mr Picard almost at once.

'This is my nurse, Sister Carmichael,' said Lady Bellamy as Agnes helped her from the wheelchair.

The consultant, a fattish man in his early fifties, held out a hand and shook Carmichael's. Lady Bellamy sat down in the chair by his desk and Carmichael stood by the wheelchair.

'And how are we? How are things progressing?' He slipped the X-rays on to the desk X-ray framed light. 'Looks good,' he said.

How many times had Carmichael heard that before! After Lady Bellamy had exchanged a few more pleasantries with her surgeon, Carmichael helped her through to an examination room and on to a couch so that he could assess the movement of her hip.

Back in the Rolls Gladys Bellamy was cheerful and appeared to be very little fatigued by the morning.

'How was it, m'lady?' asked Basil.

'Very good, Basil. I'm mending nicely, he said.'

'Home now, m'lady?'

'No, let's have lunch at the A la Carte and a nice big drink beforehand.'

'Very well, m'lady, if it's all right with Sister?' Basil said.

'Of course it is. You can lunch at the King's Arms – and don't drink,' said Lady Bellamy.

Carmichael was amused by this exchange. 'If you feel up to it, Lady Bellamy,' she agreed.

'Of course I feel up to it – and the longer I can put off meeting Herbert and Doris the better.'

Agnes had forgotten that guests were coming for the weekend.

The Rolls drew up at the restaurant A la Carte. In they went, Lady Bellamy leaving her wheelchair in the boot of the car and determinedly walking with her tripod into the dining-room.

'He said I must walk – Mr Picard – you heard him,' she said, then to the waiter: 'A double gin and tonic, please, and have what you want,' she added to Agnes, who also ordered a gin and tonic, but not a double. They made their way to a table and sat down, as it was more comfortable here than the lounge for Lady Bellamy. 'We'll have our drinks and then order,' she said to a hovering waitress.

The drinks were brought and Lady Bellamy sipped hers with appreciation. She smacked her lips. 'I love gin and tonic,' she said. Another single gin and tonic followed and then they ordered their meal. While they waited Lady Bellamy looked round the restaurant, watching the people come in, her blue eyes bright, her cheeks flushed pink – perhaps by the air or perhaps by the gin, Agnes wasn't sure.

They waited rather a long time for their soup. Lady Bellamy grew silent and Carmichael was worried that she might be tired, but suddenly she looked up at Carmichael and said: 'Tell me, Agnes, did either Alison or Nigel tell you that Edmund pushed me down the stairs when I broke my hip?'

Carmichael felt her cheeks flush, but not with the gin, and she remembered Alison's remark the first day she had come to Nettlestone Manor and been chatting in the bedroom with the girl.

'No, of course not – of course they didn't.' She lied automatically and Lady Bellamy looked at her with amusement.

'You're a bad liar, Agnes,' she said. 'As a matter of fact, of course he didn't. The longer I live, the better for him. He knows everything goes to Alison.' She smiled. 'Those naughty children.' She laughed, then looked serious. 'I suppose if he wishes anything, it would be for something to happen to Alison.'

Neither Carmichael nor Lady Bellamy referred again to her rather startling remark during their excellent lunch. It was only when the waitress had put the tray of coffee in front of Carmichael that Lady Bellamy enlarged on what she had said.

'Black or white?' Agnes asked.

'Black, please.' Lady Bellamy signalled the waiter and asked for two glasses of kümmel. When he had brought them she sipped the colourless liquid, her eyes meeting those of Carmichael.

'Hope you like kümmel,' she said. 'I'm very fond of it.'

'What? Oh yes, thank you,' Agnes replied, and Lady Bellamy sighed.

'Are you thinking about what I said of that resident ageing Don Juan, my husband?' she asked.

Agnes poured a little more cream into her coffee before she replied.

'Well, of course, Lady Bellamy, such a statement is rather amazing. Sir Edmund is . . .'

'Such a nice, quiet man, so gentlemanly, were you going to say?'

'No, I wasn't.' Carmichael could add no more before her patient broke in.

'Edmund likes to act the part of the Lord of the Manor, but

not of the responsible landowner. Not only has he ruined my happiness by killing my daughter, but he's been a constant trial with his womanizing, gambling and wilful extravagances. I have learned to live with it, Agnes, but it hasn't been easy.'

'Why didn't you divorce him?' Agnes asked, bending to pick up her napkin which had fallen to the floor.

'I don't know. There was Alison. It is my estate. For a while Edmund improved; I think he was frightened that I might divorce him. He did improve and become very civic-minded. I thought things might be better – particularly when he was knighted, that seemed to please him. One does always hope. Besides, the scandal. My family was "respectable".' She suddenly stirred restlessly. 'Let's go,' she said, 'and brave the elements and Herbert and Doris.' She put out her hand and clasped Agnes' affectionately. 'You're a comfort, Agnes. You have no one, no one you're responsible for, no one to vex you – well, that's how it seems to me.'

After they had paid the bill, they slowly walked out to the car and got in. Lady Bellamy leaned back and closed her eyes. Neither she nor Agnes spoke again until they drew up at the front door at Nettlestone Manor.

8

As Carmichael and her patient came into the hall of Nettlestone Manor they could hear the murmur of voices coming from the sitting-room. Hetty appeared from the kitchen carrying a tray on which was a silver teapot and water jug.

'I've served tea, m'lady. Sir Edmund said – '

'All right, Hetty, I'll join them in a minute.'

Agnes helped Lady Bellamy take off her coat.

'I won't go upstairs, Agnes, I'll just have tea with them all and then I can say I'm tired and you can suggest I should dine in bed.' Gladys Bellamy smiled at Agnes conspiratorially, but she did look rather tired. Together they moved into the sitting-room, where Alison was pouring tea.

Edmund Bellamy looked up as they entered, but left the enquiries and welcomings to his brother and sister-in-law.

61

Agnes Carmichael was surprised when she saw Sir Edmund's brother, surprised at his appearance. Whilst Sir Edmund's tall, well-tailored figure gave an appearance of aristocratic elegance, his brother Herbert was the direct opposite – short, red-faced, his thinning black hair combed carefully across his head but not concealing his shining scalp. His face, equally shiny, was clean shaven. He sat on the settee, one fat thigh crossed over the other exposing a short length of pale blue sock and above that an inch or two of flesh. He rose, gave a desultory greeting to his sister-in-law, then fastened his small eyes on the plate of cakes on the old-fashioned wooden cake stand that Hetty had placed beside him.

'Bread and butter first, Herbert. Remember what Mother always said.' Sir Edmund gazed at his brother, but he spoke with little humour in the remark.

'Bugger Mother,' answered Herbert. He picked up an éclair and plunged his teeth into it, then noticed Carmichael standing behind Lady Bellamy's chair and thought better of this language. 'Oh, sorry, I'm sure,' he said through the cream cake.

Agnes sat down in the chair next to her patient.

'How did you get on then, Gran?' asked Alison, getting up and putting a small table beside her grandmother, then placing on it a cup of tea and a plate with one sandwich. She waited for the reply.

'It was tiring, but it seems the hip is doing as it should, Alison. We had pictures taken.' Lady Bellamy sounded weary, but Agnes was not quite sure whether she was as tired as she sounded or if she was preparing the scenario for getting away early to her room.

Having seen her patient settled and able to reach and drink her cup of tea, Agnes had time to look at Herbert's wife, Doris, whose appearance again surprised her. She was slim and vulgarly attractive and appeared much younger than her husband – perhaps his second wife, Agnes surmised. As she drank her tea she observed with interest the way the woman, Doris, simpered at Edmund. Maybe the title had something to do with it, impressed her, Agnes thought.

'And how's work going, Edmund?' Herbert suddenly shot the remark at his brother after carefully selecting another cream cake. 'Nigel still doing most of it?'

The remark sounded offensive to Carmichael, but Sir Edmund rode it without apparent rancour.

'Of course he's doing most of the work. Why keep a dog and bark yourself?' he answered, lighting a cigarette and leaning back in his chair. 'And how is your work going, Herbert?'

His brother laughed, 'Flourishing.' He looked over at Carmichael. 'I run a pub,' he said.

Doris spoke for the first time. 'A road-house, not a pub, Herbert,' she said, rather primly.

'Right, Doris, a road-house – sounds classier, eh?' Herbert agreed.

Carmichael smiled, but said nothing. She leaned forward to pass Gladys Bellamy another sandwich, caught Alison's eye and received from her a quick, exaggerated wink.

'Just so you know we're not all landed gentry, Agnes,' Alison said.

Lady Bellamy laughed. 'Agnes is not likely to think that, Alison.'

At that moment the door opened and Nigel appeared. 'Oh, sorry . . .' he said and seemed about to retire, but Alison called out.

'Come in Nigel – tea-time.'

As the boy entered the atmosphere in the room changed.

'Oh yes, do come in.' Edmund Bellamy reinforced Alison's remark, but there was a hint of sarcasm in his tone. 'Join the family.' There was not a scrap of warmth in his invitation, but then there never was any warmth in anything he said. Only Doris seemed unchanged by the new arrival; indeed she cast an admiring glance at the boy's dark, good looks.

Alison beamed at him and patted the settee beside her. Nigel came and sat down and as he did so Alison touched his hand, quite quickly, but Alison saw that Gladys Bellamy had noticed.

The conversation ebbed and flowed, but Lady Bellamy seemed oblivious to it. Herbert had built an extension on to his road-house – The Larch Trees – and Doris waxed enthusiastic about its décor, which sounded particularly hideous to Agnes. She spoke of crimson silk-padded walls and red stools heavily outlined with chromium (only Doris called it silver), Victorian shaded lamps on all the dining tables and a circular bar. The bar appeared to be Herbert's pride and joy because he chipped in to talk about that. Agnes could picture it and could also picture

Doris officiating as the barmaid and wondered if that was her former background. Sir Edmund talked briefly of the developers who had started the bungaloid growth, as he called it, in the lower field. 'Brought in a nice few thousand though,' he added.

Nigel and Alison largely ignored their elders' conversation and talked of the horses, of whether they could find time to go for a ride together tomorrow and a little about Alison's recalcitrant car. Their voices were low and intimate.

The mention of the fact that Agnes possessed a Porsche momentarily halted the conversation.

'That's what I want, Herbert.' Doris clasped her hands, showing off her long, painted nails. 'I'd like driving a Porsche.'

'Try and get it, ducks,' answered her husband. 'Still got the Rolls, Edmund?'

The conversation then veered to cars and Lady Bellamy turned to Agnes, signalling that she had had enough.

Agnes helped her to her feet and Gladys Bellamy took leave of her guests, saying as she crossed the room that she would rather stay in her room for dinner as the day had tired her. Agnes reinforced this and they left, on Lady Bellamy's part at least, with relief.

'She's his second wife, I expect you gathered,' Gladys Bellamy explained as she reached her room.

'Yes, I thought that,' Agnes replied.

'His first wife left him – ran off with his barman. It took Herbert some time to get over it. His male ego was injured.' She laughed. 'What a family I married into.' She laughed again. 'Thank God, when I've gone Alison will be mistress of the estate, and a fitting one – I only hope she marries someone suitable who will realize the responsibilities of the place and who will love and cherish Nettlestone.'

She seemed thoughtful when at last she was in bed. 'What a day – I never thought I'd get through it,' she said, lying back on the pillows and looking wryly at Agnes. 'There was a time when I could ride most of the day and dance all night. Who would believe it now?' She shut her eyes. Then she opened them suddenly. 'Drinkies time, isn't it, Agnes?' she said.

9

After their drinks Agnes insisted that she should go and fetch the trays up from the kitchen. Lady Bellamy had agreed that they should dine up here in her room together, and Carmichael had donned her white coat and navy, silver-buckled belt. She was aware that she did this rather to distance herself from the visitors; to let them know she was there in a purely professional capacity. Also she was pretty sure that, given the chance, Doris Bellamy and her husband were the kind of people who might start asking her advice on medical problems and describing their various symptoms at length. She was safer, she felt, out of the way.

The kitchen was fairly busy and Hetty was grateful to Agnes for relieving her of the job of carrying the two trays up to Lady Bellamy's room. As she pushed open the door for the second time she heard Hetty say: 'Well, I reckon she's the nicest private nurse I've ever met – she's real decent.' She coloured as she saw that Carmichael had heard her.

'Thank you, Hetty. Some listeners do hear good of themselves.' Agnes smiled at the girl.

'What time's supper?' Basil had shoved open the kitchen door and put his head round.

'Dinner,' corrected Maud, 'and yours won't be ready for at least an hour yet.'

'Evening, Nurse,' he saluted Agnes, then turned and left the kitchen, banging the door behind him.

'Cheeky he is, cheeky,' Hetty said, spooning sprouts into a vegetable dish.

Agnes was slightly surprised. She had thought Basil lived in the village and was off duty in the evenings unless Sir Edmund wanted him, and she said so.

'No, he lives at the back of the garage. He's got his own kitchen, but doesn't make himself even a piece of toast or boil himself an egg – comes back here to get all his meals, the easy way.' Maud sniffed as if she didn't altogether agree with the arrangement. 'Put the lid on those sprouts, Hetty, and have you put a bit of butter on them?'

'No, I thought – '

'You're not paid to think, Hetty. Put a dollop on, Sir Edmund likes it and so does Miss Alison. It doesn't matter what the others like or don't like.'

Agnes took the tray from the kitchen table and escaped upstairs. As she entered the bedroom Lady Bellamy was eating her dinner with appetite. She looked up at her.

'Any turbulence in the kitchen regions, Agnes?' she asked. 'The roast beef is good. Maud's very reliable, if a bit testy at times.'

Carmichael placed her tray on the table and drew it towards her. It was not too comfortable sitting in a low armchair and eating from a table, but she liked being with her patient.

They ate in companionable silence and when they had finished the first course Agnes went down to the kitchen to fetch the sweet. When they had eaten that, Hetty appeared with coffee and took away the trays.

'In that cupboard over there,' said Lady Bellamy, pointing to a small cupboard beside the dressing table, 'you'll find a bottle of Drambuie and two liqueur glasses.' Agnes looked doubtful and Lady Bellamy smiled. 'Come now, Agnes, we should be having some if we'd stayed downstairs.' Carmichael shrugged her shoulders and went to the cupboard and took out the two small glasses. She poured some, then poured the coffee and placed a cup and a glass beside Lady Bellamy and took the Drambuie to her little table.

The sweet taste of the liqueur on her tongue brought back such a rush of memories to Agnes that she had to turn her head away for a moment and put the glass down – Brian, that hotel by the river, the restaurant windows looking out on to a summer evening, and the river flowing by. The trees bending down, their thin, trembling branches reaching right to the water and trailing like . . . Brian's face across the table, his eyes humorous and tender – caring what she wanted, how she felt. She blinked her eyes rapidly and noticed, as she picked up the tiny glass again, that her hand trembled. The detachment she thought she had attained was thinner, more delicate, more vulnerable than she had thought.

'What is it, Agnes?' Gladys Bellamy's voice startled her.

'Oh nothing, just thoughts. The taste of the liqueur took me back, you know how things do – smells, tastes.'

Lady Bellamy nodded. 'Perhaps one day you'll be able to tell me,' she said. Before Agnes had time to answer the telephone beside her patient's bed rang. Gladys Bellamy picked it up. It was Madge Hillier.

Agnes drank her coffee and tried not to listen to the telephone conversation. She tried to stop her mind from going back to memories that upset the balance of her determined detachment.

'Madge says, will we go to coffee on Monday. She expressly asked you to come. She liked you.' Lady Bellamy replaced the telephone receiver in its cradle.

Agnes nodded. 'Thank you, I'd like that,' she said.

The door of the bedroom burst open. 'Grandma, you did well to escape that meal.' Alison came in. She had changed from the dress she had worn at dinner and was now in jeans and a flamboyant scarlet, green and yellow top, one shoulder bare, her hair tied up with a scarlet topknot. 'It was awful, Gran. Doris is ghastly. She wants a Porsche now it's been mentioned and Grandpa's getting sloshed. Doris and Herbert aren't on the best of terms and Doris is going to bed.' She giggled. 'Nigel is driving me in the Land Rover to that disco in Leicester. We need a bit of fun after that lot.'

'Leicester! Darling, that's too far on these roads.'

Alison patted the end of the bed reassuringly. 'It's OK, Gran. The snow has cleared and there's a dreamboat of a DJ I want to see if I can lasso. How do I look?' She whirled round in front of her grandmother and Agnes.

'Like Top of the Pops – awful,' said Lady Bellamy, but she said it with such affection and humour that Alison bent down to kiss her.

'Mind my leg,' said Lady Bellamy and Alison flitted across the room, kissed her hand to Agnes and was gone, leaving her perfume on the air behind her.

Lady Bellamy sighed. 'A disc jockey, that's what DJ means, doesn't it? Well . . .' She was silent for a moment or two, then: 'What am I to do about Alison and Nigel? I saw her touch his hand this evening. I wonder – when I'm gone she'll need someone responsible, someone who can help her run the place.' She was silent again.

Agnes could see the way her thoughts were drifting and tried to turn the conversation in another direction.

'I didn't realize Basil lived on the estate. I thought – '

'Oh yes,' Lady Bellamy broke in. 'He has one of the cottages behind the stables, haven't you seen them yet? They're a pair; pretty stone cottages, very small, same date as the Manor, I think.' She handed Agnes her coffee cup and saucer and the small glass, which Agnes put on the tray ready to go back to the kitchen.

'Edmund making the stables into garages ruined the look of that part of the outbuildings, but I am determined to keep the cottages unvandalized. We put in bathrooms and generally modernized without spoiling them. Basil has one and Nigel lives in the other. Why do you ask?'

Carmichael made an evasive reply. 'Oh, it was just that when I was fetching the trays Basil came into the kitchen wondering if dinner was ready.' But it was not Basil she was thinking of, it was the slight young figure she had seen coming out of the front door of the house on the first night she had been at Nettlestone Manor and making his, or her, way round to the stables. Now she was more inclined to think it was 'her' way round to the stables. Perhaps it had been Alison. Agnes dismissed the thought. It could have been Nigel making his way back to his own domain. Anyway, if the young people were determined to be together there was nothing she or, she felt, anyone else could do to keep them apart.

Agnes tidied up the room, walked her patient to the bathroom and back and tucked her up in bed.

'I'm tired. After all, I've had quite a day, haven't I? I shall sleep well, I'm sure. I'm glad my hip is – what did he say – uniting.'

Agnes nodded and settled her patient's pillows.

'My hip is less painful now. Perhaps that man's right, the more I walk on it now the better.'

As Carmichael put the little silver bell by her patient's bedside she was aware how tired she was herself. Private nursing was tiring. You were responsible twenty-four hours a day, she thought, but if she was not doing it, not taking the responsibility, how could she still bear her life? Once more alone; once more bleak. No, it was better this way. She said good-night to

Lady Bellamy and, as usual, left the door ajar, went to her own room and started getting ready for bed.

Once there she could not sleep. Thoughts tumbled through her head like particles of rock running down a mountain. Lavinia – Brian – Cat's Cradle – her engagement – Derek. Firmly she switched over to the new set of names – Madge Hillier – Edmund Bellamy – Alison – Nigel – Basil – Hetty. Did it really matter genetically if brother and sister married? What were the chances of abnormality in their children? Legally wrong, of course – but if they didn't know, who could be blamed? How could it . . . ? She looked at her bedside clock. Its luminous hands showed it to be ten to three. Suddenly she heard the sound of wheels crunching over the gravel drive. She got out of bed and looked out of her window.

The thin covering of snow had nearly all disappeared. A Land Rover drove slowly round the house as if the driver was trying to make as little noise as possible. There was still enough moonlight for Agnes to see two people in the front seat. The Land Rover did not stop outside the front door, but turned slowly round the end of the house and Carmichael could hear it crunching on towards the stables. Carmichael got back into bed and lay listening for a long time, waiting to hear someone – Alison – enter the house and come up to her room. But there was not a sound.

10

The November sun had finally banished all traces of the snow when Agnes Carmichael came out of the house at about twelve o'clock the next day.

She had settled her patient in the sitting-room with Doris Bellamy and Alison. The two men, Sir Edmund and Herbert Bellamy, had decided on a walk round the estate and Nigel was in the room Sir Edmund Bellamy used as his office, typing letters for Sir Edmund to sign later.

Carmichael had come to the conclusion that the smooth running of the estate – the farms, the pheasant rearing, the upkeep of barns and fences and farmhouse, in fact all the maintenance work – was looked after by Nigel, who seemed to have a good working knowledge of management, visited and discussed repairs, and appeared to get on well with all the Nettlestone tenants. Sir Edmund, on some mornings, would walk round the estate playing, she felt, the part of the titled landowner, as Lady Bellamy had said, with rather theatrical aplomb, but as far as Carmichael could see he did little work to back his pseudo-stewardship.

Agnes was curious to see the cottage where Nigel lived. She skirted the garages. The horses stuck their heads out of the stables as she passed and she presented each with half an apple that she had got from Maud this morning for this purpose. She stood and watched them as they crunched the fruit. Agnes was little used to horses and she rather timidly stroked their noses and backed away when the grey raised his head and neighed loudly showing huge yellow teeth.

Round behind the stables Agnes found the cottages, well back from the outbuildings. They stood among the trees, solid, grey-stoned, small-windowed, the little front gardens surrounded and divided by a green-painted picket fence. Both front doors and windows were painted white. The Land Rover stood outside the left-hand cottage, the bedroom window of which was open allowing the white net curtain to blow out in the November sunshine. Carmichael wondered, had Alison spent the night here with Nigel? She certainly had not heard her come in, though she had been at breakfast this morning and, as far as Agnes could ascertain, she had come down the stairs from her room. Thank goodness, Carmichael thought, Lady Bellamy had not asked her this morning if she had heard Alison come in the night before. Indeed, she had not mentioned her granddaughter at all and seemed preoccupied with her guests.

This morning Maud had come up to Lady Bellamy's room to discuss meals and menus with her. Her rate of progress was such that Carmichael felt that soon there would be no real need for a full-time private nurse and her services would no longer be needed. Rather to her surprise, she felt that when this moment did arrive and she had to say goodbye to the Bellamys and the Manor, she would be quite sorry to leave.

Agnes had suggested to Lady Bellamy that she should take her off-duty period that day over lunch-time and go into Leicester to do a little shopping and have lunch. Gladys Bellamy had agreed and Agnes opened the garage door and backed out her car with a sense of enjoyment she had felt she would never feel again.

She drew out of Penny Stratton Lane and joined the main road. Traffic was thinner than she imagined it would be and she motored along quite slowly, admiring the sunny fields and the well-kept farms. She passed Madge Hillier's house and was pleased that she was going to meet that stout amiable lady again.

A pheasant, his colours reflecting like metal in the light, jumped out of the hedge to her left and she slowed down almost to a standstill to let him half walk, half fly across the road and into the field. She was about to go forward again when she saw something else in the hedge: a gingery form half fell, half scrambled down the little slope from under the hedge to the ditch below and did not re-emerge. Agnes thought at first that it was a dog. She braked, got out of her car and walked round it. There, in the ditch, lay a fox, its mouth open, tongue out, its sides heaving, and the noise of its breathing sounded like broken bellows. It tried to move, but could not get to its feet and turned its amber eyes towards her. It was obviously too exhausted to move.

Agnes was almost unaware of thinking what to do; she acted automatically. She opened the back door of the car, grabbed the car rug from the seat and spread it on the floor of the car. Then, with equal haste, she pulled an old plastic mac from the side pocket that she had left in the car for emergencies, covered the car rug with it and then turned again to the ditch. Gently, she picked the creature out of the water; it hung in her hands, still heaving, fighting for breath, trembling. She placed it on the mac on the floor of the car, then flung the fold of the rug over it and closed the door. Within seconds she was back in the driving seat – and only then did she see the reason for the fox's terror. Way across the large flat field were the hounds and the red-coated men on horseback; she could hear the baying of the excited pack.

They had, she believed the word was, 'found'. But she had 'found' first and a hatred against the sportsmen and their brain-washed dogs welled up inside her. She put the car into gear and away she went, with their quarry in the back, safe. She knew exactly what she would do; she would drive on and then return when the hunt had gone away. She looked in her mirror and could see the hounds now milling round the hedges and the ditch where the fox had fallen. The horses, too, and the riders, who peered this way and that, their mounts rearing and neighing.

After about half an hour of driving slowly and steadily, she turned and drove back. The rug was no longer flat, but humped as if the fox was crouched rather than lying; the harsh breathing, too, had stopped. Agnes was nervous – would it attack her? All was quiet except for a very occasional car going by. It was lunch-time and that had thinned the traffic still further. The hunt had gone, a whole hour had gone by – they had not 'found'.

She folded the rug back gingerly. The fox was sitting now and blinked in the light, then retreated to the far side of the car; its breathing was quiet, but its amber eyes were still full of terror. She spoke to it quietly, gently; it did not react. Its mouth was open, white teeth, red tongue hanging out, and Agnes realized it would not pass her. She left the door wide open and went round to the other side of the car and tapped on the window. With one fluid movement the animal slid out of the car, bounded across the ditch and through the hedge, its brush leaving little tufts of white and ginger hair on the brambles – then it was free. Agnes stood on the raised side of the ditch and watched it streaking across the brilliant winter field, disappearing at last into a large clump of trees, way in the distance.

She came back to the car, rolled up the mac in a tight bundle. The smell the fox had left was strange, musky, tobacco-like; she must take the rug to the cleaner's and throw the mac away. She opened the back windows, turned the car round and drove on to have her lunch in Leicester. The feeling of complete satisfaction she experienced was, perhaps, out of proportion to what she had achieved – but she was not sure.

She saw again that gingery creature going across the field to freedom and her heart lifted. She would enjoy her lunch, she felt. She stopped at what Doris Bellamy would have called a road-house, entered the bar and ordered an alcohol-free wine with scampi and chips.

She took the drink to a table near the window. The place was like many such places – wood-lined – and there was an imitation log fire with gas flames leaping up. There were quite a few people at tables scattered round the room. The bar was round and served two rooms, the dining-room in which she was sitting and a room the other side of it. Just as she was beginning her meal she heard a voice she knew – Sir Edmund. He was drinking with his brother Herbert. He did not see Agnes. She could hear his rather hoarse voice, but not well enough to distinguish what he was saying, although whatever it was Herbert was obviously against it. He banged his fist on the bar counter several times and then waved his hand downwards as if he was brushing whatever his brother was saying away from him.

Agnes Carmichael kept her face turned away from them and enjoyed her meal. Eventually they left. She wondered who was driving; she had not noticed the Rolls outside when she had parked. Then she saw they were making towards a grey Jaguar; that must belong to Herbert. Both men looked anything but steady as they walked towards the car. Herbert dropped the keys and staggered a little as he picked them up. They then got into the vehicle and steered it out of the road-house car-park, turned left and headed for, Agnes hoped, Nettlestone Manor. They were hardly fit, she thought, to go anywhere else.

She finished her scampi, had a coffee and thought again of the fox as she left the restaurant. Then she drove into Leicester, took the car rug into a cleaner's and put the plastic mac into a rubbish container; even then as she got back into the car she could still smell faintly her foxy refugee. Still, she didn't mind that – indeed, it proved that he really had been there. She had done something – something worth doing – and she was smiling as she sped along the road towards Penny Stratton.

That evening Agnes dined with the whole family. She noticed a tension between Herbert and Sir Edmund, and also between Alison and Nigel. The conversation was general and Sir Edmund drank steadily through the meal and relapsed into a gloomy silence before its end.

The formalities were observed at this dinner: the men were in dark suits and Doris was in a gold lamé trouser suit. Lady Bellamy, too, with Agnes' help, had dressed with care and Alison wore a red silk dress that made her look paler than usual.

The four women left the men with the port decanter and went through to the sitting-room for coffee. Agnes watched her patient for signs of fatigue, but Lady Bellamy seemed in fine form and drank her coffee and liqueur with enjoyment.

'I'm trying to get Herbert to buy me a Porsche like yours,' Doris simpered at Agnes.

'Will he, do you think?' Gladys Bellamy asked.

'Oh yes.' Doris crossed her rather thick, golden-encased thighs. 'He always gives me what I want in the end.' She pouted her lips, took a packet of cigarettes from her gold lamé evening bag and lit one. She seemed lost somehow without Herbert, or perhaps worried about how much her spouse was drinking. She hadn't long to wait; Herbert came in, red-faced but apparently sober. Nigel looked cool and smiled at Alison and came over and sat beside her. Edmund was not sober. He staggered a little as he came through the door, but made it safely to the settee.

Alison switched on the television for the news; it was almost nine.

'Agnes, be a dear and fetch my glasses,' Lady Bellamy said.

'Of course.' Agnes got up, smiling a little to herself. Lady Bellamy really needed glasses all the time but she was rather too vain to wear them when she was dressed up. Agnes made her way up the stairs thinking, I hope I'm as good as she is, but without the broken hip, when I get to her age. After a little search she found the glasses and was half-way down the stairs when she heard a crash and a scream – not quite a scream, rather a groan, but she recognized her patient's voice and flew down the remaining stairs across the hall and into the sitting-room.

Gladys Bellamy lay on the floor by the settee. Her husband, clutching the brass poker, stood beside her. Alison was on her knees by her grandmother. She looked up as Agnes entered the room.

'She fell,' she said, indicating the overturned coffee table beside her.

'A log fell out of the fire and rolled on to the rug and Gladys got up and Edmund stepped back and knocked Gladys down.' Doris added this.

Agnes Carmichael had eyes only for her patient. She appeared to her to have struck her right rib cage against the little table, for she was rubbing it with her hand.

'I'm all right, don't fuss, Agnes will look after me. My hip is all right, I didn't fall on that side. I've ruined my stockings, though.' Lady Bellamy, with Agnes' help, got to her knees, then insisted on getting to her feet – rather against Agnes'

74

advice, but when Lady Bellamy decided to do something there was little anyone could do about it.

Agnes felt curiously at a loss. She missed the familiar support of the hospital scene – the casualty department, the other nurses, the telephone which summoned a casualty officer within minutes.

'Should we call her doctor?' Doris asked, as if reading Carmichael's thoughts.

'Oh no, you won't. What rubbish, getting him out at this time of night.' Lady Bellamy's voice sounded strong and determined.

Once she was standing, Agnes could better assess whether she had done any further injury to her hip, but Lady Bellamy motioned for her Zimmer aid and with Agnes' help walked the few steps to the settee and lowered herself on to it. It was then that Carmichael noticed she had blood on her stocking, down near the ankle.

'I told you I'd ruined my stockings – new ones, too.'

On closer examination Agnes did find that she had torn her stocking slightly and that underneath was a small graze oozing a little blood.

'I'll carry you upstairs, Lady Bellamy,' Nigel said.

Lady Bellamy nodded; she seemed to trust him completely. She put her arms round his neck and he carried her as if she was a featherweight up the stairs, followed by Agnes.

Back in Lady Bellamy's bedroom, Agnes felt more able to cope with the situation. She helped her patient undress and examined the hip. All seemed well; movement in both hips was perfectly all right. She bathed the graze and put on a small dressing, but she was quietly determined to let Dr Marvin, Lady Bellamy's GP, know of the accident in the morning. She was glad to see that Lady Bellamy's remark downstairs had been right and that the other hip seemed to have received the greater impact. Gladys Bellamy could move it freely, although a blue bruise was already appearing on the thinly covered pelvic bone.

She was glad when at last her patient was safely in bed and demanding to watch the nine o'clock news – or what was left of it.

That night Carmichael did not sleep well. She continually listened in case Lady Bellamy wanted her and rang the little bell.

*

In spite of the fact that in the morning Lady Bellamy seemed completely recovered, Carmichael insisted that Dr Marvin was called and also persuaded her patient to stay in bed.

Dr Marvin arrived at eleven o'clock and examined Lady Bellamy – took her blood pressure, looked at the bruises and her hip and her grazed leg, and took her pulse at some length. Then he advised at least two days' bed rest.

'You've had a shock. Ladies of your age don't take a tumble like that without shaking themselves up a bit,' he said, replacing his stethoscope and sphygmomanometer in his bag. 'Now, please do as I say for once.'

'It will put my walking back, won't it, Agnes?' Lady Bellamy grumbled.

Dr Marvin perched on the bed. He was a short, stocky, grey-haired man. His rough tweed suit made him look more like a farmer than a doctor.

'You'll soon catch up, you're doing very well. I heard from your orthopaedic consultant. Want any more pills written up, Sister?' he asked Carmichael, who shook her head. 'OK, then. I'll see you in two days. Meanwhile, stay put.' He waddled out, waving as he went, and Agnes heard him having a word with Sir Edmund in the hall.

She felt happier now the doctor had been. It would put her patient's mobility back, she admitted that, but it couldn't be helped. She blamed herself for leaving Lady Bellamy to fetch her glasses: she should have asked Alison to fetch them. Then she realized that that was stupid; she had to leave her for some part of the day, some part of the twenty-four hours. It had just been unfortunate that she had fallen at that moment.

'Let's have some coffee now he's gone,' suggested Lady Bellamy, and Agnes made her way out of the bedroom. She was half-way down the stairs when she paused. As the doctor left, banging the door behind him, Herbert Bellamy had joined his brother in the hall.

'What did he say?' he asked.

'Oh, she'll be OK.' Edmund's manner was indifferent.

'OK, yes, but that was quite a fall. You are a cold bugger, Edmund.'

Carmichael stayed where she was in the bend of the stairs. She didn't want to let them know she'd heard this; she didn't want to intrude.

'You banged into her, you were so pissed. You drink too much, Ed.'

'That's my business, Herbert.' Edmund pushed past Herbert and went towards the kitchen to where his office was; Carmichael heard him slam the door. Herbert went back into the sitting-room and that door slammed, too. Agnes continued on her way downstairs.

The house and visitors all seemed at odds to Agnes. After the accident the brothers were both cool towards each other. Nigel and Alison disappeared directly after meals.

Next day Alison went off in her car to Leicester and came back looking upset and dejected. Nigel, too. The one person who seemed unaffected by the general temperature was Doris, who came upstairs to visit Gladys Bellamy and chattered away, though she had little to talk about other than clothes, make-up and television soaps. Gladys Bellamy was polite to her, but soon became tired and asked Doris to excuse her.

Madge Hillier was a most welcome visitor the next day in spite of the dogs. She had brought both of them this time; first they visited Maud in the kitchen then they came upstairs and jumped on the bed, luckily not near enough to hurt Lady Bellamy, who adored them.

Agnes was pleased to see Madge Hillier and stayed and drank coffee with them at their request. 'No, don't go, Agnes, unless you want to,' Gladys Bellamy had said. Agnes didn't want to. She stayed and listened to Madge's chatter about her bridge parties, her garden and the uselessness of her hairdresser.

'Look at it, Gladys.' She pulled off her tweed hat and pushed the curly hair back from her forehead. Agnes had to admit that no one would have guessed she had been near a hairdresser, but there was something attractive about the wild curls that tumbled around her head.

Madge spoke, too, of the Hunt. Her husband had been there and she told Lady Bellamy that there had been no kill. This made Agnes remember again the flash of ginger fur going across the field to freedom – temporarily perhaps, but at least with another chance.

Sitting there with the two women and the dogs, one on his back, the other drooped over the end of the bed, eyes closed, snoring slightly, Carmichael felt at ease, unthreatened. She was sorry Lady Bellamy's progress was halted, but comforted by the thought that she would be needed a little longer and for the moment would not have to move on to another place.

11

'Herbert said we ought to start at ten thirty and to be here and ready and I'm ready and he's not here and it's a quarter to eleven. He's still in there talking to Edmund.'

Doris Bellamy was seated in the hall as Agnes came down the stairs, two suitcases at her feet.

Carmichael smiled politely. 'Do you drive, Mrs Bellamy?' she asked.

'Yes, but Herbert won't let me. He won't let me touch the Jag. I don't like driving it anyway.' She pouted, got out a compact from her handbag and examined her lips. She pressed them once or twice, then got out the lipstick and drew a red line along the bottom lip and pressed them again to distribute the colour.

'Hope Gladys gets on all right. Looks like you'll have another patient soon – Alison.'

The remark stopped Agnes in her tracks on her way to the kitchen. 'Alison, why? Is she ill?'

'Oh no, not ill – but I've heard her being as sick as a dog for a couple of mornings. I reckon she's in the club.'

'Oh, I'm sure that's not true.' Agnes was startled.

At that moment the two men came out of the office.

'I won't forget this, Herbert – but it's only a loan,' Edmund was saying, his hand on his brother's shoulder.

'Oh yes, you will. You always say that – you always say it's only a loan.' Herbert grinned, then he joined his wife. 'Why didn't you get the cases put in the Jag, for God's sake. It's outside.'

Doris tossed her head. 'That's a man's job,' she said.

'Well, goodbye, Mrs Bellamy – Mr Bellamy.' Carmichael was about to withdraw to the kitchen.

'Mark my words,' Doris said and pointed a stubby, ringed finger at Agnes as she followed Herbert and the cases down the steps and got into the car.

As the Jaguar drew away another car pulled up – Dr Marvin.

'Morning, morning,' he greeted Carmichael and Edmund heartily. 'Patient all right, Sister?' He took the stairs two at a time. 'Who said you could get up?' he asked as he entered Lady Bellamy's room to find her up and dressed.

'You did. You said two days and I rested two days.' Lady Bellamy got up to greet him. She had discarded her tripod and was using a stick.

'Well, I suppose that's all right if your orthopod said so,' said her GP, and plumped himself down next to her. 'Sit down, sit down, let me take your pulse then.' He took hold of Lady Bellamy's thin wrist and looked at his watch. Lady Bellamy started to speak and he shush-shushed her, then dropped her wrist, nodded and said, 'Nice and steady then.' He looked up at Carmichael. 'Keep her as quiet as you can, though from what I know of her that'll take some doing. Sir Edmund all right?'

'As far as I know,' said Lady Bellamy, rather frostily. 'You're his doctor, not me.' There was obviously an understanding between the two of them, and when he rose to go Lady Bellamy smiled quite warmly at him. 'Thanks for coming, Dr Marvin – no need for it really. Still, you know what these nurses are!'

'I do, I do. Don't know what we'd do without them,' said the doctor. He grinned at Carmichael and made for the door and they heard him running nimbly down the stairs.

'Wish I could do the stairs like that,' said Lady Bellamy. 'Not that I could before I broke my hip.' She looked at Carmichael shrewdly. 'What are you thinking about? You look a bit preoccupied,' she said.

'Me? Oh, I was just thinking about something else,' said Carmichael; and she was – she was thinking of Alison and of Doris Bellamy's remark.

After another fairly quiet day Lady Bellamy seemed to have completely recovered from the shock and bruising of her fall. Indeed, Carmichael suspected that the enforced rest had improved rather than impaired the mobility of her fractured hip.

The following morning Lady Bellamy decided to telephone her friend Madge Hillier to suggest that, if it were convenient, Agnes and she would like to motor over for coffee that morning. The invitation was repeated with enthusiasm and they set out in the Rolls driven by Basil. The weather was cold but sunny, with no clouds and no hint of a repeated snowfall. Lady Bellamy was obviously pleased to be out and about socializing again.

'Mind your stockings when you get there with those damn dogs, and there's another now, a little one, who is apt to nip you – in play, Madge says, but I'm not so sure.' She laughed reassuringly.

Basil had greeted his mistress with obvious pleasure. 'How are you, m'lady? I heard you had a little accident.' Without waiting for a reply he added, 'Nice to see you up and about again.'

Agnes, alerted – perhaps over-alerted – by Doris Bellamy's remark, had now had time to observe Alison. The girl looked a little pale and was perhaps quieter than usual, but otherwise there was little difference in her manner and Agnes had almost come to the conclusion that Doris was dramatizing the situation. This morning, however, she had been made to think otherwise. Alison had appeared at breakfast red-eyed and had seemed to Agnes to be almost nauseated by the sight of the bacon and eggs on the hot plate, but she had drunk a cup of hot, black coffee thirstily, refusing even a piece of dry toast. She did not look at either Agnes or her grandfather – indeed, she hardly responded to their 'Good mornings'. Having finished her coffee, she pushed back her chair almost clumsily and hastily left the room.

Agnes wondered in whom the girl would confide if she was pregnant. Her grandmother? Alison, of course, could have no conception of what such news would mean to Gladys – but she would know that such a union would be a disappointment to her. That consideration alone might hold her back. Her grandfather she certainly would not confide in. She could expect no sympathy from that quarter, Carmichael was sure. Had she told Nigel, or not?

As she gave her mind to these thoughts and sat silently by Lady Bellamy the Rolls drew up to the Hillier house. The front door was wide open in spite of the cold weather and a tall, good-looking, white-haired man came down the steps to help Lady Bellamy out of the car.

'Gladys. How nice to see you.' He kissed her cheek. 'Morning, Basil.'

The chauffeur touched his cap. 'Morning, sir' he answered.

Lady Bellamy introduced Carmichael. 'Bernard, this is my

invaluable nurse, Agnes Carmichael – Agnes, Major Bernard Hillier.' Agnes liked his firm handshake and welcoming smile.

Madge met them at the door, greeting them both warmly, with her words almost drowned in a volley of barking. The two spaniels were equally welcoming and were accompanied by a rather ancient-looking Jack Russell, hound marked and slightly evil-looking of eye.

The hall was beautifully proportioned. A large stone fireplace occupied almost a third of one wall and a log fire burned with blue-topped flames. The rug in front of the fire was old and fraying and polka-dotted with small burn holes. The dogs, when quieted down, went back to this rug and sat there, looking like a Landseer painting.

As they made their slow progress across the hall, suiting their pace to Lady Bellamy, Agnes was able to look round and take in the picture the hall presented.

Opposite the fire was a large over-stuffed settee; the rose patterned cretonne cover was torn and slightly askew. A long, low table beside it was laden with copies of *Country Life* and *Horse and Hound*, a large old dog bone, a mutilated tennis ball and a truly beautiful Famille Rose bowl containing Spillers Shape dog biscuits, a packet of chocolate Good Boys and a woollen glove. A large bag of golf clubs leaned precariously against the door jamb and a Chippendale chair housed two duffle coats and a riding whip. More rugs were strewn about the floor, but most of them were wrinkled and frayed and Agnes had to take great care that Lady Bellamy negotiated them safely.

Madge Hillier conducted her visitor to a comfortable chair in the sitting-room and rang the old-fashioned bell beside another blazing log fire. Again Agnes had time to look around her. In this room, too, the pattern was repeated – comfortable untidiness and lovely furniture. Agnes thought of Lavinia and the neatness of Cat's Cradle, the beautifully polished furniture. How different people were, she thought, and how their characters affected their surroundings.

She had time to think and absorb the atmosphere as the two friends chatted about matters of which she knew nothing, but it did her good to see her patient's bright face listening to Madge Hillier. She was brought back from her thoughts by a remark made by Madge Hillier. Major Hillier had left the room.

'Yes, they were out a few days ago. I didn't ride. They lost the fox.'

Agnes hid her smile and saw again the streak of ginger crossing the field. 'Do you often catch the fox, Mrs Hillier?' she asked.

Madge shook her head. 'Not often, but the riding's good.'

The coffee was strong and hot and home-made biscuits were served with it. As they were drinking their coffee Major Hillier came back, drank a quick cup and dashed out again.

They stayed almost an hour, but before they went Major Hillier rejoined them.

'Drinks?' he suggested and poured generous measures of gin into four grapevine goblets, added tonic and produced, as if by magic, slices of lemon and ice. 'You're not driving.' He looked at Lady Bellamy. 'Doesn't Edmund get Basil to drive him in the evenings?'

There was a slight pause. 'No . . . He prefers . . .' Lady Bellamy stopped.

'He ought to watch it, Gladys,' Madge broke in. 'The other night – '

'Oh, come on, Madge, no need to go into that.' Bernard waved his glass in the air and looked a little reprovingly at his wife.

'Yes, there is, Bernard.' Gladys Bellamy's voice was slightly raised. 'Did you see him on the road? Was he . . .?'

'Well, a bit under the weather; weaving a bit; but obviously he got home safely.' Bernard was trying to play down what he had seen.

'He must ask Basil to take him. I don't know why he doesn't. Perhaps he goes to some club or other that he doesn't want Basil to know about.' Gladys Bellamy sounded a little worried.

'Well, no matter. It's all over now.' Bernard Hillier changed the subject. 'Fancy that snow in November. Unusual.' The conversation turned abruptly to other things.

On the whole it was an enjoyable and very successful visit, except for that tiny flash of disharmony when Edmund's name was mentioned.

They drove home under a darkening sky and the rain had just started as Basil turned into the drive.

Lunch was, as usual, rather a scrappy meal. Nigel, Edmund

and Alison were already in the dining-room when Agnes and Lady Bellamy entered.

'You didn't tell me you were taking the Rolls and Basil. I wanted him this morning.' Edmund had an empty plate in front of him and had seemingly finished eating. Hetty took away his plate and put a small dish of ice-cream in front of him. He waved it away.

'Cheese,' he said. A look passed between him and his wife and he added 'Please' rather reluctantly.

Lady Bellamy did not answer his remark – she chose, Agnes supposed, to ignore it. Hetty then served Lady Bellamy and herself with cold meat and hot vegetables, both of them refusing the offer of soup. Nigel, who had been eating heartily when they entered, pushed his empty plate away.

Sir Edmund turned to him. 'The lower field draininge is all to hell, Nigel. Go and look at it after lunch, will you?'

'Yes, sir, I will – and I must order grain.' He paused. 'We shall need an order for the horses, too.' He looked at Alison and smiled. 'We managed a ride this morning. I went over to Henley Bottom to look at the Gutteridge cottage. It needs a patching job on the thatch, sir.'

'Leave it. That thatcher charges the damn earth to do anything.'

'It's letting the water in, sir.' Nigel almost involuntarily looked at Lady Bellamy for support.

'Of course, Edmund, it can't be left. Get Fletcher to do it.'

Sir Edmund threw down his napkin and got up. 'Who runs this bloody estate, you or me?' he said harshly. Both Nigel and Alison looked down at their plates, but said nothing. It was then that Agnes noticed Alison had barely touched her lunch.

The mood of embarrassment swept round the table. Gladys Bellamy motioned to Hetty. 'Will you get me a bottle of mineral water, please, Hetty?'

'Yes, m'lady.' Hetty left the dining-room, casting a rather fearful glance at Sir Edmund.

'Edmund, we cannot leave work on the estate cottages undone. It has always been our pride that we looked after our tenants' well-being.'

Sir Edmund looked round to make sure Hetty had gone, then burst out, 'Bugger the tenants. They drain us of money – there's nothing for the normal luxuries of life.'

'Like horse-racing, whisky, the most expensive wines – not to speak of other things.' Lady Bellamy's face was tinged with pink, and Agnes noticed that the hand clutching the edge of the table gleamed white at the knuckles.

Edmund slumped down in his chair again, poured himself more wine and refused to answer these accusations. He muttered something inaudible except to himself.

Alison got up. 'If you will excuse me, I don't seem to have any appetite.'

Nigel looked up at her with a worried frown. 'Are you all right, Alison?' he asked.

'Yes, yes, thanks.' She placed her hand for a second on his shoulder and left the room, nearly banging into Hetty who was coming in with the mineral water.

'I think I'll go to my room for a rest, Agnes,' said Lady Bellamy, after she had sipped a little of the mineral water, which Agnes felt she had used only as an excuse to get the maid from the room while they argued.

They mounted the stairs and as they did so Agnes saw Alison disappearing into her room. Having settled her patient on the bed with a light angora rug over her and drawn the curtains, she left her and after some hesitation knocked politely on the door of Alison's room.

'Who is it?'

Carmichael opened the door slightly. Alison was sitting on the side of the bed. She looked dejected. She glanced at Agnes.

'Come in, Agnes.'

'Aren't you feeling well? I couldn't help noticing you had no lunch.'

Alison shook her head. 'I didn't feel like any.'

'Or beakfast,' Agnes continued.

'Are you spying on me – watching me?' She got up and walked across the room, sat down in front of the mirror and peered at her face.

'You know I'm not.' Agnes followed her and put her hand on her shoulder rather as she, Alison, had touched Nigel. The effect was instant. Alison covered her face with her hands and began to cry.

'You can guess, can't you? You're a nurse. I'm pregnant,' she said. 'And I feel awful in the mornings – awful.'

'Are you sure? If you feel awful just in the mornings, could it be something else?' she asked.

'No . . . Yes . . . Oh, I don't know . . . It's . . . Well, you do feel awful in the mornings, don't you? And I know I'm going to have a baby. It's so lonely not being able to tell anyone, not even Nigel.' Agnes waited. 'I can't tell him, he might hate the idea of a baby. After all, he's got no money, no real home.'

'What about your grandmother?'

Alison stood up and went to the window and looked out on the rain-washed garden. She traced a raindrop down the window with her finger and then took a tissue from her pocket and blew her nose.

'Can't tell Granny. She wants me to marry a belted earl, no less. She loves Nettlestone, really cares for the estate – so does Nigel, but he's got no money to bring to it.'

'Do you love Nigel?' Agnes asked the question almost timidly. After all, Alison might resent such a question. But she needn't have worried – Alison's face lit up and her eyes shone through the tears.

'Oh, I do, Agnes. I want to marry him, to have his baby – of course I do. I'm going to tell him this evening.'

Agnes felt an appalling sense of responsibility, and yet she knew that her own feeling was wholly to support the girl, notwithstanding that she was pregnant by her half-brother. She watched her as she stood by the window: she did look lonely, and the streaming rain on the window pane made the picture even more poignant. She made a decision.

'I'll talk to your grandmother for you,' she said, 'if you'd like me to.'

Alison turned round. 'Would you? That would be great,' she said. 'I can't.'

'Provided you talk to Nigel tonight.' Agnes Carmichael's voice was firm.

Alison came away from the window and put her arms round Carmichael. 'Thank you. You're a dear. I was getting desperate. Will Nigel be pleased or horrified, do you think?' She stood back a little and looked closely at Agnes.

'I think you two are so in love he cannot be anything but pleased.'

Alison smiled for the first time since Agnes had entered the room.

Agnes came out of the girl's room and went to her own. What had she taken on, she wondered? Still, she could only try. She thought of Alison, loving Nigel and wanting the baby. What if she learned the truth, was told that the father of the baby was her brother? Surely it was too much to bear; too much to ask a young girl to cope with.

12

Agnes felt unable to settle down to read or to look at the television that Lady Bellamy had insisted she had in her room. She looked at her watch: twenty to three. She decided to go out. She shrugged on her coat and tied a headscarf under her chin, looked in her mirror, touched her lips with lipstick, picked up her handbag and made her way downstairs.

Sir Edmund was crossing the hall just as she reached the bottom of the stairs.

'Are you going to the village, Sister Carmichael?' he asked.

'Yes, I am. I feel like a walk.' Carmichael paused and he put his hand into his breast pocket, drew out his wallet and took out a five-pound note. 'Would you get me two packets of Rennies – damned heartburn. They sell them at the general store.'

Carmichael took the note. 'Certainly, Sir Edmund.' It crossed her mind as she did so that if he drank a little less he might suffer a little less heartburn.

'I'll be back in an hour,' she said. 'Lady Bellamy is resting.'

He nodded, but without interest, and turned into his office.

It was pleasant walking along the lane to the village and Agnes was glad to be, for the moment, away from the problems of the household in which she was working. She tried, however, to keep her mind off her own anxieties, which were complicated enough. Where would she live? She had ample money to buy a house anywhere, but wherever it might be she would be alone – again.

She felt unable to visualize herself starting up a new home, a new house, new acquaintances. Making friends was, she knew, not one of her major accomplishments. When she reached the village she called in at the little general store and got Sir Edmund's Rennies without trouble from the pleasant, short, fat little lady behind the counter.

'How is Lady Bellamy?' she asked, rather to Agnes' surprise.

'Oh, making good progress, thank you.'

The woman smiled. 'Oh, I know you're her nurse. Hetty works at the Manor, she's my niece. Such a good girl – they think a lot of her.'

Carmichael could only smile again and nod. The close-knit village atmosphere rather pleased her. As she left the shop she thought, Shall I look for another cottage, or a house near a river again? No, her thoughts shied away from that. A town house, perhaps? It was a strange feeling to be without background, without an anchor, without roots – strange, but not new.

She walked on, not wishing to return straight away. She reached the end of the lane and turned right on to the Leicester road. It was not as pleasant, but she felt the need for exercise. She passed a stationary car at the side of the road. The man in the car called out: 'Excuse me, am I near the turning to Penny Stratton?'

Carmichael turned round and went back.

'Sister Carmichael, isn't it?'

Agnes did not for the moment recognize the face in the car window. The man opened the door and scrambled out of the car.

'Sister, it's Dr Patel. You remember – Casualty, Hemmington General.' He was quite excited, smiling his wide, white-toothed smile.

'Dr Patel!' Agnes felt genuinely pleased to see him. When she had worked with him in Casualty she had always liked him. 'What are you doing in this part of the world?'

'I have a job – Casualty Consultant, at least one of them, at the local hospital. Congratulations, eh?'

'Congratulations indeed, Dr Patel.' Carmichael was really pleased for him. He had been a good and willing Casualty Officer, she remembered.

'I'm down here looking for a house to bring my wife and baby. There are to be new bungalows to be built near here, they say.'

Agnes Carmichael nodded. 'That's right. Quite a lot of them, I believe,' she said.

He smiled. 'I have to find somewhere – somewhere with a big mortgage, eh?' He laughed again.

'You won't have much difficulty getting a mortgage as Casualty Consultant, I should have thought,' Carmichael said, and moved closer to the car as other traffic went by.

'Is Penny Stratton Lane near here?' he asked.

Carmichael nodded again. 'If you like, I'll come back with you in the car,' she said, 'and show you where the field is where the bungalows are being built. I don't know how many they've started; they may have finished some.'

Patel was delighted. He rushed round and opened the passenger door for her. Agnes got in and sat beside him. As she glanced sideways she noticed that he looked a little older and there was a tinge of grey in his black hair. She couldn't believe it – how long was it? So much had happened since then, since Casualty days at Hemmington General. The collapse of the hospital. Her mind leapt back over the top of Lavinia and Brian and Cat's Cradle to those days, but Patel was very much thinking of the present and she could not blame him for that.

As they drove the short way back and turned down the lane she indicated, he chatted away about his new baby, his beautiful wife, how happy he was to come to Leicester. At last they reached the site of the bungalows and Carmichael pointed it out to him. He got out of the car and looked around, but there was little to see except a field. The bungalows were mostly being built on the far side, away from the road.

'It's a nice part of the world,' Carmichael contributed and he nodded but did not seem impressed – perhaps he preferred the town, she thought. He got back into the car.

'Can I take you back to where you are?' he asked.

Carmichael shook her head. 'No, thank you. You can turn round here. Where are you staying at the moment?' she asked.

'In a room at the hospital. Not much, but good enough.' He smiled his familiar smile again, showing his white teeth. 'Perhaps you would do me the honour of having dinner with me one night – could that be?'

Carmichael was pleased at the invitation. He brought back happy memories, as well as sad ones. 'I'd like that very much; but wait, I'll give you my telephone number.' She took a small notebook from her handbag, tore out a page and scribbled on it the telephone number of Nettlestone Manor. 'I'm private nursing now.' She said it almost hesitantly.

'Oh yes, I'd heard you'd retired. Too young.' He smiled. He was always smiling, Patel, no matter how harassed he was, she remembered. She got out of the car, saying as she did so, 'I look forward to hearing from you, Dr – or is it Mr Patel now?'

He looked rather shy. 'Mr. I have the FRCS now.'

'Congratulations again, then,' she said and took her leave of him. She turned and watched as he turned the car quite deftly and drove away up the lane. It had been a nice encounter and she hoped he would ring her. She was sure she could manage one night off to have dinner with him; it would be pleasant. She started to walk home with raised spirits. She was glad she had come out this afternoon, it was a wonderful coincidence meeting Dr – Mr Patel, she corrected herself. He must have done well, he deserved it.

On her way back she went into the village church. Its quiet white-washed interior was soothing. Carmichael walked round slowly. None of the Bellamys seemed to go to church, she thought. This was unusual. She presumed they were the leading family in the village and she would have thought . . . but there was no knowing and she herself had little leaning towards religion. She made her way up and looked thoughtfully at the altar, the Crucifix, the polished brass and candlesticks, the lectern – that, too, polished bright. Someone did that, someone from the village, she expected. There was probably a busy village life, but the Bellamys seemed to take no part in it, except perhaps the local pub, where she believed Sir Edmund went pretty frequently. As she left the church she turned for one more look down the little aisle to the altar and she remembered the christening of Nigel Denton's baby, the warmth, the family. Again, as always when she remembered, a feeling of loneliness crept over her; suddenly the church felt cold and she walked quickly out of the door and into the November sunlight, and was glad of it.

As she walked along she thought of dining with Mr Patel. It would be nice to talk of the hospital where she had been regarded as a heroine, where there had been no hint of the other horrors that would catch up with her. She remembered Patel's good temper when he was called at any time to Casualty and she hoped he would have time and remember to get in touch with her.

As she drew near the entrance of the drive to Nettlestone Manor a figure emerged – Madge Hillier, her three dogs frolicking round her.

'Oh, hello there, Agnes,' she said, beaming as usual. The larger of the spaniels rushed up to greet Agnes. 'Come away, you fool dog,' called Madge. 'I've taken some magazines in for Gladys, and a bag of apples.'

Agnes stroked the dog's head and shook his proffered paw.

'Gladys was asleep. I gave the apples to Maud and left the magazines on the hall table. Perhaps you will see they get to her.'

'Of course I will, and I'm sure she'd want to thank you.' Agnes' smile was warm. Madge made you feel that way and that the country was a perfect place to be and that the world was good. Loneliness, she was sure, never cast its shadow over Madge. She strode away, calling to the dogs, who bounded after her.

Carmichael went upstairs, took off her outdoor things, slipped into her white coat and went downstairs. Sir Edmund was dozing in front of the sitting-room fire. Agnes gave him the Rennies and his change.

'Oh yes, thanks.' He took them from her, threw the two packets down beside him and relaxed again into his doze. The fire crackled pleasantly.

Agnes made for the kitchen to collect the tea tray to take up to Lady Bellamy's room. She was not looking forward to the task she had taken on; to tell her patient that her granddaughter was pregnant was hard enough, but – She tossed the thought away for a moment and greeted Maud and Hetty, who were seated at the kitchen table drinking tea themselves.

'Lady Bellamy's tray – right. Shall I put on a cup for you, Sister?' Maud got up from her seat.

'Please.' Agnes turned to Hetty. 'I met your aunt at the village store, Hetty,' she said.

The girl blushed and giggled. 'Oh, Aunt Rose.'

'She thinks a lot of you. Very proud of her niece.'

The cook put two pieces of freshly made sponge cake on the tray she was preparing.

'Thank you, Maud. I hope my belt will go on fitting me,'

Agnes said and put her fingers through the navy belt round her slim waist.

'Oh, you're not the fat kind,' answered Maud. 'I expect your mother was thin and probably your father too, weren't they? Mine were as fat as butter balls, and look at me.' She laughed and smoothed her hand over her stout abdomen. Agnes did not answer and Maud seemed not to notice.

Hetty got up to take the tray, but Agnes waved her away. 'I'll take it,' she said. 'You finish your tea.'

Maud called to her as she went through the door. 'Roast chicken and all the trimmings for dinner tonight, Sister Carmichael.'

'Good, I'll look forward to that. I know it will be delicious.'

As Agnes carried the tray across the hall and up the stairs to Lady Bellamy's room she wished again that she had not taken on this task. But then the picture slipped into her mind of Alison standing by the rain-swept window in her room, looking so young, so vulnerable, with a baby growing inside her which by law should not be coming to life – and that baby as vulnerable and defenceless as its mother and its father, both completely unknowing. Other than conceiving a child before they were married, they had done nothing wrong at all.

Agnes came to her decision as to what she was going to say as she pushed open the door of her patient's room. She knew what she would advise – right or wrong – and she would stand by it. Whether she could influence Lady Bellamy to take the same view was another matter.

She placed the tea tray on the usual table and drew back the curtains. She decided she wasn't going to mention the matter till they were both seated comfortably drinking their tea – then would be soon enough.

Lady Bellamy yawned. 'I had such a nice dream,' she said. 'What time is it, Agnes?'

'Four thirty. Tea-time,' she answered and went over and pulled the woolly tea cosy more closely round the teapot before helping Lady Bellamy from the bed to the armchair.

Agnes poured the tea and passed a slice of sponge cake to her patient. She took a piece herself. 'What a good cook you've got, Lady Bellamy,' she said as she bit into the cake.

Gladys Bellamy nodded. 'She is good, we're lucky to have

91

her. By the way, I noticed that Alison ate no lunch. I hope the silly girl is not slimming.'

Agnes seized the opportunity. 'I don't think it's that, Lady Bellamy. I think – well, I know – it's rather more serious.'

Gladys Bellamy paused with the teacup half-way to her lips. 'Why, she's not ill, is she?'

'No, she's not ill.' Agnes stopped. 'Not ill, and she asked me to tell you, to talk to you. She's so afraid that what I'm going to tell you will hurt you. She's going to have a baby!'

Lady Bellamy put her cup down very carefully in the saucer. 'A baby! Whose is it? Nigel's?'

Agnes lowered her head – she could not look at Lady Bellamy at that moment – and when she finally looked up she saw that what little colour there had been in her patient's face had drained away.

'Oh no! Not that. For God's sake, not that.' She leaned back in her chair and closed her eyes. 'It's my fault, Agnes. When his mother died in Italy we should have left him there. Edmund would have; it was my ill-conceived compassion. When his mother was killed . . .' She stopped speaking for a moment. 'That's when Nigel came here. If only he'd never been conceived.'

Agnes waited until Gladys Bellamy was more composed. 'Alison loves him very much.'

'He's her brother. Anyway, they're too closely related to have children.' She covered her face with her hands. 'What shall I do, Agnes? What shall I do?'

'Do you really want my advice, Lady Bellamy?' Agnes' tone made Gladys Bellamy take her hands from her face and look directly at her.

'Yes, I do. I'd value it. I feel unable to cope. I don't know what I'll say to her, or to the boy.'

'My advice is – nothing. Of course she will expect you to be shocked by the mere fact that she is pregnant. She feels that you expected her to marry a belted earl – that's what she said – and will be disappointed it's Nigel. But, as for the rest, my advice is, don't tell them. What good will it do? I feel they truly love each other, and that's rare enough.' As she said this she felt as if Brian was there, standing beside her. She almost saw him hold out his hand, a diamond flashing in the light. The impression was so strong that she had to get up and go over to the window; she stood and gazed into the black evening. After a moment she turned again to her patient.

'Who else knows, Lady Bellamy, about their relationship?'

'No one; only Edmund.'

Agnes came back to her chair. 'Do you think he would tell them?' she asked.

'I don't think so, not unless he was . . . I think he's ashamed of it now.' Agnes knew what she had been going to say. He drank too much. Would he let it out? That was a risk, undoubtedly.

She took Lady Bellamy's hand in hers. 'Look, Lady Bellamy, there are risks. Sir Edmund might tell. The baby might be affected. But, please God, none of this might happen.'

Gladys Bellamy's eyes were fixed on her. 'Yes, it's a risk, but if Nigel and Alison love each other . . . I know they love this place . . . probably I couldn't leave it in better hands than theirs. Yes, I agree with you. I'll say nothing.'

Both women sat quietly for some minutes. They heard someone coming up the stairs, a tap on the door – it was Hetty.

'May I have the tea tray, m'lady?' she said.

13

The delicious smell of roasting chicken filled the kitchen. Hetty pushed the door open with her backside and the tray of tea things tipped at a slight angle as she turned round. A cup rattled in the saucer, then fell on its side. Maud rushed forward and righted it.

'For goodness' sake, Hetty! That's a favourite teaset of the family's.'

Hetty put the tray down on the table, picked up the cup and examined it.

'It's all right, no damage,' she said and took the crockery over to the sink.

Maud was just putting the finishing touches to a trifle and the smell of sherry mingled with the smell of chicken. A comfortable, sizzling sound came from the direction of the oven. Maud went over to the stove and opened the door; the smell was

93

stronger and mouth-watering. She drew out first one chicken then the second and basted them with a large basting spoon. Both chickens were already brown and the bacon, draped over their breasts, was beginning to crisp. She pushed back the oven shelf and carefully closed the door. Then she crossed the kitchen, picked up the house phone and dialled.

'Basil, you in to dinner? It's chicken, ready in an hour. OK?'

She put the telephone back on its wall cradle, then went on putting glacé cherries on the trifle.

Carmichael appeared in the doorway. 'Hetty, did I leave a little saccharin box on the tea tray?' she asked.

Hetty looked, then handed her a small metal container. 'I was going to bring it up to you miss – Sister,' she said. 'Is her ladyship OK? I thought she looked a bit pale when I got the tray. I expect her hip is painful.'

Maud looked up. 'Yes, she's doing quite well, isn't she? But she tires easily, I've noticed that. It's a nasty injury, a broken hip, especially in a lady of her age.' Maud picked up the trifle and carried it across to a side table.

Hetty was still looking at Carmichael, waiting, Agnes felt, for an answer, and she thought how quickly servants were to sense a change in atmosphere. Anyway, they would all know soon enough.

As Agnes left the kitchen she was wondering when Alison would tell Nigel and when Lady Bellamy would talk to Alison – tell her she knew. Then what would happen between Lady Bellamy and her husband? She thought somehow it would not yet get into motion, the domino effect she had started, not tonight – although if Gladys Bellamy had decided that the relationship between the two young people would be better kept secret, would she change her mind? Agnes thought not; but she probably would need time to mull it over, to think of her husband's reaction when he was told.

Apparently Agnes was right. Obviously nothing was communicated that night. Dinner passed off without incident – an excellent meal, too. Perhaps, Carmichael thought with a wry smile, it was because Alison had passed on some of the responsibility for telling her grandmother to Agnes. Alison had looked at her once or twice as if she would have liked some sign from Agnes that she had already done so, but Carmichael would not rise. She would wait, she decided, to see if and when Alison kept her side of the bargain and broke it to Nigel that he was going to be a father.

Agnes enjoyed the food, too. She was aware that part of her relished the tangle of other people's relationships – and the tangle she was watching now, which was taking place all around her, was indeed a mesh of knots and snags. In her mind she stood back a little and looked at it all. The bombshell would, she supposed, explode tomorrow – or rather, to stick to her metaphor, the dominoes would all tumble one after the other. She was very curious to know how Sir Edmund would take it; it would be interesting.

As Lady Bellamy made her slow way from the dining-room to the sitting-room with Agnes by her side, the telephone rang. Hetty answered it, and her 'Just a moment please' could be heard as Agnes put a cushion behind her patient's back and settled her footstool so that she could rest her leg.

Hetty came into the sitting-room. 'Sister Carmichael, the telephone,' she said. 'A Mr Patel to speak to you.'

'Thank you, Hetty. Will you excuse me, Lady Bellamy?' She walked out and into the hall rather than use the cordless telephone. As she left the room she heard Alison say, 'Aha, a boy friend at last. I knew it.'

Agnes smiled; she was glad that Alison was in better spirits. What it was to be young and resilient. She picked up the telephone.

'Hallo, Mr Patel.' She felt genuine pleasure at hearing his voice.

Nigel crossed the sitting-room and closed the door tactfully; considerate, Agnes thought, but not really necessary and she continued her conversation, fixing a date to dine with him in Leicester, but telling him that if for any reason she could not leave her patient she would let him know. Lady Bellamy did not always stay up to dinner and Carmichael hoped a 'meal in bed' night would coincide with her dinner date. Indeed, knowing Lady Bellamy's kindness, she felt certain the arrangement could be made.

She put the telephone down and went back into the sitting-room. The conversation stopped and four pairs of eyes looked at her, enquiringly, smilingly. She shook her head.

'No, alas, not a boy friend. Just an old doctor friend.' Alison looked a little embarrassed, realizing Carmichael had heard the remark.

'Hush my mouth,' she said and giggled slightly.

The rest of the evening passed off without incident, except for Alison and Nigel having a small argument about a current pop star which ended in their going upstairs to Alison's room to play the record they were talking about.

Next morning Nigel and Alison sat in the Land Rover at the far end of the top field – aptly named, for it gave them a slantwise, downward view of the Manor, the stables and the little cottages behind them. This sideways view cut out the ugly white garage doors. The sun flooded the grey stone of the Manor. The lawns and hedges round it were lush green; the mild winter – only once interrupted by two cold days and that freakish fall of snow – had kept the grass of the meadows growing. Friesians grazed in the field nearest them. It was so quiet here they could hear the cattle pulling the grass. One looked up at them with mild brown eyes and watched as Nigel and Alison kissed.

Nigel smiled at her, put his hand on her hair and stroked back the wisps that were blowing round her face. Then he turned and gazed out on the estate.

'I love this place, Alison,' he said. 'I hope I can work here for ever – not very ambitious, is it? But to be where you're happy and surrounded by things you love, that seems to me to be important.'

Alison took his hand and kissed it. He looked down to the left where already the developers were stripping away the turf ready for more houses. His eyes clouded. 'I can hide it eventually, if I'm here long enough. I already have trees planted to screen it.' He sighed, then turned to Alison again. 'Do you think I'm stupid to care so much for a place?' He drew her to him. 'I love you, you're part of it all – part of the beauty of it all.' He kissed her lips and she responded, then drew a little away from him, her eyes troubled.

'What is it, darling? What's the matter?'

Alison hardly dared to speak, hardly dared tell him. She had tried to tell him last night, but couldn't. On his expression as she told him she felt the whole happiness of the rest of her life relied. Her eyes fixed on his face, she said, 'I'm going to have a baby, Nigel.'

He bent nearer, his face alight. 'Oh Alison, how wonderful!' Then he saw the serious look on her face. He dropped his arms that were about to clasp her. 'Aren't you . . .? Don't you . . .? Aren't you glad?'

'Yes, of course I'm glad. I'm thrilled, delighted, but I was afraid you might think it – well, think it was a burden.'

Nigel looked at her as if he could hardly believe his ears. 'A burden! Our baby! How can you say that, Alison?'

'I hoped you'd be glad – and you are, aren't you? We can be married and live here. I love Nettlestone so much, too. It will be mine one day, Grandma told me. But I don't want anything to happen to her, not for years and years and years.'

'Mother left me some money. I don't know how she managed to save it, but she did. We could buy a cottage, or at least pay a deposit.' He stopped. 'What about Sir Edmund? I hope your grandfather won't throw me out when he knows.'

'If he does, he throws me out too.' Alison felt as if all her cares had disappeared, had flown out of the window of the Land Rover and were rushing away like clouds across the sky.

Nigel started the engine of the Land Rover and turned it round. 'Back to face the music,' he said firmly.

'Together,' Alison said, equally firmly.

14

Lady Bellamy was, Agnes realized, more shaken and upset by the news of Alison's pregnancy – and even more worried about the risks of such a pregnancy and the hidden relationship – than had at first been apparent. A sleepless night hadn't helped.

'Have a day's rest in bed, Lady Bellamy,' she insisted, after her patient had complained of feeling dizzy and out of breath.

Now, clad in her dressing gown and covered by a blanket, she lay on her bed. Agnes was on the telephone cancelling the hairdresser.

'I want to talk to Alison and Nigel, Agnes,' Gladys Bellamy insisted. 'Some time today, it must be.'

Agnes looked at her watch. 'I saw them drive out in the Land Rover. I expect Alison has been telling him about the baby. She hadn't done so, you know.'

Lady Bellamy nodded. 'I know, Agnes. I spent the whole night praying I'm doing the right thing in not telling them the truth about themselves.'

'I know how you must feel.' Agnes took her patient's hand.

'Oh, Agnes . . .'

'What is it?' Agnes was startled. Was there to be more against the union of these two young people?

'I don't think it could have been Edmund who fathered Nigel. He was impotent, with me anyway. It must have been . . .' Lady Bellamy seemed to be unable even to utter his name. '. . . my son-in-law. So you see, they are perhaps even more closely related . . .' She took a tissue from the box beside her and dabbed her eyes. 'Supposing the baby – you know – there's something wrong with it.' She closed her eyes and the tears ran down her cheeks. 'It will be my fault and they will have to live with it for the rest of their lives – after I'm dead and gone. A handicapped child . . . !'

Agnes Carmichael, now sitting by her patient's bed, holding her hand, was silent, trying to think of the right thing to say, trying to be wise in a situation she hardly knew how to handle at all. It was such difficult advice to give – almost impossible. But suddenly something clicked into place in her mind: what would I say if she were my grandchild, she thought?

'Lady Bellamy, I'm not saying this lightly. You say if there's anything wrong with their child they'll have to live with it for all their lives – but suppose you tell them they must never marry, the child must be aborted, they must live with that all their lives, too, but do it without each other. To lose someone you love – for ever – is so dreadful.'

Lady Bellamy looked at Agnes and the silence in the room was broken only by the quick ticking of the little clock beside the bed.

'I think I do believe you, Agnes. I think you know as much about loss – losing those you love – as I do, and perhaps . . .'

Agnes felt she was weighed down for the moment with the responsibility she had not sought. Perhaps she should have refused to give any opinion, but she looked at Lady Bellamy and realized she had taken some of the weight off her shoulders

– and she supposed that was what nurses were for, to relieve pain and anxiety. I've done that, she thought, at least.

'After lunch, after my rest, we'll have a talk, Alison, Nigel and – would you be here, Agnes? I feel stronger when you're around,' and she put her hand out and clasped Agnes' arm. 'Do you mind? Can you bear it?' she asked, half smiling.

'Of course I can,' Agnes reassured her.

Lady Bellamy looked at the little ticking clock. 'Twelve fifteen, Agnes. What about a G and T for both of us?'

Carmichael hesitated. She didn't want to encourage her patient to drink, but she felt . . .

'I'll go and get some ice,' she said and, as she ran down the stairs and made for the kitchen, she felt very much part of this troubled family – it was a nice feeling.

After lunch, which Agnes took with Lady Bellamy in her room, she settled her patient comfortably and suggested that she take a couple of hours off.

'I might run into Leicester for some shopping,' she said.

'Yes indeed. You need to get away for a breath of fresh air, Agnes.'

'Can I get you anything while I'm in town?' Carmichael asked. Lady Bellamy shook her head.

'I'll be back by four o'clock and then I can collect those two young ones and we can have tea together?' She looked at Lady Bellamy questioningly to see if she agreed with this arrangement.

'Yes – but I don't want Edmund to think it's a family conference, Agnes.' Lady Bellamy gave a little grimace.

Agnes agreed. 'Don't worry. He'll think they're just having tea up here with you. And now, if you have a little nap it will make up for last night.'

Carmichael needed petrol, an oil check and her tyre pressure tested. She decided to take the car to a large garage in Leicester where she had noticed the agency for Porsche blazoned over the garage roof.

She drove along, feeling the usual sense of freedom the car gave her; negotiating the heavy traffic on the way into Leicester took all her concentration. The city traffic, always congested, seemed worse this afternoon and she was quite glad to drive into the backwater and comparative peace of the Porsche garage.

There were several cars at the pumps and she had to wait for some time. When at last she drew forward the attendant gave the car, rather than Carmichael, a big smile.

'Pleased with her, miss?' He patted the car bonnet. Agnes got out of the car and handed him the petrol tank key.

'Yes, very pleased. Fill up, will you, and check the tyre pressure and the oil?'

As she was about to walk away to look into the garage shop window, showing all sorts of car accessories, another Porsche, a red one, drew up behind hers. A man got out; he looked first at Agnes' car then at her.

'Snap,' he said, his wide smile turning into a laugh.

'Same letter, too, sir.' The garage attendant, filling the tank of Carmichael's car, inclined his head first to one number plate, then to the other.

'Lovely cars, I think. Do you enjoy driving yours?' The man took a slim, gold case from his pocket, took out a cigarette and was about to light it when the attendant stopped him.

'Not here, sir, please,' he said.

The man shrugged apologetically. 'Stupid of me,' he said; he put the cigarette back in his case and dropped it into his pocket.

He looked at Carmichael again and there was approval in his eyes. He walked towards her car. 'Preferred your colour, but couldn't get it, wanted it quickly. Lots of red cars about, aren't there? Common colour!' Again he laughed. 'Do you live in Leicester?' he asked. Somehow there was no impertinence in his questioning. 'No, I thought not – wrong registration.'

Carmichael gave a slight smile. 'No, I'm just staying here.' She felt acutely aware of the man's presence – his maleness. He was a big man, five foot eleven or six foot, not fat but heavily built. His hair was silver, rather than white; he wore grey trousers and a blazer-type jacket. His clean-shaven face shone with health and amiability.

'I live here – well, just outside. The town is not attractive, is it? Used to be, though, when it was smaller, less widespread.'

The attendant moved to the red Porsche and started to fill up that tank.

Agnes half felt she should walk away and snub the man. Long ago she would have been consumed with shyness and apprehension, become stiff and prim. Not any more – she felt perfectly relaxed.

'I'm at Nettlestone Manor,' she said.

'Staying with the Bellamys?' he asked.

'You know them?'

'Ye-es. Tell Edmund you met Harry Dwyer if you want to, if you can remember it. We used to play golf together.'

Agnes didn't answer. She took the key from the attendant, who had finished filling her tank, tipped the one who had checked her tyres and oil, got into the car, drew out and continued on her way. The man, Harry Dwyer, raised his hand in farewell. Agnes waved back and felt herself smiling. She had surprised herself. Was that flirting, the thing she always said she could never do – the ability she had always envied in her nurses, in other women? Well, she would never see the man again. Still, good practice, she thought, and glanced in the mirror of her car as she waited at the traffic lights. She felt she looked good; Leicester air suited her. The lights turned green and she drove on to buy herself some shoes. After all, Leicester was famous for its shoes, she thought.

She tried in three shops to get the type of shoe she was looking for, successfully in the third, and was conscious as she came out of each shop of looking at the parked cars, just in case the red Porsche was there. As she drove home she found she was still watching for it. She would mention Harry Dwyer to Sir Edmund. After all, the two men had played golf together – so he had said; she wondered if Sir Edmund had kept up the friendship. It didn't appear so, by the man's remark. Still – she put her foot down on the accelerator and felt the usual pleasure as the car leapt forward.

When she arrived home she put the Porsche in Alison's garage. As she did so, the Rolls backed out of the other garage. Sir Edmund was in the passenger seat and Basil was driving. Sir Edmund looked at Carmichael as she pulled down the garage door.

'Going to rain?' he asked. 'Got a dentist's appointment; Basil doesn't like the car to get wet.' He gave a rare smile and the car turned and passed round the end of the house and away.

Agnes was glad he would be out for what Lady Bellamy had termed the 'family conference'.

She went into the house and up the stairs to get herself and her patient ready.

15

Nigel obviously found it stiflingly hot in Lady Bellamy's bed-room. Once or twice he ran his finger round his collar as if it felt too tight. Agnes could not make out whether it was nervousness or sheer heat. Lady Bellamy noticed it too.

'Do take your jacket off, Nigel. I know it's hot in here, my old bones don't notice it.'

He thankfully took off the jacket and laid it carefully across the arm of the chair in which he was sitting, revealing a white shirt.

'I can't say this hasn't been a shock to me, Alison – Nigel.' Lady Bellamy spoke quietly, looking from one to the other of the young people. 'I suspect you already know, Nigel, that Alison asked Agnes to tell me. You have decided, I believe, that you love each other and want to marry.' She glanced across at Agnes. 'I also know that this is quite a usual procedure these days. Whether I agree with this kind of procedure or not is beside the point. You are both old enough to make up your own minds – twenty-two and twenty-three – but I feel I must ask you, Nigel, what you intend to do now. What are your plans?'

Nigel got up and went across and sat on the arm of Alison's chair. He put his arm round her shoulders. Alison looked up at him and he bent his handsome head and kissed her on the lips. It was an artless gesture prompted, Agnes felt, by his Latin blood – no Englishman would have done that. Agnes felt a little stab of envy.

'I have a little money saved to put down on a cottage if we can find one in the village. If Sir Edmund decides I must leave when he knows, I must find other work, but I would be so sorry to leave the Manor. Still, if we must, we must.'

'Hardly the life Alison is used to. Her Arts degree will be of little use to her jobwise, with a baby to look after.' Lady Bellamy interrupted him.

He flushed and Alison clasped his hand. 'We don't mind how or where we live as long as we're together, Grandma,' she said.

'Grand sentiments, my love, and maybe true – but it will be a big change for you.'

Alison sprang up and went to her grandmother. 'Please, Gran, help us. We know how you feel, but we want to get married and live happily ever after.' Tears came to her eyes. 'This isn't a sudden thing, Grandma, I've loved Nigel ever since he came here. I know you hoped I'd marry Ted Thurston or Dickie Egremont. They're rich, but they're so stupid. Nigel loves Nettlestone, really loves it. He's proved that, hasn't he, by the way he's worked?'

Nigel came over and gently drew Alison away. 'Don't try and influence your grandmother, Alison, she must say what she thinks is best. We'll manage, whatever anyone says.'

They went back to the armchair and waited silently.

'Would you like me to leave you now, Lady Bellamy?' Agnes asked, but Gladys Bellamy shook her head at Carmichael and she settled back in her chair and listened.

The old lady was silent for a few minutes. She pleated and unpleated the fringe of the blanket covering her, then at last she looked up.

'Nigel, how would you like to rent Top Field Farm? As you know, Tom Halstead is leaving. You could manage the rent if you keep your job here, and I'll see to it that you do.'

Nigel's face flushed again. He looked at Alison, but didn't answer.

'Oh Gran . . .' Alison was about to say something.

'You, young lady,' continued Lady Bellamy, 'you will be a farmer's wife with a baby. No Maud to cook for you, no Hetty to wait on you.' The words did not sound harsh; she looked at them both with such love.

Suddenly she opened her arms and both young people went over to the bed and she clasped them to her. Her eyes that looked at Agnes over Nigel's shoulder were wide and troubled.

'We shall be so happy, Grandma,' said Alison.

Gladys Bellamy's eyes remained fixed on Carmichael. 'Please God everything will be all right for you,' she said.

'What about Sir Edmund?' Nigel asked.

'Wait a little – leave all that to me,' Gladys Bellamy said firmly. 'Time enough, nothing need be said yet.' She looked at Agnes. 'Where is Edmund, by the way?' Then she looked at Nigel.

103

'I don't know, Lady Bellamy,' he answered.

'I met him as I came in. He was going to the dentist,' Agnes answered and Lady Bellamy looked slightly relieved.

'I must catch the post. Thank you, Lady Bellamy,' Nigel said.

Alison kissed her grandmother and followed him out.

'They certainly are in love, there's no doubt about that.' Gladys Bellamy sighed.

'When do you think they will marry?' Carmichael asked.

'That's another problem. Ideally as soon as possible, but I've got to tell Edmund – reason with him. He's bound to . . . I've got to somehow ensure his silence regarding their relationship. I expect it can be done.' She suddenly looked very tired and leaned back on her pillows. 'I'll have my meal here, please, Agnes,' she said. 'I'd like to be alone.' Carmichael agreed. 'You dine with the family, and for goodness' sake warn Alison and Nigel to keep their love for each other hidden. Edmund must not suspect until I have told him.'

'How can you get him to co-operate?'

Lady Bellamy opened her eyes. There was a bitter expression on her face that Agnes had not seen before. 'There are ways – you can probably guess,' she said. Then suddenly, 'I'll rest till dinner-time.'

Agnes left the room, her opinion of Sir Edmund lower than ever. What a man to be married to, she thought as she made her way kitchenwards to tell Maud that Lady Bellamy wanted a light meal in her own room.

The atmosphere at dinner that evening was rather strained. Nigel and Alison avoided speaking or looking at one another more than was absolutely necessary. This careful avoidance would have been amusing if the reason behind their behaviour was not so serious. Luckily, Sir Edmund had overstepped his usual consumption of whisky; maybe, thought Agnes, because of pain after his dental appointment. For whatever reason, it made him oblivious to the conversation around him.

In the sitting-room after dinner Nigel sat on the settee beside Sir Edmund and attempted to talk about estate matters. Alison sat in the armchair on the opposite side of the fireplace.

'I hope your visit to the dentist wasn't too painful, Sir Edmund?' Agnes felt her remark was banal and stilted, but the after-dinner coffee was being drunk in almost complete silence.

'What? Oh, painful in a way. He wants to charge me £400 for capping a few teeth. Blasted robbers, these tooth men.'

Alison got up and turned on the news, which was again watched in silence except for a few explosions of rage from Sir Edmund when taxes or financial affairs or references to the City were mentioned.

After it was over, Nigel rose and said he wanted to write some letters and left the room. Just a quick, fleeting glance passed between the two lovers.

At twenty to ten Agnes went upstairs. She felt she had left Lady Bellamy long enough. As she mounted the stairs she remembered her date to dine with Mr Patel the following evening. She wondered if her patient would be well enough to have her dinner downstairs or if she would decide again to have it in her room. As she helped Lady Bellamy to get settled for the night she noticed how pale and tired she looked, and decided that anyway tonight was no time to ask her.

When at last she switched the bedside light off and was about to leave the room, Gladys Bellamy held out her hand, took Carmichael's in hers and pressed it.

'Thank you, Agnes, for everything,' she said.

Carmichael smiled and returned the pressure, then said softly, 'Good-night, sleep well,' and went quietly along to her own room.

She, too, felt tired and drained. It had been quite a day for all three of them.

After she'd had a bath and got into her nightdress and dressing gown she suddenly felt restless and wide awake. She wondered whether she should creep downstairs and make herself some Ovaltine, then she decided against it – she had no wish to encounter Sir Edmund or, for that matter, anyone else.

She put out the light, pulled back the curtains and stood by the window. It was a clear, frosty night; the stars pierced the blackness of the sky. Only one light was visible, on the top of the rise to the right of the house. Top Field Farm, she understood, was somewhere about there; perhaps where the light was was where Nigel and Alison were to make their first home. Farm life – Nigel was used to working around a farm, but Alison? She wondered, as Lady Bellamy had pointed out, how a cosseted young woman, used to being waited on by servants, her meals prepared, would stand up to being a mother with its attendant anxieties and broken nights, as well as being a farmer's wife.

Agnes shivered. The room was warm, but by the window it was quite cold. Just before she turned away the light went out and only the stars remained.

As she got into bed and thankfully clasped her hot water bottle, she decided that when she was off duty one day she would either drive or walk up to Top Field Farm; it would be interesting to see it.

As she lay in the dark, her thoughts still occupied with the young people, she suddenly felt irritated by her involvement. What were they to her? Once she left and went back to London, how many times would they think of her? A Christmas card, perhaps? But if she pushed the Bellamys and their problems and personalities out of her life, out of her thoughts, what would come flooding in to fill the vacuum? No. She cast around for something else to occupy her thoughts. Strangely enough, the space, when she succeeded in making it, was filled not by her own past tragedies but by a tall, silver-haired man beside a red Porsche. She turned on her side. Why think of him? she thought – ridiculous; but in spite of that, the remembrance of the approving glance he had given her stayed behind her closed eyes, and with that strangely persistent image she drifted off to sleep.

16

'Of course, Madge, I'd love to. It must be two years since I've seen her. Yes, do come.' Gladys Bellamy put the telephone down and turned a pleased face to Agnes.

'There. I'm glad I decided to get up and dress.'

Carmichael watched her walk across the room using two sticks. Yesterday, she thought, may have stimulated her into action. When she had entered the room earlier on this morning her patient had greeted her by saying, 'I've got to make more effort – the least thing and I stay in bed. I need a cattle prod.'

The hairdresser was due at eleven o'clock. 'Thank goodness I shall look decent, my hair is a mess.' She ran her fingers through it. 'What time is it?'

As if in answer the hairdresser put her head round the bedroom door. 'Eleven o'clock on the dot, Lady Bellamy, and here I am. '

The hairdresser was a pleasant, cheerful girl, whose own hair was hardly an advertisement for her work. It was blond and crunched and stuck out from her head in the fashionable 'spring curls', which fell forward into her eyes as she worked. She and Lady Bellamy went through into the bathroom, the girl carrying a large bag and a case which Agnes guessed contained a hairdryer.

'Madge Hillier and her daughter from Paris are coming for drinks.' The information was given over Lady Bellamy's shoulder as she walked into the bathroom. 'Would you tell Maud to do something about tasty pieces, Agnes?'

'Yes, I will. Shall I let Sir Edmund know they are coming?'

'Yes, do – and Alison, please.'

Carmichael could just hear her patient's voice now over the sound of running water.

She went downstairs. In the kitchen Basil was drinking coffee, the usual pair of muddy wellingtons by the back door. Hetty was not there; she was, as Maud put it, 'doing the bedrooms' with the cleaning lady, Mrs May.

'Cup of coffee, Sister?' Maud asked.

'Thank you, though I really came to tell you about the Hilliers coming to drinks, and Lady Bellamy says can you do some tasty pieces.' She smiled as she said it, but Maud didn't.

'Oh Lord, I believe I'm out of cheese.' She went to the cupboard and took out a packet of Ritz crackers, then to the refrigerator. 'Oh no, I've got enough, so that's all right. What else, though?' She went back to the cupboard. 'Crisps? No, I haven't got any. I'll have to make some cheese straws.'

Hetty came into the kitchen. 'Any coffee, Maud?' she asked.

'No, we've got guests coming for drinks. Open that jar of olives and put some in that little glass dish. No, not that one, the fluted one.'

The back door opened and Harold kicked off his wellingtons, sidled up to the kitchen table and sat down. 'No cake?' he said, looking at Basil.

'No cake,' Basil replied.

Maud smacked down a mug of coffee in front of the boy.

Hetty helped herself from the percolator, then popped an olive into her mouth and made a face.

'Ugh,' she said. 'I don't like these – can't see what they see in them.'

Maud exploded. 'Don't eat them. They're expensive and of course you wouldn't like them, you don't know about that kind of thing.'

Harold put a tentative hand towards the dish of olives and Maud slapped his wrist with the handle of the cheese knife. 'You leave those alone, too,' she said.

Mrs May came in. 'What's going on?' she asked, seeing Maud put pieces of cheese on the crackers. 'Those for us?'

'No, they're not,' Maud said loudly.

'All right, I only asked. No cake?' Mrs May looked at Maud hopefully.

'No cake,' said Basil and Harold in unison.

Maud, her temper fraying visibly, slammed down a tin of biscuits on to the table.

'Cocktail onions, Hetty. Come on, my girl, it's twenty to twelve.'

She was mixing flour and grated cheese in a large bowl. 'Who's coming, Sister, just the two of them?'

'No, Mrs Hillier's daughter as well.' Carmichael finished her coffee.

'Oh no, not that French piece,' said Maud. 'We'd better open the tinned oysters.'

'I've seen her. What a looker!' said Basil. 'I could do with a bit of that.'

'Forty-five if she's a day,' said Maud.

'I don't mind.' Basil got up. 'Come on, Harold, back to the grind.' He made for the door and thrust his feet into his wellingtons. 'Your biscuits are stale, Maud.' This was his parting shot and the door banged after them.

'I'm thinking of making those two make their own coffee. Basil could do it in his cottage. I don't see why I should have to. Hetty!' Her voice rose to a scream as Hetty, having opened the flat tin of oysters as directed by Maud with the key supplied, overturned the lot, all over the floor. The oil spread on the lino. Hetty bent down, scooped the oysters up and popped them into a little dish which she had in her other hand.

108

'They'll never know,' she said, looking guiltily at Agnes, who turned away to hide a smile. 'You have to eat a peck of dirt before you die.' Hetty giggled. 'My aunt says that.'

'Probably she's right,' said Agnes and was rewarded by a scandalized look from Maud.

'And you a nurse, Sister?' she said, but did not insist that Hetty threw the oysters away.

Carmichael left the kitchen, but before she went upstairs she knocked on Sir Edmund's office door. He was seated at his desk, looking out of the window. The room smelled of tobacco and slightly of whisky.

'Lady Bellamy asked me to tell you that the Hilliers are coming for drinks, Sir Edmund.'

He looked at her in rather a vague way. 'Who?' he asked.

'Major and Mrs Hillier and their daughter.' Agnes repeated her remark a little more loudly.

'Oh, right,' he said and relapsed into his torpor again.

Alison was arranging the flowers in the sitting-room and Agnes repeated her message. 'Oh thanks, Agnes, I must put some more make-up on.' She looked at Agnes and grinned. 'Our Marcia, she's quite a humdinger; I mean, wrong side of forty, but looks right side of thirty. Know what I mean?' She laughed.

Upstairs Lady Bellamy was seated under the dryer while the blonde girl gave her a manicure.

'Take that beastly white coat off and come in for drinks, Agnes.' She did not realize how loudly she was speaking because of the dryer humming around her ears.

'Thank you.' Agnes was not quite sure she wanted to be included in all the family's social engagements, but Lady Bellamy seemed to want her and after all, she thought, she was on 'duty'.

She went to her room and, taking her cue from Alison, cleaned her face and made it up again, more carefully this time. Usually in the morning she just put on a little foundation cream, some powder and lipstick. She was interested to be meeting the daughter from France. She must, she thought, be quite something to make Maud open the oysters and Alison go and put on more make-up. She took off the dress she was wearing and slipped on a demure navy and red dress she had not yet worn at Nettlestone. It was a Chanel; when she had paid for it Agnes had felt a stab of guilt at the price but now, when she looked at herself in the dressing-table mirror, she was very well satisfied. It had cost a lot, but it looked as if it had cost a lot. She would wear it for dinner with Patel, she thought, then remembered she must ring and put him off for the moment.

She went downstairs to the hall telephone, rang the hospital and soon had Mr Patel on the other end of the line. After a brief conversation in which she explained that she found it rather difficult to leave her patient in the evening, they compromised and made an arrangement for lunch in two days' time – Lady Bellamy's after-lunch nap made Carmichael feel happier about going off duty then. She put down the telephone. She looked forward to meeting Patel again, but was glad she would not have to ask Lady Bellamy for an evening off instead of the usual midday break.

She hurried upstairs again to help Lady Bellamy into her dress. The hairdresser was packing up and exhorting her client not to smudge her nails.

'What a lovely dress; you look so nice.' Agnes smiled as she helped her patient into her dress. It was a cleverly cut woollen dress in French blue. Its full pleated skirt hid the deformity of her hip, which still showed as she walked.

'Look at my beastly shoes,' Lady Bellamy grumbled. 'I hate flat shoes, Agnes. Will I ever be able to wear high heels again?'

Agnes doubted it, but she did not want to spoil the occasion by saying so. 'Oh, I expect so, Lady Bellamy,' she said, opening the door for the laden hairdresser who, with a cheerful goodbye, made her way downstairs and out of the front door to her car, which was parked right outside to, Agnes suspected, Sir Edmund's annoyance if he had seen it.

Lady Bellamy patted her hair, carefully applied a little rouge and lipstick and then, as she reached for her perfume, she gave a little wince of pain.

'Damned hip,' she said. 'I hope Maud has managed to find something to go with the drinks.'

'I'm sure she has.' Agnes handed her her tripod, but she waved it away and motioned for her stick. Together they went down the stairs and into the sitting-room.

Maud had put out dishes of crackers, olives and onions, cheese straws and the rescued oysters. Edmund had already poured himself a stiff whisky and was, unusually for him,

110

popping in some ice cubes from the ice bucket on the drinks trolley.

'Maud has done well at such short notice.' Gladys Bellamy seated herself with Carmichael's help and looked at the array of glass and silver dishes on the fireside table. The log fire blazed.

Alison walked in. She, too, had changed into a dress.

'Alison, you look so much nicer in a frock, darling,' Gladys Bellamy remarked as Alison came and kissed her grandmother's cheek.

'Have to put something decent on with Marcia around.' Alison grinned.

At that moment wheels crunched on the gravel and a car door banged, then another. After a short pause the door opened and Hetty announced the guests.

Major Hillier, preceded by his wife and daughter, walked in. Madge Hillier was in her usual tweeds, so was her daughter, but there the similarity ended. Marcia de Curzon was introduced to Agnes. She looked, in spite of her country clothes, every inch a Parisienne. Her legs were long and elegant, her slender feet clad in immaculate brogues that looked as if they had never walked on a country road or been brushed by a blade of grass. Facially, too, she did not resemble Madge Hillier. The high cheek bones and the white magnolia-like skin and dark-lashed eyes owed much to cosmetics. Agnes noticed with fascination how she popped an olive into her mouth and sipped her drink without the slightest damage to her lipstick.

When she was introduced to Carmichael her eyes took in the navy and red dress and Agnes sensed her appreciation.

'I've lost my gloves. I bet I dropped them in the car, or else they fell, fell off my lap into the road somewhere.' Madge felt in her ample pockets. 'I know, don't tell me. I know what Marcia's going to say.'

'Don't tell you what? What were you going to say, Marcia?' asked Lady Bellamy curiously.

Madge replied with a high put-on voice, 'A Frenchwoman puts her gloves on in the bedroom, an American puts her gloves on in the hall and an Englishwoman puts her gloves on in the street.'

Her daughter laughed, showing perfect white teeth. 'Or drops them in the street,' she said, with an affectionate look at her mother.

They were all seated and talking when there was a tap on the door and Hetty opened it.

'Excuse me, m'lady,' she said, 'there's a gentleman come for Sister.'

'Well, who is it, Hetty?' Lady Bellamy asked. 'Did you get his name?'

Hetty looked at the card in her hand. A card, Agnes thought, was unusual for Patel – anyway, what would he want with her? She had only just phoned him. But it was not Patel's name that Hetty read from the card in her hand. 'Mr Harry Dwyer,' she said.

Outside in the cold Harold was forking straw and horse muck into a wheelbarrow. Basil was leaning against the Rolls watching him.

As the red car drew up in front of the house and the dark-suited figure emerged from it, he leant forward to see properly and whistled softly.

'Will you look at that!'

'What?' Harold followed Basil's gaze. 'Who's that, then?'

'That, Harold, is Harry Dwyer – Mr Harold Dwyer of the golf club. He as good as kicked the old man out of the clubhouse – drunk and disorderly, our Edmund was.'

'Really? Well, that's nothing new.' Harold banged his fork on the end of the barrow and prepared to wheel it away.

Basil straightened up and walked casually towards the red Porsche. When he got there, Harry Dwyer was just banging shut the door of the car.

'Morning, sir,' said Basil. 'You calling on the family?'

Harry Dwyer turned. 'Basil, isn't it?' he said.

'That's right, sir.'

Harry Dwyer smiled and tapped his car key on the fingers of his other hand. 'No, I'm not calling on the family, if you must know.'

He mounted the steps, rang the bell and Basil waited, full of curiosity, as Hetty opened the door.

'Yes, sir?'

'I want to see your guest – the lady with the grey Porsche.'

'Oh, Sister Carmichael. Come in, sir.' The door closed behind him.

Basil went back to where Harold was filling a fresh load on to the wheelbarrow.

'Well, that's a turn-up for the book,' he said.

'What is?' Harold was not really interested and did not stop forking.

'Dwyer calling on Sister. Wonder what that's for? He must know her. Well, well, wonder how that will go down?'

Harold took no notice of him and Basil continued. 'Sir Edmund's going to be pleased.' He laughed. 'Good job there's a party going on or fighting might break out.'

The impact made by the newcomer's entrance was immediate. Carmichael was surprised; Lady Bellamy, too, seemed startled and she looked from the man's face to her husband's.

The Hilliers, Madge and Bernard, looked incredulous. Marcia and Alison were the only two who seemed neither surprised nor put out – nor, indeed, affected by the entrance.

'Oh, I'm sorry. I only wanted a word with . . .' He glanced towards Carmichael, who came forward.

Sir Edmund had regained his composure. 'Oh, do come in, Dwyer. Let me get you a drink.' His voice was loaded with sarcasm, which Agnes was at a loss to understand. The Hilliers glanced at each other and Major Hillier raised a hand to Dwyer and muttered, 'Hallo old man.'

'I'm sorry to intrude in this way, it's just that . . .' He turned to Agnes. '. . . the keys of our respective petrol tanks have been muddled. I have yours and I presume you have mine. Mine has a particular mark on it and when I got this I saw . . .'

'*Cherchez la clef*,' Marcia said, drawing Harry Dwyer's attention to her – but it did not remain with her for long.

Edmund had turned away. 'The usual, Dwyer?' he asked.

'Oh, thank you.' Dwyer continued to look away from Marcia towards Agnes. 'Stupid boy at the garage; it's his fault, I'm afraid.' He smiled at her, took a key from his pocket and gave it to her.

'Here you are.' Sir Edmund handed him his drink, looking rather as if he hoped it would choke him. 'Ice and lemon, I remember you liked.'

'Do sit down, Mr Dwyer,' Lady Bellamy said, with her usual charming smile. He sat, drank the gin and tonic and refused the olives handed to him by Madge. The atmosphere was not easy and almost at once, having put down his empty glass, Harry Dwyer rose.

'Perhaps you would be good enough to check.'

'Of course. I'll just get my coat, it'll be cold outside.' Agnes was glad to get out of the room. Whatever were they all so embarrassed about, she wondered?

As she came downstairs, having donned her coat, Harry Dwyer emerged from the sitting-room and closed the door behind him. He looked at Carmichael.

'Well, Daniel in the lions' den,' he said, smiling.

'Why? Why the lions' den?' asked Agnes.

'Nothing really – a little difference of opinion some time ago. Why Sister Carmichael?' He put a stress on the word 'Sister'.

'I'm looking after Lady Bellamy. She had an accident.'

'I'm sorry.'

They walked round to the car in silence. Agnes unlocked it and handed him the petrol tank key which she kept in the little ashtray.

'You'd better try the one I gave you in yours,' he suggested.

She inserted the key and turned it. 'Yes, that's mine. Thank you so much for bringing it back.'

He smiled at her. 'Had to – couldn't get at my tank. Nice to see you again, anyway. Excuse me, but . . . a nurse with a Porsche and looking like you do . . . That's badly put, but that dress – so charming.'

'Well, we're not all as poor as church mice.' Carmichael locked the car and let him pull down the garage doors. They walked round to the front of the house and to his car.

He got into his Porsche. 'May I – may I telephone you?' he asked.

Agnes Carmichael hesitated. 'If you wish.'

'Dinner, perhaps?'

'Perhaps, if I can get away.' She smiled and walked away from the car towards the door of the house. As he drove by the Manor door she raised her hand and he gave a short, sharp toot in reply.

Agnes paused at the top of the steps before she pushed open the door, looking after the red brake lights of the red Porsche. Then she went back into the hall, slipped out of her coat and returned to the party in the sitting-room.

114

As she entered, Alison spoke quickly as if to fill in a silence or change the subject.

'Have you got a drink, Agnes?' she asked.

Agnes shook her head and went over to Lady Bellamy. 'I'm so sorry about that mix-up. We should have sorted it out in the hall.'

'That's all right, Agnes.' Gladys Bellamy looked mildly amused. 'I'll tell you about Harry Dwyer later.' She gave a slight wink at Agnes.

Alison brought a drink to her and took her arm. 'Come and talk to Marcia. She's interested in us yokels.'

Marcia laughed as she heard the remark. 'I was a yokel, you know, not all that long ago,' she said, handing her empty glass to Alison. 'Be a dear and get me another one.' As Alison walked away she patted the seat beside her. 'Do sit down and talk to me – I love your dress.'

'It's nice of you to say so. I'm a little unsure about buying clothes. I think it was a reasonable choice, though. I can't wear fussy clothes.'

'Neither can I – I hate them anyway. Do you diet?'

Agnes shook her head.

'I have to, my husband likes thin women. Never marry a man with that preoccupation.'

Carmichael smiled. 'I'm not likely to,' she said.

'That man – what was his name – Dwyer? I think I remember him. Lucky the garage man mixed the keys.' She accepted the drink Alison had brought her and cast a glance at Carmichael, one delicately plucked eyebrow raised. 'Do you think it is a plot to see Agnes again?' She said this almost cattily.

'That's not like you, Marcia.' Alison grinned at Marcia, then turned to Agnes. 'Did he ask to see you again?'

'Don't be so *effrontée*,' said Marcia, laughing.

'I'm not. I believe he did plot it.'

Carmichael got up, still smiling. 'I think I'll just go over and see if my patient is comfortable.'

'*Touchée*,' said Marcia and rose to her feet as she saw her mother and father rising also to say goodbye.

Sir Edmund accompanied his guests to the door and Agnes watched as he guided Marcia with his hand on the back of her slim waist. He did not come back into the sitting-room and

Alison left, too – presumably in search of Nigel, as it was nearly lunch-time.

Agnes sat down beside Gladys Bellamy. Lady Bellamy sighed. 'I envy Madge sometimes,' she said. 'Her happy-go-lucky nature, her daughter, her husband.'

Agnes knew what she meant and what she envied. There was nothing to say in answer, though, so she changed the subject.

'I'm sorry there was that mix-up about the car keys,' she said.

'It was not your fault. Harry Dwyer is not a bad fellow. He's captain, or he was captain, of Edmund's golf club and he had to ask Edmund to resign after an incident at the club. Edmund was – well, why go on about it.'

Agnes took Lady Bellamy's hand. 'I'm sorry, I had no idea. It must have been embarrassing for you.'

'Where my husband is concerned I'm used to embarrassment, Agnes,' she said quietly.

Edmund came back into the room. He looked rather suspiciously at his wife and Agnes. 'Lunch is in,' he said.

Agnes helped Lady Bellamy to her feet and they went through to the dining-room.

17

The artificial flames leapt round the make-believe logs in the grate. Two or three men and a couple of women were standing at the bar laughing and talking and drinking. Agnes had just eaten a salad sandwich and Patel a ploughman's lunch. Now they were waiting for the waitress to bring them their coffee.

As Carmichael listened to Patel talking with lively enthusiasm about his new post, how lucky he was to have got a consultancy, the happiness he felt in his marriage and fatherhood; as she watched his brown face full of expression and animation, his confident smiles, his brown eyes full of optimism, she was glad for him – but she was also filled with memories of hospital life, the terrible things that had happened at the hospital at which they had both worked.

Patel spoke of none of these things and Carmichael was glad that it was so, that his new life had obliterated Hemmington

General, and now he was a consultant in a Leicester hospital with a wife and child to think about and work for. He showed her photographs of his rather fat wife and their tiny baby; he was full of pride. His eyes were fixed on her as she looked at the photographs to gauge her reaction.

The waitress put their coffee in front of them. Carmichael turned back the tab on the tiny pack of cream, tore open the small brown bag of sugar, added both to her cup and watched the cream swirl round turning the coffee from dark, almost black, to fawn. She felt curiously isolated. How could she talk to Patel? What could she say of her life? She had found it easy to listen, but to talk . . . Patel was not part of all the things that had happened since her retirement. He knew nothing of how she had almost had a family life like his and how it had all been snatched away from her. No, it was better if she was silent about that.

Suddenly, as she finished her coffee, she realized that she did not want to talk about herself at all. He had too full a life to listen anyway. He had hardly asked a single question about her life or plans.

'Thank you for a nice lunch, Mr Patel.' She gathered up her coat and he helped her on with it. Then she picked up her gloves and handbag. She felt she was leaving abruptly, but there was nothing more to talk about – that was how she felt. As if he sensed something of her feelings, he put a hand on her arm.

'I would be most honoured if you would come and see my department, just a quick tour.' He smiled, his eyes questioning, looking as if he felt he had perhaps offended her. She could not refuse.

They got into their respective cars, drove to the hospital and parked in the consultants' area outside Casualty.

The department was newly built and was most interesting to Agnes Carmichael – a night stay ward of six beds, well monitored: how she would have appreciated that when she was a Casualty Sister. Dressings dispensers, syringe and needle dispensers, all to hand, no cupboards to go to, all ready just to be taken.

The doctors' office and the Sister's office brought back memories. The Casualty Sister welcomed her and Patel.

'Do come in, Sister Carmichael,' she said, after Mr Patel's

introduction. 'I'm really proud of my office. Before the department was built I only had a sort of cubby hole. Do sit down.'

Agnes shook her head. 'I must go back to my patient.'

'You're private nursing, I believe?' Was her voice patronizing?

'Yes, I'm nursing Lady Bellamy in Penny Stratton.'

'Lady Bellamy. We looked after her when she came in with a fractured femur – she was admitted and pinned, I believe.'

'That's right, and she's doing very well,' Carmichael said.

'She presented us with these two chairs.' She pointed to her own swivel chair behind the desk and the other near where Agnes was standing. 'Such a nice person, I thought, to do something like that, to remember us. Often they forget all about Casualty when they get to the ward.'

'She is a nice person,' said Carmichael.

A quick peep into the three small theatres and then into the dark theatre and the plaster room, and Agnes bade farewell to the Sister and to Mr Patel.

'Thanks again for lunch. I did enjoy talking about old times and hearing all your news,' she said.

He smiled widely and shook her hand firmly. 'My pleasure, Sister Carmichael.'

Driving home she was conscious of feeling depressed and deprived and she shook herself irritably. What did she want? Another casualty department, hospital life again? That was all over. She had money; could, when she got round to it, buy a new house for herself. The very thought of that made her almost cringe. She grasped the steering wheel, accelerated and the car leapt forward. No good, she thought. No matter how fast I drive I can't get away from my own loneliness, my own self.

Then, as usual, as almost always, consolation came. Supposing she were not rich, supposing she were married and unhappy, supposing she had children who were drug addicts? Supposing, supposing . . . By the time she reached the turning into Penny Stratton Lane she was feeling more cheerful.

She needed some tissues and stopped at the village shop. The same plump little woman greeted her, Hetty's aunt – Aunt Rose. This time she was more talkative than ever and chatted away. Most of the chatter went over Carmichael's head – until: 'Our Hetty can look after herself, though, Nurse, don't you worry.'

'Look after herself?' Agnes asked, pausing with a pound coin still in her hand.

'Yes, that's right. Take care of herself – I mean, that man, though he's a Sir he's a dirty old devil, Nurse.' She looked at Agnes with a grim face. 'Hetty says she soon told him where he got off. Tried to put his hand up her clothes, he did.' She took the pound coin and handed Carmichael her change. 'Doesn't matter how old they are, once a dirty old man always a dirty old man, I say.'

Agnes smiled with a touch of primness and left the shop without answering. As she got into her car and seated herself she smiled more broadly. You might have married someone like dear Sir Edmund, she thought, and put the car gently into gear and made her way towards the Manor. 'I'd rather have a Porsche,' she said aloud.

As she drove into the garage area Basil was just backing the Rolls out. Carmichael drove the Porsche into Alison's garage and was about to lock it when there was a resounding crash. She hurried out. Luckily, Basil had backed the Rolls far enough out for it not to be damaged by the falling door.

'Bloody door. Excuse me, miss,' he said, touching his chauffeur's cap. 'I've been asking his bloody Lordship to get me another cable spring in Leicester for weeks. I would put it in the door if only he'd get it – only costs a tenner. But no. I'm not offering to get it myself because he won't pay me. I've done things like that before. I know 'im.' He went and picked up a large thick piece of wood that had fallen down, opened the garage door with some difficulty and wedged the wood under it. 'That'll do for the moment. Must have touched it when I backed out.'

Carmichael tried her own garage door. 'Mine seems all right, Basil,' she said.

'Oh, they don't often break – rust most likely.' He got into the car and turned it. 'Taking his nibs to the races,' he said through the open window, then, touching his cap again in salute to Agnes, he drove round to the front of the house.

Carmichael at that moment gave the garage door very little thought, but later it was to loom large.

Alison and Nigel were in the hall as she entered. Alison was just replacing the telephone receiver. 'Oh bother, Agnes, I didn't hear you drive in. That was Mr Dwyer wanting to speak to you.'

Agnes made a face.

'He said he'd ring you up again this evening. He's keen, Agnes, isn't he?'

'No, of course he isn't. He just likes someone to take out, that's all.' Agnes smiled at her.

Nigel pinched Alison's arm affectionately and reprovingly. 'Don't be cheeky, Alison,' he said, touching the end of her nose with his forefinger. Alison immediately kissed him.

'Well, he must be keen. I reckon he switched the keys at the garage and now he's ringing Agnes up.'

'Come now, Alison – switched the keys!'

Carmichael smiled at her again and started up the stairs.

Nigel stopped her. 'Take no notice, Miss Carmichael, she's teasing you.' His smile was sweet and humorous. He wore his love and happiness in Alison like an aura.

Agnes paused and looked at them both. Nothing, she thought, must spoil that relationship – nothing must come between them.

She wondered, as she went up the rest of the stairs to her room, just when Lady Bellamy would decide to tell her husband of the impending marriage and Alison's pregnancy. How would he take it? She shivered suddenly, although the hall and her room were both warm.

Agnes went into Lady Bellamy's bedroom and found her still sleeping. She had had a bad night, so Carmichael decided to let her sleep at least for another half-hour or so. She looked at her watch: it was twenty to four.

In her own bedroom she donned her white coat and silver-buckled belt and then went down to the kitchen. Alison and Nigel had disappeared from the hall.

In the kitchen Hetty, Maud Spencer and Harold were grouped round the kitchen table, on which was spread a large sheet of paper.

Maud explained. 'It's the plans of the bungalows and houses, Sister, on the lower field site,' she said. 'There are eight kinds of bungalows, some are bigger than others. That's the one I want.'

Agnes looked with some interest where her finger pointed.

'Two bedrooms, sitting-room, kitchen, bathroom and cloakroom – spacious garage.' Maud said this aloud with some pride.

'You haven't got a car, Maud,' said Hetty.

'I might get one, miss. But anyway, I'd get more than £5 a week if I let it.'

'I thought you'd got a cottage, Maud?' Agnes looked at the cook curiously.

'Well, I have, but it's thatched and old-fashioned and dark. I think I'd like a change, something more modern. I like modern things.'

'It's ever so pretty, Maud's cottage,' volunteered Hetty. 'Just like a picture on a biscuit tin.'

Maud looked wistfully at the plans. 'It's going to cost quite a lot of money,' she said, 'and of course I've got to sell my cottage.'

'Where is it, Maud, your cottage?' Agnes asked.

'It's in the village, in a lane at the back of the church.' She began to roll up the sheet of drawings.

'Lady Bellamy's tea, please.' Agnes smiled at Maud.

'Oh, I'm sorry, Sister. That's where daydreams get you.' She assembled the tray, made the tea and Agnes took it upstairs to her patient.

Lady Bellamy was just emerging from the bathroom when Agnes took in the tea tray.

'Aren't I clever? I was really in no dire need, but I felt I must try and get around a little on my own.'

Carmichael watched as Lady Bellamy limped across to her armchair, leaning heavily on the walking aid.

'Soon you'll be able to do without me,' she said, bringing over the cushion Lady Bellamy liked at her back.

'Oh Agnes, don't say that or I shall refuse to move at all.'

Carmichael laughed. 'I'm here for as long as you wish, Lady Bellamy,' she said. 'Remember you start physiotherapy next week.'

'Oh Lord, I forgot she was coming. I hope she's not like the hospital one – she reminded me of a sergeant-major and she had a moustache.'

Carmichael poured tea and handed a cup to Lady Bellamy, whose levity suddenly seemed to have left her, to be replaced by an anxious, worried look.

'I will have to tell Edmund about those two children – next

121

week probably. Nigel apparently wants the wedding soon – you can understand that.'

Agnes sipped her tea. 'How do you think he, Sir Edmund, will take it, Lady Bellamy?' she asked.

'God knows; I tremble to think about it, Agnes.' She looked up at Carmichael and suddenly smiled. 'I need you here more, or as much, for that crisis as I do for my hip.' Then, as if she had only just remembered that Agnes had been out to lunch, she asked, 'Oh, did you have a nice lunch with your doctor friend?' The conversation veered away to a lighter note as Carmichael told her about Mr Patel and his wife and baby and his search for a house. She told of her visit to the hospital, and mentioned how pleased the Sister was with the office chairs.

'Oh that,' said Gladys Bellamy. 'They were so kind, it was the least I could do.'

18

The next two days passed uneventfully and outwardly peace-fully, but Carmichael could tell that her patient was not peaceful in her mind. She was obviously dreading telling her husband about Nigel and Alison – fearful, as she confided to Agnes, of Sir Edmund's reaction and how he would use the knowledge once she had given it to him.

'Next week I'll do it – when I've got used to this awful woman,' she said. This 'awful woman' was the physiotherapist, who had arrived at eleven o'clock the day after Agnes had lunched with Mr Patel.

She was a large woman, with fair hair in rigid waves. Lady Bellamy was certain it was a wig, but Agnes doubted this. She had light blue eyes behind round spectacles and very definitely belonged, as she put it, to the 'old school'. Her opening remark to Lady Bellamy, almost on arrival, of 'Now dear, let's see what we can do, shall we?' did not help to start the relationship off on a good footing.

'Is that the royal "We", do you think she means?' grumbled Lady Bellamy after Miss West's first visit and departure. 'And how dare she call me dear!'

Carmichael debated whether to have a word with Miss West, who was coming twice a week, or let the situation sort itself out. She decided on the latter course. Miss West did not look the type of person with whom to cross swords.

'She will do you a lot of good and get you walking sooner and better – and you must do your exercises.'

Lady Bellamy looked at Agnes and they both laughed. 'You medics stick together.'

Agnes nodded. 'Of course we do. How else could we cope with patients?' she said lightly and went to fetch some coffee, turning a deaf ear to her patient's suggestion that she would need a little whisky in hers.

That afternoon, having settled Lady Bellamy for her after-lunch nap, Carmichael set out to walk to Top Field Farm. She was interested to see what might, and probably would, be the first home of Nigel and Alison.

She was beginning to enjoy walking and the ascent up to the farm was gradual. However, the lane, rutted by farm machinery, was not easy walking. When at last Agnes emerged from between the two hedges and arrived at the outer perimeter of the property she was pleasantly surprised by the front aspect of the farmhouse. Built of the same grey stone as Nettlestone Manor, it was similar to a house drawn by a child, two steps up to the white front door flanked by a window on each side and another similar two windows above, with a third one situated over the door. The slate roof gleamed with the wintry sun shining on the recently rain-spattered tiles. It looked square, homely and solid, standing at the top of the rising field which gave it its name – Top Farm. The field below it was Top Field.

A white fence surrounded the front garden and a brown dog barked at her as she went by, rushing to and fro along the fence but not attempting to jump over.

The back of the farm was as attractive as the front, with exactly the same arrangement of windows and door, only the back door was brown and wide open. A kennel occupied one side of the back door and a chain was dangling. Quite a large piece of ground was given over to a vegetable garden, but at the moment it was almost empty of vegetables, with only one or two cold-looking cabbages.

Agnes smiled a little to herself. Somehow she found it difficult to imagine Alison digging and weeding and planting carrots and cabbages – but perhaps Nigel could be relied upon to do that. As she drew away a woman appeared at the back door, looked at her curiously and closed it.

Talking to Lady Bellamy Agnes had found out that the farm consisted of just over a hundred acres and supported fifty-five dairy cattle. After walking still further, Agnes came to the outbuildings. She imagined Nigel having to tend the cows as well as doing his job as bailiff, but probably they would get a cowman. It would be too much for him to cope with – the estate, especially with Edmund doing so little, and the farm and a baby. Agnes thought aloud as she made the full circle and came through the fields where some of the Friesians grazed, the winter sunshine on their backs again giving the impression of a child's drawing or a toy farm. A chicken run at the back of the house was obviously used only at nights, for the brown chickens ran loose about the vegetable garden.

Agnes started her walk back to the village with a pleasant picture in her mind. Drawing near Penny Stratton she suddenly came to the decision to go and look at Maud's cottage. She glanced at her watch: it was only ten past three – plenty of time.

Behind the church, Maud had said. Agnes found a small slip of a lane, almost a passage, down by the side of the church between the churchyard and a large red brick house which even in November had an immaculate, if flowerless, garden in front. The rather dark little pathway, overshadowed by the church and house on each side, opened out into a wider lane going from left to right. Agnes got her first sight of Maud's cottage. She knew it must be the one for it stood alone behind the church. On each side there was a stretch of grass and on the left side another narrow lane.

Agnes' first thought was, How could anyone who owned such a cottage dream of selling it? Then she remembered that Maud had probably lived in it all her life and longed for a modern kitchen with wide windows, double glazing, pine kitchen units, pastel bathroom with plastic curtains, electric fires, central heating – everything convenient, Carmichael thought.

Agnes knew Maud was back at the Manor, so she could draw near the cottage and even peer in – as far as she knew, Maud lived alone. She opened the low white gate and walked up the flagstoned path, then stood and looked at the thatched cottage.

'Just like a picture on a biscuit tin.' She remembered Hetty's words, and the girl was right. The small casement windows, the brown latched front door, the square garden. The thatch looked in good repair, a fine chicken wire-like mesh stretched over the parts Agnes could see – 'To keep the dormice out or the birds from nesting,' she whispered to herself. She hastily looked round her to see if anyone had heard her, but there was no one in sight. She walked round to the back. Even in late November she could smell lavender, or was she bewitched? The paths in the back garden were grass, well edged, and the garden itself, though suffering November blues, was obviously well tended. No garage; still, room to build one, thatched like the cottage. 'A garage – and what am I thinking?' she said to herself, and with a quick walk round the vegetable garden tried to dismiss any thought that had come into her head of owning the cottage. The vegetable garden was minute and the bean poles still standing. Walking rapidly back to the front of the cottage she closed the gate quietly behind her and, without looking over her shoulder, started to walk back to her patient and tea. But nothing could dismiss or black out the image of that snug, biscuit-tin cottage.

As she entered the drive at Nettlestone Manor, a little weary after her walk, the Rolls passed her with Sir Edmund sitting by Basil. Basil touched his cap, Sir Edmund raised his hand.

She went in and up to her room, changed her shoes, came out and peeped into her patient's room. Lady Bellamy was awake and yawned.

'I've had a lovely nap. I seem to sleep better after lunch than at night. I haven't told Sir Edmund yet,' she said.

'I know, I met him coming in. I've been walking, I went to see Top Farm.' Agnes smiled at her as she helped her up. 'You're walking better,' she said.

Lady Bellamy stopped in her tracks to the bathroom. 'Now, don't you try selling that Miss West to me – she's only been here once,' she said.

'I wasn't, Lady Bellamy,' Carmichael protested. Having installed her in her chair she suggested tea.

'Yes, have yours with me, won't you?' Lady Bellamy smiled and her smile was very warm.

As Agnes made her way down to the kitchen she thought, 'What a routine I have got into in this house and how soothing it has become,' and she wondered what would have happened if routine had not rescued her. She wondered if she should tell Maud that she had seen her cottage, but decided no, not today, perhaps never. She would think about it. After all – Leicester. Why Leicester? Who did she know here? Who cared about her? But then, who really cared about her anywhere, so why not this part of the world? Why not decide to live here? It was the same as anywhere else. During her short stay in this flat, neat, green county, she had grown to like it. She was not keen on Leicester, too big a town for her, but she only need use it for shopping. She stopped herself with determination and tried to banish the cottage and where she would live from her mind.

Maud and Hetty were, as usual at this time, drinking tea. There was no sign of the rolled-up maps that Maud had acquired showing the bungalows she so liked.

'Been walking, Sister?' she asked.

Agnes nodded.

'Thought so. I just took a couple of stale cakes out to give to the horses and I saw your garage was shut. Himself was out, though.'

The old-fashioned bell jangled and Maud looked up at the equally old-fashioned row of little circles in the box-like bracket on the wall.

'Oh, he's in, that's the sitting-room. Tea tray, Hetty, relish sandwiches. There's yours, Sister.' Maud handed Agnes the tea tray for Lady Bellamy's room. 'She's worried, her Ladyship, worried about something.'

'Is she, do you think, Maud?' Agnes replied.

The two women's eyes met and it crossed Agnes' mind that Maud, a down-to-earth countrywoman, might have noticed some change in Alison and suspected she was pregnant. Anyway, it would be obvious in time.

She took the tea tray, left the kitchen, crossed the hall and made her way up the stairs.

For some reason that she could not place or understand she suddenly thought of Anthony, who would have been her stepson had Brian lived. Oh well! Thank God for routine, she thought, and pushed open Lady Bellamy's door.

'Tea, Lady Bellamy,' she said.

*

126

After tea, Gladys Bellamy decided, as she usually did, that she would like to see the news on television and started searching round in her chair, as she usually did, for her glasses.

'Are they by the bed, Agnes?' she asked.

Carmichael smiled. Lady Bellamy and her glasses were two things most easily parted.

'No, Lady Bellamy.' Agnes held up the glasses on the bedside table. 'Only your reading glasses are here.'

'Oh dear, I must have left them downstairs last night after dinner. If you remember, I didn't come up to bed until quite late. Would you be a dear . . .?'

'Of course.' Hetty had already fetched the tea tray, so Agnes ran down the stairs unhindered and crossed the hall into the sitting-room. Sir Edmund was seated by the fire reading the *Guardian*, but Agnes could sense his eyes under their bushy eyebrows watching her.

'I'm looking for Lady Bellamy's glasses,' she explained.

'Oh yes.' He cleared his throat, turned a page of the paper and shook it into place. 'Can't see why she doesn't keep them on; she can't see without them and God knows it doesn't matter what she looks like in them.'

It was not a particularly pleasant remark, but then, Agnes thought, he wasn't a particularly pleasant man. Not only was the remark offensive, the tone in which it was uttered was, too. Agnes chose to ignore it and went on thrusting her hands down the sides of the cushion of the chair in which Lady Bellamy had sat the night before.

'That Porsche – did you buy it new?' Sir Edmund lowered his newspaper on to his knees.

Agnes was so startled by the sudden remark that she answered almost without thinking. 'I did. I did buy it new, Sir Edmund,' she said, looking directly at him and ceasing for the moment her search for the spectacles.

He reached for a cigarette and looked at her just as directly as she was looking at him, over the top of his half-glasses.

'Seventy-three thousand, or something near that, is the price of a Porsche?'

Agnes did not reply.

'A lot of money for a nurse, eh?' He gave a sort of sneering smile. 'Grateful patients, I suppose – you get quite a lot left you

127

one way and another, looking after the old and decrepit, I'm sure.'

Agnes felt her face flushing and anger rising in her, but then she saw the edge of Lady Bellamy's glasses sticking out from the far cushion in the chair and retrieved them. Then she spoke.

'I really think that is an impertinent remark, Sir Edmund.'

He put his hand up and smoothed his moustache; he was still smiling. 'I'm sure you do, but it's true, isn't it?'

Again Carmichael felt too furious to answer him. She walked across the room and was conscious of his expression as he watched her go, a mixture of satirical amusement and triumph. He shook the paper, raised it and resumed reading.

Agnes had to pause outside her patient's room to regain her composure before she entered. Then she managed to smile, switch on the television to the right channel for the six o'clock news, hand Lady Bellamy her glasses and excuse herself.

She went into her own room, closed the door behind her and sat down on the bed. She felt cold, angry and somehow defiled. Perhaps, she thought, she should not have bought the Porsche. Perhaps it had been stupid, ostentatious, showing off, perhaps. But it had been a gesture to comfort herself, she supposed – and why was she making excuses for that man downstairs?

Then gradually the mixture of feelings subsided. She got up and went over to her bedside table and picked up the picture of the blind white cat. As she looked at it, the small creature who was responsible for her fortune, she began to feel better. Her heart stopped pounding with fury and resumed its normal rate. She put the little silver-framed picture back.

Sir Edmund Bellamy had invaded her privacy, hinted that she cared for her patients for ultimate gain – money. He would regret what he had said, she would see to that. She did not know at the moment how he would regret it, how she would make him regret it, but she would.

She went to the wardrobe and took out a dress; she would put the matter out of her mind for the present. She looked in the mirror and noticed that across her upper lip and over her forehead sweat glistened, so much had the scene downstairs upset her. She decided to have a shower before she dressed for dinner.

At dinner Alison and Nigel seemed more relaxed and happy than they had been for some time, although they tried hard not to look at each other. Agnes felt that telling their secret to

Alison's grandmother had relieved them of responsibility. She was careful not to mention her visit to Top Farm in case her curiosity to see the place should rouse suspicion in Sir Edmund.

She felt regret at having put on the new, expensive dress. While she had been helping Lady Bellamy dress, the latter remarked how nice Agnes looked. Edmund Bellamy, by suggesting she nursed her patients in the hope they would leave her money, had made her wish to spite him by showing off her exclusive wardrobe. He was goading her.

'This fillet steak is not as tender as it should be, Gladys.' Sir Edmund's remark interrupted her thoughts.

'Mine is very nice, Grandpa,' broke in Alison.

'Oh, really? Well, I hope Sister Carmichael's is as good – after all, she is used to the best.' Sir Edmund did not look at Agnes, but she could see the puzzled glance Lady Bellamy cast at her husband.

Agnes cut through her steak, the knife making a screech on the plate. 'Mine is perfect, thank you, Sir Edmund, but then I perhaps have a sharper knife.' She looked directly at him; he raised his eyes to hers; they narrowed slightly. He hates me, she thought, and she felt a thrill of pleasure. She wished she could use the knife in her hand, slit the pulsing vein in his neck, watch the red blood flowing out and with it his evil power to destroy the happiness of the people around him. But that was not her way; she had always used a subtle approach to killing . . . waited till the opportunity was presented. Up to now that opportunity had not failed to come. Agnus wondered, did the menace show in the eyes that she focused on him? His eyes dropped before hers.

That night Agnes lay awake, gazing into the darkness for a long time. She was well aware that what Sir Edmund had said was totally untrue. She had never in her nursing career ever thought of monetary gain from her patients and the legacy from the old lady whose blind cat she had rescued had come as a surprise from which she had never really recovered.

But the expensive car – very expensive – the clothes, the perfume: had she gradually become educated to pick the best, or was it an instant reaction to cover some deep inadequacy that her childhood and lack of love had left her with? She had nobody, so she had to have things – was that it? And the objects that she bought – had they to be better than anything other people had? She shook her head from side to side on the pillow. No, that couldn't be right. She gave to charities, but then that was easy enough when you had it to give.

She sat up suddenly and the cold draught from the slightly open window made her shiver. No, that was not the way to think. Most people, nearly everyone she knew, had someone to love – someone who loved them that they were responsible for, one for the other.

She had things. She suddenly began to feel more comfortable. Children go away, leave home, forget their parents. Husbands could be unfaithful, wives too. Friends – they die or go away and you never hear from them again. But money – it is cold, soulless and unresponsive, but it does comfort and protect. She closed her eyes and pictured the silver, gleaming Porsche, snug in its garage.

'Your money is growing all the time, Miss Carmichael.' She could hear the lawyer's voice, see his face, round eyes behind glasses.

She lay down and suddenly felt secure, and thought of something she had heard an American say on the television one night. 'A man is as good as his bank balance.' Well, that applied to women, too, she thought. She snuggled down in bed and felt herself dropping off to sleep.

19

'I've decided to talk to Edmund and tell him, today I think – it's no good putting it off any longer, he's got to be told.' Lady Bellamy looked at Agnes with anxious eyes. 'I've asked him to come and have a cup of tea with me.' She limped across the room and Agnes felt terribly sorry for her.

'Do you want me to be here, in the house, I mean?' asked Carmichael.

Lady Bellamy shook her head. 'No, thank you. It's kind of you to suggest it, but I'd rather handle this alone. I have a feeling I know how he'll react. Well, I can guess.'

Carmichael touched her patient's hand as she passed her. 'I'll go into Leicester then and do some shopping, but I shall be thinking of you.' She really meant it.

Miss West had been and gone, leaving Lady Bellamy with an over-bright 'Cheerio, then. You're doing very well indeed,' which Agnes had to agree with. Lady Bellamy had improved since the physiotherapist had been coming, but today she had hardly reacted to the woman's brightness, she had been too preoccupied.

When tea-time arrived Agnes left her patient in her armchair by the small table in her bedroom, waiting for tea and her husband. Lady Bellamy crossed her fingers and waved them at her and Agnes did the same back, but she felt that the optimistic gestures had little justification. She knew that Sir Edmund could easily harass her patient and the young people if he felt so inclined.

Carmichael went to her room and changed, then set off into the November afternoon sunshine with a heavy heart. She walked round the back of the house, got into her car and made her way out of the drive and on to the road.

By the time she reached the town she had to put on her sidelights, and as she planned to be in Leicester for longer than usual to give Lady Bellamy plenty of time to talk to her husband, she decided to put her car in the large central town car-park and walk round the shops: maybe she would get a cup of tea somewhere.

Although it was getting dark, Agnes rather enjoyed her slightly longer off-duty break, but she could not forget what might be happening at the Manor and how Sir Edmund might be behaving. She wished she was there to support Lady Bellamy should she need it, but this she reasoned, as she abstractedly looked in the shop windows, Lady Bellamy had clearly not wanted. She had doubtless been dealing with crises brought about by her husband all through her married life and she could probably deal with this one as she had the rest. Agnes tried to dismiss all thoughts of what might be taking place at Nettlestone whilst she was away.

She spent some time looking round the shops for a candlewick dressing gown. She wanted one in green, which was not an easy colour to get. At last she found one in a large store in Leicester's main street. In the small fitting room with the long mirror in front of her she looked at herself. The dressing gown fitted well and the wrap-around was ample – Agnes hated skimpily cut things. She tied the belt and smoothed down the lapels. Yes, she would have it. She was just taking the gown off and picking up her handbag to go out of the fitting room when she heard a familiar voice.

'OK. I think it makes me look fatter, but if you think it slims me down I'll take your word for it.'

Agnes got out of the little box of a room at the same moment as Madge Hillier came out of the next-door one. Madge greeted her with her usual warmth and enthusiasm.

'Hallo, Agnes, nice to see you. I've just bought a suit. What have you bought?'

'A dressing gown.' Carmichael held up the green candlewick gown.

'Nice you're so slim.' Madge smoothed her skirt over her ample hips. '"Madam takes it up so" – that's what one of the sales girls said to me.' She gave her loud, jolly laugh and put her hand on Agnes' arm. 'Come and have a cup of tea with me. I don't want to go home yet, there's a man cleaning the Aga and I want no part of it.'

They paid for their respective purchases and emerged from the store to find a fine drizzle wetting the pavements and reflecting the lights from the shop windows.

'Oh, it's colder.' Madge drew her tweed coat more closely round her.

She and Agnes hurried along the pavement to a small tea shop tucked away in a little lane off the High Street. It was a cosy, warm little place and smelled of hot scones, which Madge recommended.

'I'll be mother.' Agnes knew she would say that, and smiled.

When the tea and scones arrived Madge ate heartily, then rather to Agnes' surprise she brought up the visit of Harry Dwyer at the Bellamys' while they were there for drinks.

'That was a difficult moment for you, Agnes,' she said. 'Harry was so sorry; he came to dinner last night and spoke about it.'

'I didn't quite understand what it was all about. As you say, it was rather . . .' Agnes poured more tea for both of them, as Madge seemed to have forgotten her role as 'mother'.

'Oh, thanks,' said Madge, as Agnes proffered her the refilled cup.

The waitress put a plate of assorted cream cakes on the table.

Madge took an éclair and sunk her white teeth into it: the cream bulged out at each side. She laughed as Agnes refused to take one.

'I knew you wouldn't,' she said. 'I'm dreadful, that's why I'm so fat. No self-control. Don't know that I care, really.'

She drank her tea thirstily and with gusto and put the cup down with a clatter into the saucer.

Everything Madge Hillier does, thought Agnes, is full of life and vigour. I should think she lives life pretty fully. She tried to imagine her as a girl as she looked across the table at Madge's wrinkleless face.

'Harry Dwyer wants to meet you again, Agnes. Did he telephone you?' Madge asked. Agnes did not reply and Madge went on. 'He's a nice fellow – the Bellamy affair was unfortunate. Edmund drinks too much. The golf club put up with some rather unsavoury scenes; then after the final one he was asked to leave. Harry Dwyer happened to be captain – nasty job for him to have to do.' Agnes again said nothing; she felt embarrassed that her professional attachment to the Bellamys had taken such a personal slant. Madge Hillier realized this. 'I can understand how you feel, Agnes,' she said and changed the subject. 'Harry used to be fond of Marcia at one time – before she was married.'

At twenty past four by the café's electric wall clock Madge Hillier started to collect her handbag and shopping bag. 'I must go. He'll have finished the Aga by now, I hope.'

Madge insisted on paying the bill. As they went out into the street they found that the rain had stopped.

'Goodbye. I'm glad I met you, I hate having tea alone.' Madge gave her a swift kiss on the cheek – an unexpected gesture, and Carmichael felt surprised by it. She parted with Madge and made her way along the street to the car-park.

As she approached she had to orientate herself to the rows and rows of cars shining under the lights in the car-park – densely packed rows, red cars, blue, green, black, grey, gold, fawn, every colour was represented, and there in the third row was her Porsche, gleaming silver, its rakish body looking quite unique. Beside it, leaning against the driver's door, was Harry Dwyer. Carmichael paused, but he had seen her and waved a hand as she continued to approach.

'I knew your car, Miss Carmichael.' He patted it and smiled his rather wide smile at her, showing white uneven teeth.

Carmichael felt herself blushing as his eyes regarded her with cool candour mixed with admiration. She was not sure whether the latter was for her or for her car. She pressed the little switch in her hand that unlocked the car door and he opened it for her. She got in.

'May I have a word? I just wanted to – Oh damn!' This remark was caused by the spattering of rain that had started again. 'I'll come round.' He disappeared from Agnes' vision for a moment, then reappeared by the passenger door and put out his hand to grasp the handle. Agnes touched the control again and he slipped into the passenger seat and closed the door behind him.

Carmichael waited, her hands resting on the steering wheel.

'I was so sorry about the débâcle at the Bellamys'. I only intended to see you and swap the keys. Unfortunate!'

'Oh, I had forgotten all about it,' Agnes said, easily.

'Well, it was unfortunate, nevertheless. Bellamy's not a bad chap, I suppose. Takes a bit too much now and then, but – '

Agnes stopped him firmly. 'I really don't want to know any more, Mr Dwyer,' she said, perhaps more crisply than she had intended.

'No, of course not. I quite understand. I wondered if I could make up, perhaps, for that silly business with the key. I thought perhaps you'd have dinner with me. I know a nice little place.'

Agnes was ready with a firm 'No' – then, as she looked out at the rain dancing on the silver bonnet of her car, for some reason she changed her mind. Why not? she thought. Why not? She turned and faced him squarely.

'Did you switch those keys at the garage?' she asked.

Harry Dwyer's face changed and for a moment he looked like a naughty schoolboy caught out in a misdemeanour.

'Well . . .' He smiled. 'Actually, yes.'

As Agnes looked at him she was aware that she did not believe him. She laughed outright. 'Very well, the day after tomorrow – the evening,' she said, as if she was making a business date. 'Where is this place?'

'Oh, I'll fetch you, around seven o'clock. No trouble.'

She shook her head. 'No, I'll meet you there. Where is it?'

He looked slightly crestfallen, then he brightened up. 'Horse and Groom Road-house. You go – '

Agnes stopped him. 'I've seen it, I know where it is. Seven thirty?'

He looked at her. 'You know your own mind, don't you? May I call you Agnes?'

'Yes, you may and yes, I do know my own mind. This is, of course, if I am able to get away from Lady Bellamy's – if she is well enough to be left. If not, I'll telephone you.'

He agreed to this and opened the car door. 'I'm glad I switched those keys, though.' He closed the car door firmly, but without banging it. His face as he said goodbye was distorted by the raindrops on the glass, then he disappeared, possibly, Agnes thought, to his own car somewhere in the car-park.

She backed the car out and turned it. She was surprised that she had accepted his invitation, but anyway, she thought, as she steered carefully out of the car-park into the busy Leicester street, what did it matter? Lady Bellamy would, presumably, be pleased – and at the thought of her patient she edged her way through the traffic with a little more impatience, wondering again how Sir Edmund had taken the news, what his reaction had been and how Lady Bellamy had stood up to it all.

20

Carmichael ran up the stairs into her own room and took off her coat. It was slightly damp, but she did not bother to hang it up, so great was her impatience to see Lady Bellamy.

As she had crossed the hall she had glimpsed Sir Edmund Bellamy sitting beside the fire, legs stretched out, a glass of whisky by his side. His air of complete relaxation gave her a feeling of foreboding. He looked as if he thought he had got the better of the argument. This foreboding was confirmed when she opened the door of Lady Bellamy's room.

She looked up as Carmichael entered.

'How did . . . ?'

'It was terrible, Agnes. Edmund behaved like a lunatic at first. I thought he was going to strike me.' She almost broke down, turned her head away and blinked her eyes rapidly.

135

Carmichael sat down beside her and took her hand. Lady Bellamy recovered her composure and told Agnes the details of the whole confrontation.

'I knew the moment Edmund sat down there, opposite me, that he suspected I was going to talk about Alison and Nigel. I do think, though, that the pregnancy took him by surprise and he immediately said, "But they're related. Nigel is my son."'

Lady Bellamy beat the arm of her chair gently with her clenched fist. 'I made a mistake, Agnes. I told him Nigel couldn't be his son, he was impotent. His reply . . .' She paused for a moment and looked away from Agnes again. 'He said, "I was only impotent with you, Gladys".' She looked up. 'That may be true,' she went on. 'Anyway, he wanted – still wants, I suppose – to consider he's sired another son, and one that lived this time. That's one reason he sent for him when he was old enough to come back.'

'But their relationship – how did he take that?' Agnes asked.

Lady Bellamy grimaced. 'Better than I thought he would. The child, the baby – well, he was silent when I first told him about that. Then he asked, "Do they want it, does Nigel want it?" And when I said, of course he does, they're in love and they want the baby and to marry, that seemed to have a quietening effect on him. He got up and started to pace about the room. He was smiling slightly and, knowing him so well, I almost guessed what he would say next. He stood over me. I don't know whether it's my comparative helplessness with this hip or what, but I felt almost frightened of him – very vulnerable, anyway.

'"Do you want them to have the child and be happy – and marry? What's the chance of kids born in this way being idiots, Gladys?" I looked up at him, Agnes. He was still smiling. Of course I want them to be happy and pray that their child or children will be normal and healthy, I answered him. I still had to look up at him and that made it worse – I felt physically frightened. Then he walked away again and looked out of the window. "OK, I don't mind, if Nigel wants the kid." He turned round and looked at me. "It will cost you money, Gladys. I want ten thousand a year on top of what I get now to keep my mouth shut."'

Agnes Carmichael felt herself completely repelled – a hatred

136

for this man who could blackmail his wife and use the situation that was obviously causing her much pain for his own gain.

Lady Bellamy's head drooped onto her hand; she looked very upset.

'What did you say?' Agnes asked.

'I agreed – what else could I do? I knew that whatever I said it wouldn't move him, he'd use me and the children. Oh, the estate can do it, I suppose. I can put the farm rents up a little and the field next to the one we've sold, the developers want that – well, we may have to let them have it. I hate to see any of the estate eroded, but Edmund won't give way, I know him.'

Agnes could do or say nothing to help her patient. This news was no medical matter, something she could handle with two painkillers and a glass of water, with reassuring words that the pain would lessen.

'Will he keep his word, Lady Bellamy?' she asked.

'Oh yes, Agnes. When he's sober Edmund will keep his word as long as he gets the money.' Gladys Bellamy's voice was bitter. 'For God's sake, pour me a stiff gin, Agnes,' she said. 'I won't go down to dinner tonight; I couldn't. Edmund will know why, but just tell the children I feel tired.'

Agnes Carmichael agreed and got up and mixed a strong gin and tonic. Perhaps, she thought grimly, it was not a correct nursing procedure, but it was the only treatment she could think of for a woman who was being treated so by her husband.

She sat down again and watched Lady Bellamy sip her drink. 'Did you mention their living in Top Farm?' she asked.

'Yes, I did and it didn't seem to interest him much. It doesn't matter one way or the other, though, I can cope with that. It's lucky it's becoming vacant; it will suit them for a time, anyway.' She sighed deeply and leant back in her chair and closed her eyes. 'I'll go to bed, Agnes, if you'll help me. I feel I've had enough for one day.'

Agnes was glad to see her patient safely installed in bed and eating a light meal, though she had at first refused it.

'Go down and have your dinner, Agnes. Then, if you will, come up and tell me about your visit to town. Did you get what you wanted?'

'Yes, and I met Mrs Hillier and Mr Dwyer.'

Gladys Bellamy smiled. 'I'm glad,' she said. 'I'd like to hear about it after your meal. Anything to take my mind off this wretched business.'

Agnes made her way downstairs to join the others for dinner. She went with reluctance – she felt she never wanted to speak to Edmund Bellamy again after his accusations about her receiving money from patients, and now this. But it had to be done. After all, the young people must not suspect that anything was wrong. They must know that their grandmother had told Sir Edmund about the baby, but of course that was a small worry.

Sir Edmund was in high spirits and obviously slightly tanked up. He hurried through the meal and excused himself before they went through to the other room for coffee.

'Where's Grandpa off to?' asked Alison, as they heard the front door bang behind him.

Nigel looked at her quizzically. 'Got a date with Maisie, I expect,' he said, without malice.

Alison nodded agreement.

'Who is Maisie?' asked Agnes.

Nigel reddened. 'Oh sorry, Agnes, I shouldn't have said that.' He looked embarrassed, but Alison smiled.

'It doesn't matter, everybody knows about it – she's the barmaid at the pub Grandpa goes to. He fancies her. She's all curls and cleavage.'

Agnes looked incredulous.

'Oh yes. He's still quite a lady's man, believe me.'

Agnes took her second cup of coffee from Alison. That, too. Poor Lady Bellamy, Carmichael thought. How can she bear it all, and for all these years?

She left the two young ones together and went up to her patient. Lady Bellamy looked better. Maybe her drink and the meal and resting in bed had helped her.

Agnes related the happenings of her afternoon in Leicester – her tea with Madge Hillier. Then she showed her the dressing gown. She even made Lady Bellamy laugh a little as she related Harry Dwyer's admission that he'd switched the keys at the garage. His invitation to dinner also delighted Lady Bellamy. 'He really likes you; you must let him take you to dinner. When is it?'

'The day after tomorrow, if you can manage without me in the evening,' she told her. Lady Bellamy agreed at once. Agnes hesitated at first but, seeing that it would please Lady Bellamy, she decided she would go.

After that she felt it was better for her patient to have an early night, so she left her with the bell close beside her and went to her own room.

It was still early and she didn't want to sit with Nigel and Alison, who so obviously loved being alone together and could manage to be so only rarely. She read for a while, then lay in a bath trying to let the hot water relax her. There were so many thoughts chasing through her mind. Lady Bellamy's story of her awful afternoon – Madge Hillier – Harry Dwyer. She smiled at the thought of her patient's pleasure in the fact that he had invited her to dinner.

She got out of her bath, slipped into her nightdress and dressing gown and as she was putting her feet into her slippers she heard the tinkle of the little silver bell. It was the first time Lady Bellamy had used it to summon her. She went quickly to her patient's room.

'Forgive me, Agnes, but I just had to ask you, please tell me if you can.' There were tears in her eyes. 'What are the chances of those two having a malformed or retarded child? Please, dear, tell me the truth if you can?'

Agnes was silent for a moment or two before she replied. 'Lady Bellamy, I truly cannot answer that, because I don't know. There are tests that can be done when the child is conceived, I believe, but it's not my field. I would tell you if I knew.'

'I know you would, Agnes. It's just such a big responsibility letting them go on with this. Would it be better to tell them? The awful part is, we can't ask anyone – a doctor, I mean.'

Again Agnes took time to answer. 'I think it's better to let them go on. After all, unrelated parents have retarded or deformed children. I think it's better to let it go – to let it be as it is,' she said. 'After all, their relationship is not . . .' She paused. 'They may have the same father, but they have different mothers. That could count for something genetically, I think.'

'It might break their hearts if I parted them, Agnes.' Lady Bellamy sighed. 'You've helped me more than I can say. Good-night, my dear. It's the first time I've ever used this.' She held up the little silver bell and smiled.

Back in her room Agnes filled a hot water bottle and got into bed. 'Don't get too involved with your patients.' Wasn't that what she had always told her nurses? 'I ought to have added, "Do as I say, not what I do,"' she said aloud, then closed her eyes determinedly and tried not to think any more.

21

Next morning the sky was overcast, the fields and hedges were hardly visible through the misty haze of rain and low threatening clouds. Carmichael closed her bedroom window directly she got out of bed. She shivered as she looked out over the grey landscape – 'No flowers, no sun, no hope, November,' she quoted to herself as she dressed.

She tiptoed into her patient's room. Lady Bellamy was still asleep, her room dark. The weather and the drawn curtains had no doubt been responsible for the fact that she had not wakened at her usual time. Agnes decided to let her sleep – probably, she thought, the worry caused by the clash with her husband and the plight of the two young people had given her a disturbed night.

She heard voices in the dining-room. Nigel usually breakfasted with Sir Edmund and they sometimes used the time to discuss estate matters. Alison was there, too; she heard her voice as she passed the door. She decided a cup of coffee or tea and a slice of toast in the kitchen would suffice this morning. Indeed, she decided, anything would be better than a meeting with the odious Sir Edmund.

The kitchen, as usual, was warm and cosy and smelled of toast, bacon and eggs and percolating coffee. The central light was on and Basil was seated at the table eating toast copiously spread with butter and marmalade. Carmichael told Maud that Lady Bellamy was not to be disturbed at the moment and Maud nodded and suggested coffee for Agnes. She accepted and sat down at the table.

The atmosphere in the kitchen was more than usually cheerful for such an early hour in the morning. Maud could sometimes be a trifle tetchy this early in the day, but her face was wreathed in smiles. She was just pouring Agnes' coffee when Hetty came in.

'They're all at sixes and sevens this morning, that lot,' she grumbled. 'Himself said the bacon wasn't crisp enough and he asked Nigel to do something in the office and Nigel said he had to go up to Top Farm because of the removal and Alison wanted tea, not coffee.' She then appeared to notice Agnes Carmichael. 'Morning, Sister,' she said. 'What about the news, isn't it great?'

For the moment Agnes thought the news of Nigel and Alison's impending wedding must have leaked out, but no.

'Maud has sold her cottage. What about that?'

'Subject to contract, don't forget that, Hetty,' said Maud. 'There's many a slip between cup and the lip.'

'Get off, Maud,' said Basil, speaking with his mouth full. 'You'll have the Fletchers in there, it's ideal for them.'

Carmichael felt a slight stab of regret and congratulated Maud.

Hetty left the kitchen carrying Alison's tray of tea.

'Don't know why that girl has decided to change all of a sudden,' said Maud. Then to Agnes, 'Yes, it's true. If the sale goes through I can move in with my sister in the village and give them vacant possession almost at once, and that's what they want. Then, when the bungalow is finished I can move in there. I got much more for the cottage than I thought I would.'

Agnes congratulated her again – and indeed felt very pleased for her. She finished her coffee and toast and went upstairs to check on Lady Bellamy. She was still asleep and snoring slightly. The frilly nylon net she wore to keep her hair in place was slightly askew and one hand was under her cheek. She looked very old and very vulnerable.

Agnes went back to her own bedroom, made her bed and tidied the room. She felt curiously at a loss, as if she was living in a vacuum – perhaps it was the sale of the cottage, perhaps she really had thought . . . but she had this strange feeling that she did not exist. All around her were people with relationships, troubled or ecstatic; everybody seemed to exist in pairs – Nigel and Alison, Edmund and Lady Bellamy, Madge and her husband, Maud and her sister, Hetty and her aunt, Agnes Carmichael and nobody. She suddenly dreaded going back to London to the Nursing Co-op where she knew no one and where everyone shut the door of their flatlet or disappeared during their off-duty times, presumably to join families or husbands.

Agnes stood at her window and looked out at the landscape. The sky was lighter now and the misty rain was clearing. Yes, it was the sale of the cottage, probably, that had brought on the feeling of depression. Perhaps she should have . . . Well, it was no use thinking that, regrets were always stupid.

She would go for a walk after lunch no matter what the weather was like; that was if Lady Bellamy did not want her. She must get out, walk. She would explore Penny Stratton a little more fully. Perhaps she would find another cottage that was for sale, or a house. Perhaps . . . perhaps . . . Her thoughts were interrupted by the silvery tinkle of Lady Bellamy's little bell. She hurried from her room and went along to her patient.

Bathed, dressed and fortified by breakfast, Lady Bellamy seemed more cheerful than Agnes would have expected.

'I've got a bit of telephoning to do this morning, Agnes dear,' she said. 'My lawyer, my accountant, I have to make appointments and I want to put Miss West off this afternoon. I want to go to Leicester, alter Edmund's allowance, talk to my accountant and my bank manager about it, tell my lawyer about the children's marriage and get them some legal standing in the estate. Remember, I told you Alison will inherit if I die first and she will have a heavy burden to support Edmund while he lives.'

Agnes passed her the telephone and the telephone book and Lady Bellamy settled down to make appointments with the three men she had mentioned and make her excuses to the physiotherapist. Agnes left her to do this in private and, at Lady Bellamy's request, went downstairs to tell Sir Edmund that she would be wanting the Rolls after lunch. He was in his office filling in a ledger.

'I'll bet she does,' was his answer to Carmichael's message. 'Yes, tell her that's OK and I hope all the arrangements will be as planned.' He went back to his writing. On the desk in front of him was a large, ornate, brass inkstand. It looked heavy and lethal. Agnes felt at that moment she would have loved to pick it up and fell him with it. She turned on her heel and abruptly left the room.

She had put on a mac and headscarf before she came down to speak to Sir Edmund and now she went through the kitchen and out of the back door to find Basil. He was cleaning the windscreen of Alison's car. The rain had almost stopped.

'Lady Bellamy needs to go to Leicester this afternoon, Basil,' she said.

Basil looked up from his task. 'What time, miss?' he asked.

'Not quite sure yet, Basil.' Agnes went along to the stables, but the horses were not there.

'Miss Alison and Nigel are out. They rode up to Top Farm, I think, and are coming back via Maud's bungalow to see how it's getting on.' He laughed.

'Who are the Fletchers who have bought Maud's cottage, Basil? Are they local people?'

'The Fletchers? Oh yes, nice old couple; well-feathered, too, but their house is too big for them now the children are married and gone away. Conkers Lane they live, next door but one to Hetty's aunt's little shop.'

Agnes nodded. 'I see,' she said and at that moment Basil's telephone rang and he hurried into his cottage.

She felt as she went back to Lady Bellamy that the village and the county were becoming familiar to her in rather a strange way. The Fletchers, the Bellamys, the Hilliers, Harry Dwyer, Hetty's aunt, Maud Spencer, Basil – Agnes Carmichael of Penny Stratton, she thought to herself, then aloud, 'Spinster of this Parish.'

'Two thirty we'll set out, if you don't mind, Agnes,' said Lady Bellamy as Carmichael entered the room. 'I've told Basil to bring the car round.' She laughed suddenly. 'Miss West wasn't too pleased, though.'

At two thirty promptly Basil drew up the Rolls at the front door of the Manor and Agnes helped Lady Bellamy into it.

The afternoon visits to lawyer, accountant and bank manager were rather boring for Agnes. She helped her patient up to the various offices and waited outside. At about four thirty Lady Bellamy emerged from the last visit, her lawyer, and once in the Rolls she instructed Basil to take them to the Hilliers.'

During the drive Agnes asked Lady Bellamy if she knew the Fletchers.

'Oh yes, indeed. She's a great bridge player. Nice people.'

Agnes told her they had apparently bought Maud's cottage.

'Well, that's a good idea; there's only the two of them now. So Maud has sold her cottage. Well, I'm glad for her.' She went on, 'I've settled everything I can, Agnes. Edmund will get his ten thousand a year, but I've spread it to quarterly payments. If

I let him have it all at once he'd just bet it away or spend it somehow. My lawyer couldn't understand why he had to have it, and I couldn't tell him. My accountant couldn't understand, either. The bank manager asked no questions, which was a relief.' She said all this while they were waiting at the garage for Basil, who was paying for petrol. When he re-entered the car Agnes and Lady Bellamy continued to talk about Maud's move.

At the Hilliers' they were greeted with the usual warmth from both human and animal occupants. Agnes was touched by the way they greeted her, as a friend, not as an employee of the Bellamy family.

The fire blazed in the untidy book- and newspaper-strewn room. Agnes loved the disorder of the house, yet knew it was something she could not stage. She was tidy by nature and as she moved the colour supplement of the *Sunday Times* and the copy of *Bartlett's Quotations* from the armchair she was invited to sit in, she realized it would not be possible to achieve this almost sweet disorder.

Agnes wondered if Lady Bellamy would say anything to the Hilliers about Alison's pregnancy or her approaching marriage – it was obvious that the Hilliers were close and old friends. However, she didn't.

Madge Hillier darted into the kitchen and Bernard and Gladys Bellamy talked about farm and estate matters. In a very short time Madge came back wheeling a rather rickety trolley, on which was a tarnished silver teapot and a plate of delicious hot buttered scones.

'There you are, all made by my own darling hand,' she laughed, 'and strawberry jam made with the last of our strawberries.'

The scones were delicious. 'How do you do that, Madge?' Gladys Bellamy asked.

'No problem. I can make scones in a flash. Flour and water and stuff.' Madge laughed. 'Mind, they're hot.'

After tea Lady Bellamy got up with difficulty. Agnes could see that she was stiff and tired. She helped her.

'Oh, I forgot to tell you,' Madge exclaimed as they were making their way towards the front door. 'Do you remember Tracy Matthews – Marcia's friend? She came to your house several times, pretty dark girl.'

'Yes, I do. Why?' Gladys Bellamy asked.

144

'She's getting a divorce. She married an old flame of Marcia's, a Roman Catholic, she's Church of England. These mixed marriages never seem to work, do they? Poor girl.'

'Oh dear, I'm sorry.' Lady Bellamy did not refer to the remark till they were in the Rolls and the Hilliers' front door was closing. 'That's a cheering parting shot, Agnes. Do you think it's true?'

'No, of course I don't.' Agnes did not enlarge on the subject in front of Basil and it was dropped.

'Well, a good afternoon's work done, I suppose – if you can call it good.' Lady Bellamy eased her hip on the car seat.

'Does your leg hurt?' asked Agnes.

'Well, not too bad. Probably all the better for not having our Miss West pummelling it about.'

'Now, I don't think that's quite true, Lady Bellamy,' said Agnes, but she smiled all the same.

The moment she awoke the next morning Carmichael wished she had not made the dinner date with Harry Dwyer. Why was it one did these ridiculous things? she grumbled to herself as she dressed and got ready to attend to Lady Bellamy's needs. At the time you think it's a pleasant idea, then when the time arrives you wish you hadn't to go.

Once her patient was dressed and ready for her breakfast Agnes went down to the kitchen to fetch the tray and, having settled Lady Bellamy with it, she herself went down to the dining-room.

Nigel was at the hot plate helping himself to bacon and eggs and mushrooms. Alison came in as he was carrying his plate to the table, closed the door behind her, went up to Nigel and they exchanged a long kiss. Then, rather to Agnes' surprise and pleasure, Alison turned round, put her arms round her and kissed her, too.

'Grandpa and Grandma and you all know about us now, thank goodness,' she said. 'So we don't have to be afraid any longer wondering if they can see us.' She went and stood by Nigel.

Then he spoke. 'And a lot of this straightening out and helping Grandmother and us over what might have been a time full of disharmony is due to you, I think.' Nigel kissed Agnes' hand. As he said this, the word 'disharmony' and the kissing of her hand made his Italian origin seem more marked to Carmichael and on impulse, although Agnes was not a demonstrative person, she kissed Alison back and pressed Nigel's arm.

'I'm so glad for both of you,' she said and meant it. Though the burden of what hung over them would never disappear, at least they loved each other and she hoped they would never suffer the spectre that seemed to be hanging over her head more and more as she got older – loneliness.

Sir Edmund came in and grunted a 'Good morning', helped himself to breakfast and retired, as usual, behind his paper. His very presence seemed to dampen the feeling of joy and love so obviously shared by the young couple.

The meal proceeded in silence. Edmund, helping himself to mustard, maybe because his hand shook slightly, dropped the lid of the mustard pot with a clatter on to the polished table. In the silent room it made a sound like a pistol shot.

Alison looked up with a start.

'It's all right, it's all right. No damage done,' Sir Edmund said irritably, as if someone had accused him of carelessness. He left the room first and as the door closed behind him Alison looked across at Agnes Carmichael.

'You're having dinner with Harry Dwyer this evening, aren't you?'

'Who told you that?' Agnes smiled.

'Gran, of course.'

'Yes. I rather wish I wasn't.'

'Why?' Alison asked in surprise.

'Oh, I don't know. I was thinking upstairs, one makes these arrangements, then wishes one hadn't.'

Alison poured herself more tea. 'Oh, you'll enjoy it. You must get sick of us and all our problems.'

'No, I don't,' said Agnes positively.

Lady Bellamy was seated at her dressing table. She had squeezed a tiny drop of Vitapoint into her hand and was lightly brushing it over her hair.

'Hairdresser this afternoon, Agnes, thank goodness,' she said, speaking to her through the mirror.

'Yes, and talking of hairdressers, I don't know what to do with my hair. It looks awful.'

146

'It doesn't, your hair is so beautifully cut it always looks nice, but if you feel it doesn't, let Hester do it. She's quite good.'

Agnes was pleased at the thought. 'She may have another appointment to go to, Lady Bellamy,' she said.

'Oh, she'll probably squeeze you in, especially if I cross her hand with silver. I must get those letters off verifying the arrangements I made yesterday. I'll do that this mornng; I hate writing letters.' She went over to her little bureau and made a face as she sat down on the hard chair in front of it. 'Cushion, I think, Agnes dear,' she said. 'Will you take the letters to the post office? The one in the village will do. I've no stamps and I don't want to ask Edmund for them.'

'Of course I will. I'd like the walk,' Agnes replied and Lady Bellamy got up with some difficulty while Agnes popped the cushion underneath her.

The walk to the village shop which housed the post office was interesting to Agnes because it meant she could get a glimpse of the Fletchers' house. After posting the letters she went along a little further to the gate of the house and noticed that the board read *Hunt & Palmer, Estate Agents, Thorne Road, Leicester. For Sale, Enquire within.* She went and rang the bell.

'Oh yes. Do come in.' The white-haired lady who opened the door smiled pleasantly enough, but looked slightly harassed. She whisked Agnes through into what she presumed was the dining-room. 'It's just that we haven't had anyone to see the house until this afternoon, and now there are two of you. My husband is just . . .' She looked towards the stairs. 'If you will wait a moment – Oh, here he is.' A grey-haired man ushered a tall, imposing, dark-haired lady into the room where Agnes sat, rather self-consciously, at the dining-room table.

'And this is the dining-room.' He looked towards his wife as if asking her to explain the presence of the strange woman.

Mrs Fletcher made rather a faltering introduction. 'This is Mrs – er – Mrs Emanuel. This is . . . ?'

'Agnes Carmichael.' Agnes supplied the name.

'Miss Carmichael,' repeated Mrs Fletcher.

Mrs Emanuel inclined her head towards Agnes Carmichael, flashed a heavily lipsticked smile at her and wafted a hand.

'Hallo,' she said. Then she looked round the dining-room. 'Rather small, isn't it?' she said. 'I like to entertain quite a lot.' Her accent was American.

147

'Well, we seat about eight round the table,' said the grey-haired man Agnes assumed was Mr Fletcher, rather defensively.

With another glance round the room they left. Mrs Fletcher murmured something and followed.

Agnes waited for about ten minutes. The front door closed and she heard a car start. Then in walked Mrs Fletcher, full of apologies and explanations, and proceeded to conduct Agnes Carmichael over the property.

'It's an attractive house,' Agnes told Lady Bellamy on her return to Nettlestone Manor. 'Three bedrooms, two bathrooms, dining-room, sort of little morning room, a large sitting-room and kitchen. I think it's the garden that is largely responsible for their move; it's very large for them and partly sloping – difficult.'

'Would you like it, Agnes? Would you like to live in Penny Stratton?'

Agnes looked directly at Lady Bellamy, then looked away. 'Yes, I believe I would. I'm not sure,' she said. 'I don't want to go south again and I don't care for London. The little I have seen of Leicestershire I rather like.'

Lady Bellamy put her hand on Agnes' arm. 'You've come through something very sad and hard. At least you would have friends here.' She squeezed Agnes' arm lightly. 'Don't forget that.'

Carmichael shook her head, but could not speak. The kindness of her patient had made the tears prick behind her eyes.

There was time for a short rest for her patient before the hairdresser came. Yes, she could fit in Sister Carmichael.

At tea-time Alison was briefed about the help Lady Bellamy would need when she was retiring and Agnes went to her room to change.

She put on a little more make-up than usual, some perfume, and she was ready. She had confided to Lady Bellamy, as she had to Alison, that she rather wished she had not made the date, but both Alison and her patient brushed this aside.

'Oh, come. Harry Dwyer is quite a presentable man – you will enjoy going out. It will be a change for you.'

When Agnes was at last speeding along the main road to Leicester and the Horse and Groom, the silver car purring, she began to feel a little more cheerful anticipation – she had not been out to dinner with a man since . . . She thrust that thought aside. The yellow lights made the road like gold and the sky like black velvet.

The Horse and Groom was lit with fairy lights outside and it looked quite attractive. She drove into the car-park and noticed, four cars away from her, the red Porsche. She got out, pressed her remote control to lock the car, and made her way across the gravel and in through the doors of the road-house.

22

Harry Dwyer was standing waiting for Agnes in the large red-carpeted foyer. He came forward smiling. 'Good evening, Agnes, lovely to see you. Would you like to leave your coat here?' He indicated a coat rack, took the garment from her and hung it up.

'Now.' He pointed to the left. 'Would you prefer a drink in the Huntsmen's Bar or the Saddle and Bridle Bar, there?' He pointed to his right.

Agnes chose the Huntsmen's. They went down four steps into a rather dimly lit bar and walked to a small table.

'What will you drink?' He seemed to be well acquainted with the surroundings, which rather pleased Agnes. He walked away towards the bar and Agnes watched him from the table. He was shorter and rather fatter than she had remembered. She looked round. It was a large room and the bar itself was horseshoe-shaped. Harry Dwyer stood with his back to her; the bar was crowded. Agnes took the opportunity to take her compact out and check her lipstick.

'Here we are.' Harry placed the drink she had asked for in front of her and what looked like a large gin and tonic in front of his seat. The lemon in his drink was hidden for a moment by some bubbles as he added the tonic. A waiter approached their table with a 'Good evening, sir,' and placed two dishes, one containing olives and the other crisps, on their table.

'Evening, Jeff,' Harry replied. 'Thanks.' He pushed the dishes closer towards Agnes. 'I've recently had dinner with the Hilliers. I believe you have met them. They were there when I . . . Great couple, terrible dogs, one covered me with mud.' He laughed, good-naturedly. 'Have you met the dogs?'

'Yes, I have. I like the Hilliers and I like their house, there's something so welcoming about it.'

He agreed. 'The dogs are bit too welcoming. I'm a cat man myself. My wife used to breed Burmese, I've still got two. I make fools of them, spoil them.' He took a large gulp of his drink.

Agnes was about to ask more about the cats when their attention was drawn to the far side of the bar. A glass splintered on the tiled floor and an angry voice exclaimed: 'What the hell do you think you're doing? Barging into people.'

A quieter voice answered. 'Sorry, old man, but you lurched against me.'

'Lurched? What do you mean, lurched?' The voice was easily recognizable to Harry Dwyer and to Agnes. It was Edmund Bellamy.

'Oh Lord, here we go again. I suggest we beat a retreat.' He picked up his glass and Agnes' and they left the bar, crossed the foyer and went into the other bar. Even then they could hear the sound of raised voices.

'I didn't see the Rolls parked outside,' Agnes said.

Harry Dwyer shook his head. 'If Basil's not driving him, and he usually isn't at this time in the evening, he parks it round the back. Poor old chap, he prefers to do his drinking anonymously.'

Agnes was sorry the incident had occurred at all. After a few moments she glimpsed Sir Edmund walking across the red carpet of the hall and heard the front door of the hotel bang behind him.

'He's gone, thank goodness,' she said. 'He sounded rather troublesome.'

'Well, we can forget about him now. I hope he gets home safely.'

'We can try,' said Agnes, but she could not help worrying about Sir Edmund driving in the state he was. He might go on to another pub and crash the car, and she would not be there to comfort and support Lady Bellamy.

'I know what you're thinking,' Harry Dwyer said, 'but Edmund has driven home more times than you can imagine with a load on. That old Rolls knows the way home by itself. Don't worry.'

Agnes tried to put the thought of Sir Edmund out of her mind and the rest of the evening was more enjoyable than she had expected. The food was good. She refused any other but non-alcoholic wine and, rather to her surprise, Harry Dwyer shared it with her. He had travelled a great deal and talked well. He spoke once or twice about his late wife. He had a son who was married and in advertising and was an enthusiastic hang-glider. Harry Dwyer had apparently tried it once, but in his own words, 'It had frightened him to death.'

Agnes Carmichael felt she had little in the way of conversation to exchange with him. When he asked her about her life she said, 'I've done a lot of work in the South of England, mostly attached to hospitals, but I thought I'd like a change. Lady Bellamy is actually my first private patient.'

'She's a dear person,' Harry said.

'Indeed,' Agnes answered.

'Do you like this part of the world?' he asked.

'Yes, more than I thought I would,' Agnes answered, without much enthusiasm.

'I know,' he grinned. 'Everything north of Potters Bar is "on safari" to you southerners.'

Agnes smiled. 'Something like that, I suppose.'

She allowed herself a kümmel with her coffee and was surprised when she glanced at her watch to find it was ten past ten.

'I said I wouldn't be late back, Harry. I feel I ought to go. It's been most enjoyable. Thank you.'

Having helped her on with her coat, Harry said, 'I'd like to do this again, or lunch perhaps, whichever you prefer.'

Agnes hesitated. 'Yes, that would be nice, but of course I'm not sure how much longer Lady Bellamy will be needing me.'

'Oh!' He had obviously not thought of that. 'And what then?' he asked.

Agnes felt her spirits sink. 'I go back to London – to the Nursing Co-op,' she said.

'Well, we must meet again before that sad event.'

They walked out into the cold night air and on the way back to her car he said again, 'I may ring you, then?'

She got into the driver's seat before she answered him, then looked up at him. 'Please do. I would like that,' she said.

She saw him again – he was the first to drive out of the broad entrance to the car-park. He waved and turned for the town centre and she turned left towards Penny Stratton.

It was only after she had been driving for ten minutes that her headlights lit up the car in front of her. It was the Rolls and it was weaving from side to side. She slowed down, deciding to leave plenty of space between herself and Sir Edmund Bellamy.

23

A turn in the road hid the Rolls from Carmichael's view for a minute or two then, as she reached the bend herself, the car came into view again. This time it was on the wrong side of the road and hardly moving. Agnes wonderd if Sir Edmund had passed out. Suddenly he must have wrenched his steering wheel; the car crossed the white line in the middle of the road and almost landed up with its bonnet in the opposite hedge, but it straightened and proceeded a little way without swerving.

It looked as if Sir Edmund had been startled at finding the car on the wrong side of the road and he was now driving dangerously close to the rising grass verge, the ditch and the thorny tangle of the briar hedge that divided the road from the adjacent fields. An approaching car flashed by them, its dipped headlamps lighting up the asphalt. Another bend, and Carmichael saw the Rolls lurch a little as the driver hit his far side wheels on the rise of the verge. She slowed her car still more. The rate at which she was having to drive irritated her, but she was fearful of overtaking Sir Edmund while he was driving so erratically.

Lights from a car behind her appeared suddenly out of the darkness and drew closer and closer to the Porsche's back bumper. The driver hooted once, twice, then the blue car drew out and overtook her. She glimpsed a woman's white face gazing at her in annoyance from the passenger seat window, then the car gathered speed and passed her and the Rolls, which was still well tucked into the side of the road.

Carmichael debated whether she should do the same and pass Edmund Bellamy at speed – indeed she flashed her indicator automatically, although at the moment there was no car behind her. Then, out of the gloom, way along the road, a figure was lit up by the headlights of Sir Edmund's car, walking towards them. The Rolls continued to hug the hedge. The man, for Agnes could now see the figure clearly, was youngish, wearing blue jeans and a black plastic jacket, the zip of which was shining in the car lights. The Rolls drew closer, lighting up the man's black hair, red healthy face and rather large moustache. That was the last Agnes saw before the Rolls hit him. Sir Edmund had appeared to put his foot on the accelerator, for the car had leapt forward. Agnes thought for a second it had swerved enough to miss the man, but it had not. He rose in the air as the wing of the car struck him, then he fell backwards on to the verge. The Rolls passed and he rolled down like a doll, like a puppet, into the road. The Rolls sped on.

As Agnes drew to a halt beside the fallen man she saw the red tail lights of Sir Edmund's car: the Rolls had now moved over to the middle of the road again. Another bend and it disappeared.

Agnes got out of her car and went to the man Sir Edmund had so callously left behind him. He was lying on his back, legs spread-eagled. He turned his head and his eyes – glazed – looked at her. He clutched his stomach, his head fell sideways and he lost consciousness. Agnes left the headlights of the Porsche trained on him and tried to stop the next passing car. It flashed past her, accelerating rather than stopping. After two more had raced by she realized they were frightened it was a trap. She had heard of people doing this and then mugging the person who stopped to help. She regretted bitterly she had no telephone in the car, the one thing she had thought a useless luxury – for who had she to telephone?

Another car coming the other way refused to stop, in spite of Agnes' waving. She decided she had to get the man to hospital herself – she felt the nurse in her taking over completely. The Porsche was as near as she could get it to him. She opened the door, took out the rug, rolled it under the man as gently as she could, then taking the top two corners she pulled him towards the open door. Surely, she thought, someone would stop as

153

they saw her trying to – but the cars still went by and nobody stopped.

Inch by inch, and handling the man as gently as she could, she got him to the car door, then lifted his shoulders. By the time she had managed to get him into the car and settled on the floor, his head on one side, she was conscious of the perspiration running down her neck and down between her breasts – not from heat, for it was a cold evening, nor was the exertion very great for the man was thin and light, but from sheer anxiety and fear that she might make his injuries worse. His pulse was rapid and his breathing shallow, and she was fearful that meant internal bleeding.

She turned the car and sped back to Leicester and to the hospital. As she drove in she felt she had never seen a more welcome word than CASUALTY in lights over the door at the right of the hospital entrance. She drew up to the door, parked on the spot marked AMBULANCES ONLY, got out and dashed into the Casualty Department.

'Please help me,' she said to the Sister sitting at the desk just inside the deserted department. 'I've got an injured man in my car outside – I think he's very bad, Sister. It's a hit and run, RTA. I'm a trained nurse, Sister Carmichael.'

The Sister seemed to take the situation in quickly and turned to a nurse who had just walked out of a curtained area. 'Get two porters and a trolley,' she said and followed Carmichael out to her car, standing shining, the engine still running. The Casualty Sister leant in and looked at the man, put a hand on his wrist, then on his neck. Agnes Carmichael felt a surge of relief. Two white-clad porters lifted the man out with some difficulty and laid him on the trolley they had brought with them. The familiar red blanket was draped over him and at a word from Sister he was pushed through the doors that opened as they approached.

Carmichael switched off the car engine, locked the car and followed the trolley. It went through two further doors, which closed behind it. A nurse appeared.

'Waiting room, please,' she said and pointed to a door marked 'Waiting Room'. Carmichael went in and sank down on one of the plastic chairs. In a corner stood a large fish tank in which tropical fish darted about, the bubbles bursting through the water at one corner. Agnes watched it; there was nothing more she could do. Once it would have been her province, her responsibility, to do what the woman she had just seen would be doing – phoning the surigcal registrar, getting a drip ready, cutting off the man's clothes, taking his blood pressure, alerting the theatre. She put her head in her hands; she felt exhausted and redundant. She watched the fish and tried to regain her composure. Fifteen minutes dragged by.

After about ten more minutes she felt better. From where she sat she could see the glass doors that led into the department, but they were opaque. Figures moved about behind them. The other end of the waiting room led out into the hall from where she had come. That door suddenly opened and a woman, her hand wrapped in a towel stained with blood, was led in by a man. He looked at Carmichael, went to the further door and pressed the bell push.

'Sit down, dear,' he said and the woman sat down in a chair, still clutching her hand. She looked at Agnes.

'Cut my hand opening a corned beef tin, it slipped.' She was white-faced and sweating slightly.

A nurse put her head round the door. 'Yes?' she said.

'It's my wife, she's cut her hand.' The nurse nodded.

'Come through,' she said.

Agnes gave her no marks for courtesy or feeling. The door shut behind the man and woman.

Agnes got up and rang the bell that she had not noticed until the man had used it, in spite of a small sticker over it which said 'Please ring'. There was a pause, then another nurse appeared.

'Can I help you?' she said.

'Yes, may I use the telephone?'

'Sure. It's outside, just by the door, in the hall.' As she was about to close the door again the Sister appeared.

'Oh! You're not leaving,' she said. 'You'd better stay.'

'No, I just want to telephone.'

The Sister turned as if to go back into the department, then changed her mind.

'Could you come through and see me after you've telephoned?' she asked.

'Of course. How is he?'

Sister came forward a little. 'Did you say you were a nurse?' she asked.

'Yes, private nurse, but I was Casualty Sister.'

'Oh well – he's pretty bad. In theatre at the moment. His injuries are – well, go and telephone, we can talk afterwards.'

Agnes made her way out into the hall. First she went outside and reparked her car: she was very conscious that an ambulance might need the space. That done, she went to the telephone.

'Oh Agnes, how awful for you. Yes, thank you, I'm quite well. I'm in bed and Alison has been wonderful. But what about you? When will you . . . ?'

'I don't know, Lady Bellamy. I've got to see the Sister and maybe the police if they come, I don't know. Sister says the man is in the operating theatre.'

After the conversation had ceased Carmichael went back through the swing doors, into the waiting room and through the far doors into the Casualty Department itself. She sat down at the desk where she had first seen the navy blue-clad Sister sitting, and waited.

After only a minute Sister came out from a curtained cubicle where, presumably, the woman with the cut hand was being attended to.

'Bad news, I'm afraid – er – Sister Carmichael, isn't it?' Carmichael nodded. 'They've just rung. He's dead. Died on the table. Ruptured liver, spleen. Must have taken some whack – the car must be a bit bent. The police are coming.' She sat down tiredly. 'Where did you train, Sister?'

Carmichael told her.

'Retired?' she asked, uninterestedly.

'No, I'm not retired.' Agnes bridled slightly. At that moment a door in front of Sister's desk opened and a young policeman, followed by a policewoman, came in.

'We've got a photograph, found on the victim.' Casualty Sister pushed a small, square photograph towards him across her desk. He picked it up. 'This is Sister Carmichael, who witnessed the RTA, Constable.'

'Oh hallo, Sister, you're a nurse then?'

'Yes.'

'That your Porsche outside?'

'Yes, it is. I couldn't get anyone to stop – on the road, I mean – so I brought him in myself, but his injuries . . .' She stopped speaking and picked up the photograph which the policeman had put back on the desk. It was of a woman holding a baby.

156

The woman was plump, fair-haired, smiling. The child in her arms was about a year old and as fair as his mother.

Agnes closed her eyes for a moment against the picture.

'What can you tell us, Miss – er – Carmichael?' asked the young policeman. They had both sat down, the constable and the woman constable, opposite her at Sister's desk. 'What can you tell us now it is fresh in your memory?'

Agnes was still silent. She thought of Lady Bellamy, the pain on her face when she moved across the room, her blackmailing husband, the problem of Alison and Nigel, the coming wedding and the pregnancy.

The young policeman's pencil was poised over his notebook.

'Of course, you'll probably have to make a full statement tomorrow at the police station, but what can you tell me about the car that knocked the man down? What kind of car was it, can you remember? You didn't get his number?'

Agnes was still silent. If I tell him, she thought, how will they ever prove Sir Edmund was drunk? He's home now, probably sleeping it off. What will they do to him? Two years barred from driving, perhaps? Fined one, or perhaps two thousand pounds. Basil will drive him if he's banned himself – his wife will have to pay the fine – at his age it's unlikely they will send him to prison. No, I can do better than that, she thought. She broke the silence at last.

'I really can't help you very much,' she said. 'I was driving along and I saw the man lying by the roadside, he was on his back. I stopped the car, got out, took my car rug and covered him. Then I tried, unsuccessfully I'm afraid, to stop a car going either way. I thought they could phone for an ambulance, but none of them would stop – at least five cars went by.' The policeman wrote busily and she went on. 'I put the rug under him and managed to get him in my car. I thought someone would see me and stop and help – but no, they didn't.' Suddenly Agnes felt faint – dizzy.

The young policewoman got up, came across to her and put her hand on her shoulder kindly. 'I know, they won't now. The public just won't stop, in case – in case it's a set up. They're afraid, afraid that they might stop and then get attacked. It has happened.'

Carmichael nodded, then she shivered slightly. The Casualty Sister looked at the policeman reproachfully. 'I think she should lie down for a little. After all, she did get him here – she's had enough for one night.'

He nodded. 'I suppose so,' he said.

Agnes got up and the Sister took her arm and led her through into the night stay ward, off the large curtained casualty area. Agnes lay down thankfully.

'I do feel a bit shaky,' she said.

'I'm sure you do. I'll get you a cup of tea.' The Sister bustled off.

Agnes lay on the bed. She decided she would stay for half an hour or so, then she would drive home. She was half amused that the police had obviously examined her car to see it was not she who had struck the man; they would presumably be looking for any damage. Well, they wouldn't find any. She wondered about Sir Edmund – would there be much damage to his car and what would he do about it? Did he know, or was he too drunk to remember that he had hit the man? She smiled gratefully at the Sister as she took the cup of tea from her.

'That poor woman and baby,' she said. 'There was nothing on the man to say who he was. There was some money in his pocket and some keys, but nothing else – no letter, no driving licence, nothing except that photograph.' She sighed.

'Yes indeed,' Agnes replied. 'Poor woman. They won't even be able to let her know till they find out who he is.'

'The trouble is they don't punish these hit and run drivers enough, if they do catch them. He or she was probably drunk.'

'Very probably,' said Agnes, sipping the tea. She was feeling calmer now. 'Very probably.'

'I must get back. You'll be all right?' Sister asked Carmichael.

'Yes, I'll be quite all right, and thank you for being so kind.' Agnes smiled at her and the Sister left the room.

After half an hour, Carmichael felt better. She got up and went through the department, being careful to take her cup and saucer with her and place them on the desk. The Sister came out of another cubicle; obviously they had another casualty in, but to Carmichael – considering that the hospital was so large and in a busy area – the department seemed very quiet.

'You're having a quiet night, Sister,' she said.

The woman nodded. 'Thank goodness – it's a change to have a quiet night here, especially when the Leicester races are on.' She laughed. 'Do you miss working in Casualty?' she asked.

'I do and I don't.' Both women laughed. 'It was nice when I was working there, but it's more restful, I suppose, to be out of it when you get older.' She looked at the woman with a trace of malice in her eyes. Carmichael hadn't yet forgotten the Casualty Sister's remark, 'Retired?' She must, she thought, look older than she realized.

'I'll go now, if you don't mind. I feel quite up to driving.'

The Sister nodded. 'OK. Well, you gave your name and address and everything to the police. They'll probably be in touch with you, I don't know. As you didn't see the other car maybe they won't, but as you found the man injured they might. Anyway . . .'

Carmichael put her hand out impulsively and shook the Casualty Sister's hand warmly. She felt it was, in a way, an old-fashioned gesture, for the Sister looked slightly surprised.

'You have a new Casualty Consultant here, Dr Patel – Mr Patel now, I believe. He worked in a hospital I was at.'

'Really? How did you get on with him – he's Indian, isn't he?' There was something in the Sister's voice that Carmichael did not like.

'Very well indeed. He's a very good doctor and very willing and able.' She regretted the fact that she had said it almost defensively.

'Oh well. I suppose we'll get used to having an Indian in charge.'

'He's Pakistani, actually,' said Carmichael.

'Well – I never know the difference.' The Sister laughed again, but not as easily this time. There was something in her change of mood that made Carmichael think that Patel might not find his Casualty Department a bed of roses.

'Good-night then, Sister, and thank you again,' she said and left the department.

Outside the night was cold and the sky clear and full of stars. Carmichael stood there for a moment and looked up at them. The same stars, she thought, were looking down on that woman and that baby somewhere, somewhere in England. She didn't yet know that she had lost her husband and the child had lost its father. She went down the small ramp to the ambulance area and walked to her car. It stood shining as usual – opulent, safe, friendly. She got in and closed the door with its rich thud. She sat a little longer before starting the engine. She realized that she felt exhausted, not physically but mentally. The responsibility of the sick man; that had been the exhausting factor. In the old days, surrounded by her Casualty Department and her nurses, it would not have tired her at all. She started the car, drove out of the hospital gates and headed back to Nettlestone Manor.

24

The Hilliers arrived unexpectedly the next morning whilst Lady Bellamy was putting the final touches to her make-up.

'That sounds like Madge's car,' she said, looking up at Agnes.

'Yes, it is – Major and Mrs Hillier,' Agnes said from her vantage point at the window.

'Good, Edmund will take care of them.'

'How are you, Gladys?' Madge Hillier greeted Lady Bellamy as Agnes walked with her slowly into the sitting-room. As she helped her to her chair the little clock on the mantelpiece chimed twelve o'clock.

'I'm getting better every day, thanks to Agnes here.' Gladys Bellamy did look better and was walking more easily, using only a stick.

'And thanks to Miss West,' said Agnes, gently.

'My dreaded physiotherapist,' Gladys Bellamy said, laughing.

'Whisky, Bernard?' Edmund Bellamy asked.

'Thanks, Edmund.'

Madge asked for the usual gin and tonic.

'Nasty business, that man knocked down last night – the bastard left him to die. The radio said he did die, too. Someone got him to hospital. I didn't hear much of it, just bits.'

'That was Agnes. She had to take him. He was left lying by the roadside.'

There was a slight crash. 'I dropped the ice.' Edmund's voice sounded a degree shaky.

'Unfortunately I couldn't get help, no one would stop,' said Agnes quietly, conscious that Sir Edmund was looking at her, the tilted ice bucket still in his hand.

'How awful for you, Agnes,' Madge exclaimed. 'I think you

were brave to stop. I wouldn't, not on that road at night, not if there were six bodies in a row.'

Agnes smiled slightly. 'Well, there was only one, Mrs Hillier.'

'Agnes had to go to the police station this morning to make some kind of statement about it all. Poor Agnes, she has had a time.'

'Your drink, Gladys.' Sir Edmund proffered her a gin and tonic and looked at Agnes again.

'Just mineral water, thank you, Sir Edmund,' she said.

His eyes remained fixed on her face. 'Did he tell you who he was, this fellow?' he asked. 'Did he see who hit him?'

'No, he never spoke. I believe he never regained consciousness.'

Edmund Bellamy, she could see, had difficulty in suppressing his relief. He handed her her drink and sat down.

'How's the wedding coming along?' Madge Hillier obviously wanted to change the subject.

'Slowly. Nigel and Alison are determined to make it a quiet affair. Village church, of course.'

'Top Farm is empty, I see,' said Bernard. 'Is Nigel looking after the stock?'

'No, the cowman is staying,' answered Sir Edmund and the conversation then became general.

'That was your gorgeous Porsche outside?' Bernard looked across at Agnes. She liked both him and his wife. No envy, no questions; they were easy.

'Yes, I left it there when I came back from Leicester this morning. Nigel and Alison were just coming out on the horses so I left it there for the moment. I'll take it round to the garage later.'

Agnes wondered what effect this remark would have on Edmund. Basil usually got the Rolls out about now for a polish or a look at the engine. When she had gone off to Leicester earlier the Rolls had been in the garage, so he must know she could not have seen the damage that could have been caused by the accident.

When she had awakened this morning and got dressed she had done everything like an automaton. She had felt seriously disorientated; even when she started her car and drove out it was as if for a moment her life had gone into rewind. Perhaps it was the visit to the Casualty Department, the familiar smell, the lights, the uniform. Well, that was over for ever and ever for her.

The visit to the police station had been uneventful. She had repeated her story: seeing the man hit, stopping, getting him to the hospital, trying to stop the cars, his one groan, and then nothing. No, she had said again, she could not identify the car that had struck him other than it was dark in colour. All her attention had been on the prone figure. They had been sympathetic, polite and kind, and had complimented her on her action. They had quite understood, but had impressed on her that if she remembered any more – as sometimes, they said, people did in such a situation – she should go back and report to them immediately, and she had promised she would do so. No, they had said, the man had not yet been identified, but the woman's picture was going to be out on television, etc, etc.

Agnes felt that as far as Sir Edmund was concerned she had him firmly on her hook if he threatened her patient in any way at all. If he demanded more money, or threatened to say something at the wedding or wreck the lives of these two youngsters – then she would confront him!

After a little while Agnes excused herself to go and put the car away. As she went out of the front door she felt Sir Edmund's eyes following her. He must realize she would see the Rolls now.

As she had predicted to herself, Basil was washing the Rolls.

'Morning, Sister,' he said. 'Like me to give yours a bit of a wheel wash?' He pointed to the wheels of the Porsche as she stopped outside the garage; they were muddy.

'Thank you, Basil. I'd be grateful.' She decided to leave her car outside and got out and approached him.

'Look at that. Look what his nibs did to the garage door last night.' He pointed. The white-painted door frame had a large piece of wood splintered out. 'Look what he's done to the wing – dratted man. In his cups again, I know.'

Agnes looked at the car. The outside wing was buckled and even showed some flakes of white paint from the garage door frame. Clever Sir Edmund, she thought – clever Sir Edmund.

'He's done that before. Why he doesn't leave it outside and let me put it away in the morning I don't know. Silly bugger.' The last two words were said under his breath out of deference to Carmichael's presence, but she heard them.

162

'Why doesn't Sir Edmund let you drive him, Basil?' she asked.

'Never 'as done, not when he goes out at night. I could tell you why, miss, Sister, but I won't – not seemly.' He stroked the damaged wing as if the car was alive. 'The wrong sort of people have good cars,' he said then, realizing what he'd implied, he looked at the Porsche. 'Present company excepted of course, Sister,' he said. He looked embarrassed about his remark.

'Of course, Basil,' said Carmichael and made her way through the back door and into the house.

Back in the sitting-room the Hilliers were preparing to leave. Madge pressed her arm as she passed her and said gently, 'I still think that was brave, what you did last night. I tell you, I wouldn't dare stop. Maybe it's because you're a nurse, eh?'

'Maybe,' answered Agnes and she glanced at Sir Edmund. There was a little smile on his face – was it triumph? He looked at her and his eyes narrowed slightly, then he busied himself with saying goodbye to the Hilliers and seeing them to the front door.

He doesn't care at all that he killed that man last night; he doesn't care for his wife; he feels nothing for her injury; he feels no compassion for Alison or Nigel. Agnes was so preoccupied about her feeling regarding Sir Edmund that she did not hear Lady Bellamy's remark that lunch was ready until she said it for the second time.

25

'I don't believe it – a car remembering? It's against nature.' Basil banged his mug down on the table.

'I tell you, Basil, it's true. Miss Carmichael's car can remember the last person who sat in the seat and adjust the seat accordingly.'

Hetty giggled. 'So if you've got a large bum . . .'

'That's enough of that, Hetty,' said Maud, refilling Basil's mug.

'What's that about my car?' Agnes Carmichael walked in. It was elevenses time and Lady Bellamy was in the sitting-room talking to her husband. Carmichael, as she was passing the sitting-room, had heard him say: 'Well, it's got to be paid, Gladys, whether you like it or not,' so she had beaten a retreat to the kitchen.

'Well, what are they for anyway, in the car, these computer things? I tell you, one day they'll take over the world. Coffee, Miss Carmichael?'

'Yes, please, Maud – and I'll have it here with you, if I may.'

'Right, I'll take your cup off the sitting-room tray then, shall I, Sister? I've put three on,' Hetty said.

'Yes, do.' She turned to Basil. 'Thank you, Basil, for washing the Porsche.' She slid a five-pound note across the table while Maud's back was turned.

'Oh. Ta,' he said and the money disappeared in a flash.

'I heard what you were saying. Those commuters are the work of the devil.' Mrs May came in from the butler's pantry, where she had been cleaning silver.

'Computers, not commuters. That's people on trains,' Basil said, holding his cup out again for more.

'That's two cups you've had already,' said Maud, nevertheless pouring more.

'Well, is it rationed now, then?'

'Coffee, Mrs May?'

'Yes, please. Well, I know a girl – at least my friend knew a girl – who worked in an office on one of those commuters and her eyes went green, dark green, and then she went blind.'

Maud paused, a piece of cake half-way to her mouth. 'No! Did she get compensation?'

'No. She tried, but it was no use, they wouldn't pay.'

Hetty regarded her with eyes like saucers. 'Come on, Mrs May, there's computers at the Town Hall.' She made for the door with her tray.

'Well, that's as may be; but mark my word, there'll be a big sale for white sticks if they go on with them.'

'It's true they do give some people headaches, but I don't know about blinding them,' said Agnes mildly.

Mrs May was undaunted. 'Oh yes, Sister, they do. They peel the cover off the back of your eye – commuter blindness, that's what it's called.'

There was silence while the kitchen digested this fact, then Basil changed the subject.

'Old Captain Forsyth's a gonner, then?'

'Yes, poor old chap.' Maud turned with more interest to Basil as he made the remark. 'Poor old soul. He was lonely, that man.'

'No wonder,' said Mrs May. 'He was a right dirty old man. I know, I worked there.'

'You did, for how long?' asked Hetty, who had returned from the sitting-room.

'Three hours – and that was too long.' Mrs May pressed her lips together and took another piece of cake. 'That house is in a pretty state, I bet.'

Agnes was interested. 'What house is that, Maud?' she asked.

'It's the Dower House that belongs to the estate.'

'Where is it?'

Maud explained. Apparently the Dower House was situated a good way down the lane that ran beside Maud's cottage.

'Haven't you ever seen it, Miss – Sister?' she asked.

'No, I've never been down that lane.'

'He rented it, Tim Forsyth. He never did anything to the garden. They kept on telling him he must keep it up, but he didn't. It's a real wilderness, a jungle. Nice little house, though.' Mrs May explained. 'He was senile, that's my opinion.'

'Did he threaten your honour?' asked Basil, winking at Agnes.

'That will do – no filth in my kitchen.' Maud's voice was threatening.

'He chased me round the 'all with a feather duster. If you can call that normal behaviour in a grown man . . . ?'

Hetty choked over her coffee. 'Why can't I meet someone like that?' she spluttered.

Mrs May sniffed. 'I know what I know,' she said. 'Those cats will starve to death. Two of them, Siamese, slinky animals.' Mrs May supplied more information. 'He was queer all right – Siamese cats.'

'How can he be queer and chase you with a feather duster?' said Hetty. 'If he was queer, he'd be after – ' A look from Maud silenced her.

Agnes got up, thanked Maud for the coffee and left the kitchen. She crossed the hall and entered the sitting-room. There was an immediate silence, although she had heard Sir Edmund talking rather loudly when she had shut the kitchen door behind her.

'I just want to slip into the village, if that's all right, Lady Bellamy.'

'Of course, Agnes.' Her patient looked at her; she was pale and seemed nervous.

'Are you all right, Lady Bellamy?' Agnes asked.

'Of course she is,' Sir Edmund snapped, obviously furious at the interruption.

Agnes left the room, went upstairs and put on a thick coat and a headscarf: the morning was chilly. As she crossed the hall again to the front door, not wanting to go through the kitchen, she paused, unashamedly listening.

'Well, look here, Gladys, I've got to pay him five thousand. That will shut him up.'

She heard Lady Bellamy's reply. 'Edmund, you will get the first instalment of the extra money you've demanded – a quarter of ten thousand – next week. I've arranged it with the bank.'

Sir Edmund's voice was raised in protest. 'For God's sake, I'm not paying that away on a debt. He wants it all now.'

'Well, I can't raise any more at the moment, Edmund.' Lady Bellamy sounded weary. Agnes stayed where she was to hear his reply.

'Gladys, I don't want to do this, but unless you cough up the five thousand I want now, I'm not staying quiet at this damn wedding, I warn you.' There was a pause. 'What do they say, "Speak now or for ever hold your peace", is that it?'

'You wouldn't do that, Edmund. You say you're fond of Nigel, you say he's your son, how can you even think of it?' Agnes heard the clink of ice going into a glass.

'Maybe I'd like to get him out of your granddaughter's clutches.'

Agnes had heard enough. She felt now it was time for her to have a showdown with Sir Edmund Bellamy, but first she had something important to do.

She drove to the village shop and there she purchased two big tins of Whiskas, which she asked Hetty's aunt to open for her. She also bought a little dish, a bottle of milk and some cat biscuits. The little plump shopkeeper looked at her curiously.

'Going to feed some cats?' she asked.

'That's right,' said Agnes and did not enlarge on the subject, but she felt Hetty's aunt watching her intently as she drove away.

After a little trouble she found her way to the back of the church and to Maud's cottage and started down the lane beside it. She had not gone far when the road veered sharply to the right, became a little rougher and more rutted. She motored on, and then she saw it: The Dower House. It was a low, grey stone house, tall chimneys at one end, the garden like a jungle. She drove up near the fence, got out and pushed at the gate; the base of it was choked with weeds. She slipped round it and went up to the front door, tried it, but it was locked. She peered in the downstairs windows, but they were all closed and she could not see much inside. The dirty curtains were half drawn. She stepped over the trailing brambles and skirted round unpruned rose bushes. A November garden, she thought, that had never known summer care.

She went round to the back of the house and found one window slightly open. She called – nothing. A bird twittered, but there was no other sound except the wind rustling in the tops of the trees. Then suddenly a Siamese voice – unmistakable – answered her. She stood in the desolate back garden as two Siamese cats squeezed through the open window, jumped to the ground and stood squinting at her. She opened her carrier and took out the two tins of Whiskas and turned the meat out on to the flagstones. The cats stopped their talking and fell to. They were obviously very hungry.

While they were eating Agnes examined the house more closely. The slate roof glistened in the sunlight; the grey stone blended with the fields and hedges around it. It nestled, that was the only way Agnes could describe it to herself – the house nestled against the slight rise behind it. In a way it resembled Nettlestone Manor, a small edition.

She returned to the cats. One was sitting on the windowsill washing its face, the other still sniffed round where the food had been. They both looked up at her as she approached. Agnes sat down on a small wooden bench by the back door. She took out of the carrier the little dish, filled it with milk and put it down for them. Only one drank, then they both jumped up on the sill, squeezed through the open window and were gone.

Agnes got up. She felt the deep satisfaction she always felt when dealing with an animal, particularly a cat in need of help. She would come back tomorrow, feed them and maybe get to know them a little better.

At the end of the house was a garage with a wooden door. She used the run-in to it to turn her car. She went slowly past the house. It drew her strangely – or was it the cats? She couldn't be sure. The Dower House, Captain Forsyth. He certainly hadn't done much for the garden, or probably the house inside either. Did he love cats? Why two? Maud was the one to ask. She drove back with a greater feeling of anticipation and lightheartedness than she had felt since Brian's death.

26

Agnes drove along the road, into the drive at the Manor, round the house and into the garage, but did not go in the back door. She was anxious to see if her patient and Sir Edmund were still downstairs in the sitting-room – if so, she did not want to interrupt them again.

Crossing the hall her suspicions were confirmed; the sitting-room door was closed, but Sir Edmund's voice could be heard quite plainly. Then she heard the softer voice of Lady Bellamy. They were still there and by the sound of it still arguing. The conclusion Carmichael had reached about their relationship precluded the thought that they were merely chatting amiably.

She made her way through to the kitchen, where the appetising smell of vegetable soup, one of Maud's specialities, pervaded the air.

Hetty greeted her. 'Hallo, Sister. Been out?'

'Yes, I have.' Agnes wanted to speak to Maud, who was busy stirring the large saucepan of soup.

'They're having a row, him and her, in the sitting-room. I heard him say . . .'

'That's enough, Hetty. You're not supposed to hear things, much less repeat them.' This was Maud, her back still turned to them. Hetty made a grimace at Agnes, which Maud caught just as she turned from the stove. 'Sister Carmichael doesn't want to hear it either,' she said.

'No, I don't, Maud, but I do want to ask you something.'

'Oh yes, Sister, what's that?' Maud proceeded to lay cold meats on a circular plate – ham, sliced chicken, tongue, beef, thinly cut. She paused in her task and looked up at Agnes. 'What's that, Sister, you want to ask me?' she said.

'Will you tell me more about the Dower House, Maud?'

'The Dower House. Well, it's part of – '

'The estate,' Agnes finished for her. 'Yes, Maud, you told me that, but tell me about Captain Forsyth. Was he married, did he live there alone or . . . ?'

Maud put the last piece of meat on the plate and proceeded to put out peeled tomatoes, lettuce and sliced cucumber round the edge. 'Yes, his wife died about five years ago, I think. She was a nice lady, quiet. She died of cancer. He nursed her right up to . . .' She paused and put the plate on a tray, then broke some eggs and proceeded to make mayonnaise, beating vigorously, dripping the oil in slowly. 'He was a writer, wrote mysteries, murders, under another name – don't remember it, though. Lady Bellamy said they were very good, she used to get them from the library.'

'You don't read murders, though, do you, Maud? You say they frighten you.' Hetty picked up a big platter to take it to the dining-room.

'Yes, they do frighten me.' She went back to her mayonnaise, which was beginning to thicken, as she whisked it. 'I think he sort of lost heart about his writing when his wife died. Janet, that's what he used to call her; they say he didn't write any more – let everything go.'

'Yes, I went there this morning to feed the cats. They were hungry.'

'Did you?' Maud went over to the stove and moved the saucepan slightly to one side. 'Those funny cats, they used to come and see me sometimes when he forgot to feed them. Their eyes – they're blue and sort of crossed, aren't they?'

Agnes nodded.

'That's because they're Siamese, isn't it?' asked Maud.

'That's right, Maud. But hadn't he anyone to look after them, go to the cottage, perhaps, or relatives to take them in? Poor things.'

'Don't know. Shouldn't think so, never heard of any relative or anything. You heard what Mrs May said – he was a bit peculiar, strange. Lady Bellamy said somebody was coming to clear the cottage; maybe they've done it already, I don't know.'

'Well, the cats are still there and they're lovely. It was

wonderful to feed them.' Agnes could see again those thin, beautiful creatures, their blue eyes squinting at her.

Maud sniffed. 'They kill birds, cats do,' she said, taking hot rolls out of the oven. 'These are just going in, Sister; lunch will be ready.' She took the heavy saucepan off the stove and poured the contents into a big tureen; she had already put the mayonnaise into a silver jug. Five small soup dishes went on the tray beside the tureen.

Hetty came back through the door and was about to pick up the tray.

'Rolls go up first,' called Maud.

Agnes left the kitchen following Hetty. 'They have had a row,' whispered Hetty, 'whatever Maud says.'

'Never mind, you shouldn't talk about it, Hetty.' Agnes' voice was mildly reproving.

In the dining-room Lady Bellamy sat at one end of the table and Sir Edmund at the other. Alison sat opposite the door and Agnes took the chair across from her. She looked anxiously at Lady Bellamy as she sat down. She thought her patient looked ill. Her husband looked angry. Alison seemed unaware of any atmosphere, isolated and separated, thought Agnes, by her love and happiness.

'Did you get what you wanted in the village, Agnes?' Gladys Bellamy smiled at Carmichael.

'Thank you, I did – just what I wanted.' Agnes smiled back. 'I must tell you about it after lunch. Thank you, Hetty.' This as Hetty ladled soup into the bowl in front of her.

'We've fixed the day for the wedding, Agnes. Two weeks' time.' Alison's eyes were bright, her cheeks flushed with the joy of letting out her secret.

'Goodness, that's soon,' said Agnes.

'Well, why should we wait? Top Farm is empty, we can get it ready and decorate and stay here meanwhile.' She smiled happily. 'We're only asking the family, the Hilliers and you.'

'At least it will be cheap.' Sir Edmund took a swig of sherry and poured some into his soup. His voice sounded surly, disagreeable, but nothing could quell Alison's happiness, even a remark like that in a tone like that.

'Cheap, dear Grandpa, I'll be Nigel's wife and that's all I want.'

There was a short silence while Hetty collected the soup bowls and put plates in front of everyone for the cold food.

'Nigel's wife. Well, I suppose all will go forward,' said Sir Edmund, helping himself to ham and chicken. 'Still, remember there's many a slip . . .' He looked up. 'Isn't that right, Gladys?' he said.

Agnes sensed the threat in his voice and she wondered just what had transpired between the two of them when they were talking in the sitting-room before lunch. Well, after lunch she would go upstairs with Lady Bellamy and, if possible, have a talk to her. She knew that her patient would want to tell her what her husband had said or threatened or demanded, and she herself wanted to talk about the Dower House.

All Carmichael's plans for a talk with her patient were set aside by a visitor. Sir Edmund had returned to the sitting-room after lunch and Alison had gone to the stables to give Jilly, the mare, a canter, when a peal on the doorbell interrupted Lady Bellamy's slow progress up the stairs.

Agnes answered the door. It was Madge Hillier standing in the winter sunshine, backed by her large, dirty Daimler. The colour of the car was disguised by its covering of Leicestershire mud. She slammed the front door behind her.

'Cold outside, but very nice. Just thought I'd drop in and see if you'd like a run, you haven't had much fresh air lately.'

Agnes looked at Lady Bellamy who, to her surprise, assented. 'Yes. Is Agnes included in the invitation?'

'Surely,' said Madge heartily. 'Bernard's out, shooting – not that he hits anything. I don't think he can see all that well lately, but he won't wear his glasses; he may bag a couple of local inhabitants.' Her hearty laugh shook the hall.

'Well, come on, Agnes, we'll put on warm things. Madge's car isn't completely draught-proof.'

'Oh yes, it is, and warm. Nigel fixed the heater for me. It's like a greenhouse on wheels.'

She was right. As they bowled along the lanes warm air belted out of the heater, making the car so hot that Lady Bellamy took off her scarf.

'It's not going to catch fire, is it, Madge?' she asked.

'No, he did it very nicely. The cigar lighter shows red all the time, but I'm sure it's all right.' She beamed at Lady Bellamy sitting beside her. 'How are things at the Manor, Gladys?'

171

Lady Bellamy glanced back at Agnes. 'We-e-ll, Nigel and Alison get married in a fortnight's time.'

'That's nice,' said Madge, completely without surprise.

'Very quiet wedding. You're asked, and Bernard.'

'When's the baby due?' Madge looked rather archly at her friend, then laughed. 'Well, Gladys, you know Penny Stratton – the postman told Alice!' Alice was Madge's live-in maid. 'Alice told your Hetty, who told her aunt, who told her husband, who told Bernard.' Her laugh rang out again. Agnes felt it was a joy to be with her and Lady Bellamy looked better, too. 'Anywhere you want to drive to? Do you want to see the site? The houses are going up fast, it's a bit of a mess.'

'No, I don't.' Lady Bellamy was adamant.

'Well, anywhere you want to go, just say. What about you, Agnes?'

Agnes was quick to seize the opportunity. 'Please, Mrs Hillier, could we go to the the Dower House? I'd like to see the cats there. I saw them this morning.'

'Right, back we go then, but I warn you they may have gone – two Siamese, aren't they?' Agnes nodded. 'I saw a big pantechnicon go down the lane just before lunch, past Maud Spencer's cottage. Nothing much down there but the Dower House. I expect they were going to clear the house.'

Agnes' heart sank. 'Never mind,' she said. 'If you don't mind we'll go, just in case.'

Madge took a corner on two wheels and the water and mud in the ditch splashed up over the window and windscreen.

'Sorry,' she said and righted the car expertly.

Agnes noticed that Lady Bellamy's face was more animated than she had seen it for a long time. 'I haven't seen the Dower House since Janet Forsyth died,' she said. 'I used to love it when I was a child. I loved to play there.'

Madge started down the lane, driving with more consideration as it grew more rutted. Round the bend they went – and there it was, a large van facing them, with *Marriott and Harris, Removals* in red letters on a cream background. The men were just closing the two big back doors of the van as they drove up.

'You'll have to back up, missy,' one of the men called out. Madge did so, again with more expertise than Agnes would have credited her with. She turned into a field, the gate of which was open. After a few minutes the removal van drove slowly past, the man acknowledging her with a wave of his hand, then it disappeared up the lane.

Madge revved up to get her back wheels out of the muddy field and they went down and parked at the gate. Agnes got out of the car and went round to dissuade Lady Bellamy who, in spite of the state of the road, was determined to look more closely at the Dower House. Would the cats still be there, Agnes wondered, or had they gone? She felt somehow that everything – though what everything was, she wasn't sure – depended on them being there. With difficulty Agnes persuaded her patient to stay in the car.

'Oh, how I'd love to go in.' Lady Bellamy gazed longingly out of the car window. Agnes was already half-way up the path.

'Stay there, Gladys.' Madge Hillier swung her legs out of the car and thrust herself upright. 'Stay there for a minute. If things are as they were I'll get you in there in no time.' She strode up the path, passed Agnes, her heavy brogues making little of the weeds and brambles. 'Just there, that's where it used to be.' She pointed to a spot just left of the front door. 'Want something to dig with.' She looked round and at last picked up a piece of flower pot and began to scrape away the earth. 'Oh dear, it must have gone. He must have taken it away,' she said, but went on scraping, this time in a slightly different place. 'No – eureka! here it is.' She scuffled away the earth and picked up a large key.

Agnes looked at the front door. 'But it's a Yale lock, Mrs Hillier, that's – ' she said.

'This is for the back door. Janet buried it, just in case she got locked out. She did once – poor Janet.' Madge went back to the car. 'Got the key, Gladys, look! Want to come in?'

Lady Bellamy hesitated, looking at the path and then at Agnes.

'Oh, come on. We'll see you don't fall, won't we, Agnes? You stand at the front door and I'll go round to the back, through the house and let you in. Won't be a moment,' she said, after she and Agnes, one on each side, had helped Lady Bellamy up the path. Lady Bellamy's face was alive with anticipation.

'I used to come here when I was a child,' she said, 'and to see Janet, of course. But then it belonged to someone else.'

They heard a rasping sound and a bang, then Madge's voice. 'Damn and blast.' Something fell to the floor with a sound of breaking glass. 'Dratted milk bottles, what a place to leave them.' Madge's voice again.

Lady Bellamy laughed outright. 'Madge was always clumsy,' she whispered.

The front door opened. 'Come on in,' said Madge, and in they went.

The entrance hall was small and dark, narrowing into a short corridor, at the end of which, facing the front door, was a window. It was almost completely obliterated by ivy, giving a green, almost underwater tint to the surroundings.

To the left the oak door was open and gave a glimpse of a room whose main feature was a large, brick fireplace, full of grey ashes. To their right was another smaller room, which presumably had been the dining-room, its window looking out obliquely on to the lane. This window, too, was covered with ivy. The floors of the rooms were pine, unpolished and uncared for. Bits of paper littered the floor; they blew about in the draught caused by the back and front doors being open. Pieces of newspaper made a swishing noise and a cardboard box skittered towards them.

The kitchen – Agnes looked at this with interest. The sink was blocked by what looked like tea leaves and the tap dripped rhythmically into a pool of brown water. A blue plastic pail, with no handle, under the sink also contained dirty water and an even dirtier floorcloth.

The three women looked around them. 'Poor devil. Is this how Tim Forsyth ended his days, in this squalor? He used to be rather a smart, dapper man, do you remember, Gladys?'

Gladys Bellamy nodded sadly, too. Madge opened a kitchen cupboard and a jar fell out. As it hit the work surface the lid flew off revealing solid instant coffee. There were more tins and jars, some dirtied and rusted, some newer looking as if they had just been purchased. A kettle on the stove was covered with grease.

'He wouldn't have anyone in to help him; we did try,' Madge said, her normally happy face sad. 'I called quite a few times, so did Bernard, but after Janet died he never opened the door, or if he did he only opened it an inch and said he didn't want anything, he wanted to be left alone – that he was writing. Even the telephone we tried, but either he didn't pay the bill or had

174

it cut off, I don't know.' She sighed. 'Oh well, perhaps we didn't do enough, but what's done is done.'

Lady Bellamy went through the back door into what had been, she said, a charming garden. She sat, with a little help from Agnes, on the bench beside the kitchen door. The November sun shone down, quite warm, on them.

'I must find the cats,' Agnes said and she called and called, but there was no sign of them.

'Perhaps they're frightened or perhaps the men took them,' Lady Bellamy suggested. 'Perhaps there was some arrangement that they should be put down or given to someone.'

Madge said, 'Come on, Gladys, we'll get back to the car. You'll be more comfortable and Agnes can call them. Perhaps they'll come if there's only one person – after all, they did this morning.'

Agnes nodded and Lady Bellamy agreed.

Once the two women were in the car Agnes went again to the back door and called. For some time nothing, then suddenly she glimpsed two blue eyes and a pointed brown mask, cream head and brown ears. First one, then two sinuous bodies, slender and graceful, emerged out of the tangled undergrowth and slowly approached her. When they were quite close they started to talk – the loud, insistent, melancholy dialogue which only Siamese cats seem able to attain.

Agnes put out a tentative hand to touch the head of the nearest one, but he drew back. Too familiar, she thought, not ready for that. They looked up at her, their tails upright, as if they already recognized her. There was a sudden crash from inside the house as the draught blew something over, and they both fled away back into the undergrowth.

She went into the house and closed both the doors, then looked again at all the rooms. Opposite the kitchen, there was a small room – but she couldn't imagine what it was used for. She went up the stairs for just a quick look, because Madge and Gladys were waiting for her. There was a bathroom – not quite as dirty as the kitchen – one small bedroom and two larger ones. She came down the stairs again. They were still carpeted, but the carpet was worn and dirty. Then she went out, closed and locked the back door and checked that the window was still open so that the cats could get in and out at will. She could still

175

see them both in the undergrowth, looking at her. She went round the house, down the front path and out to the car.

'Did they come?' Madge asked.

'Yes, I fed them.' Agnes felt enormous satisfaction.

'Ti-ming and Ti-sing, those were their names. Janet had them – they must be about seven, something like that. Janet doted on them.'

'And Captain Forsyth?' asked Agnes.

'I don't know. I never heard him speak to them, but he must have fed them. It's five years now since . . .'

Gladys Bellamy confirmed more of the cats' history. 'They won prizes, then Janet had them doctored. What's going to happen to the poor things now?' she wondered.

Madge laughed. 'I know. I've got a good idea. Agnes ought to move in with them, then we'd all be happy. The cats would be and we'd be happy to have Agnes around,' she said, starting up the car.

'That's exactly what I would like to do, Lady Bellamy,' Agnes said.

For a moment there was silence, as if they were taking it in, then, 'Do you really mean that?' Lady Bellamy asked.

'Yes, I do. I love the house as well as the cats.'

'Well, if you do want the Dower House there is no one I would rather rent it to.' Gladys Bellamy put her hand towards Agnes over the seat and Agnes grasped it. It was as if the agreement was made.

What have I done? What have I done? thought Agnes. But she knew – and she was glad.

Agnes sat in the back of the car and listened to the two women chatting away in the front. She was determined that the time had come to have a talk to Lady Bellamy about her usefulness now to her as a nurse. She also wanted to hear, if possible, what Sir Edmund had said to her and if he had made any threats about the wedding or made any more demands about money. If so . . . She thought again of the man lying helplessly beside the road. He was dead – but even dead he could be very useful. After all, she had, during her nursing career, known several witnesses of road accidents who had been so shocked that it was not for some time afterwards that they had remembered the make of the car, or its shape, or colour, or general appearance, and sometimes they had even remembered part or all of the number plate.

Yes, she would be more than interested to know just what attitude Sir Edmund was taking!

27

They had arrived back at the Manor as darkness was falling and Agnes thought how pretty the house looked against the evening sky. Lights were on in some of the rooms, and the windows shed an amber glow on to the gravel. It was not quite dark; a little daylight still remained.

'Come in and have a cup of tea, Madge.'

'Love to.' Madge slammed the door of the Daimler and with a clatter one hub cap fell off. 'Damn and blast,' she said and bent to pick it up.

'Leave it, Madge, I'll ask Basil to fix it.'

At that moment Nigel walked round from the back of the house. He looked at the hub cap and then at Madge – they both laughed. He picked it up, fixed it on to the wheel and gave it a sharp kick. 'That'll hold for the moment. Is the heater all right, Mrs Hillier?'

'All right! We've practically had to do a striptease. No, it's fine, but you can't turn it off, Nigel.'

'I'll have another look at it.' Obviously Madge and Nigel were old friends.

'Coming in for a cup of tea with us?' Madge asked.

'Yes, please.' He looked at Lady Bellamy for confirmation and she nodded, smiling.

In the sitting-room Nigel sat down in his stockinged feet; he had left his wellingtons at the front door. He got up and handed round the cups which Lady Bellamy was pouring out.

'I hear you're getting married in a fortnight's time.'

Nigel paused for a moment and looked at Lady Bellamy, who obviously was about to speak.

'I've asked the Hilliers to the church. You don't mind, do you, Nigel?'

'No, of course not.' He sat down and wiggled his toes in his thick woollen socks; his left big toe protruded through the wool.

'Looks as if you need to get married,' said Madge, pointing.

He laughed. 'Can't see Alison darning socks.'

'Top Farm, isn't it?' Madge asked.

'Yes, we're working on it now, it's great up there. Cows are my favourite stock and there's a cowman who we are hoping to be able to keep.'

Agnes had not seen Nigel so relaxed before. In his working clothes, corduroy trousers, thick jumper, open-necked shirt and the green anorak which he had taken off and thrown over the back of the chair, he looked less Italian. His hair was dark, but as he came near Agnes to take her cup for a refill she noticed, with some surprise, that his eyes were grey.

'What do you want for a wedding present, Nigel?' asked Madge.

He looked slightly embarrassed. 'A combine harvester would be nice,' he said, laughing. Then, more seriously, 'Alison was wishing she had a food processor. Is that too expensive, Mrs Hillier?'

'No, I'll talk to her about it and ask what kind she wants.' Madge Hillier finished her tea and then stood up. 'I must go and start my old man's dinner.'

Nigel got up too. He looked at his watch. 'I'm going to fetch Alison, she's at the hairdresser's. I've got to go in the Land Rover because her car has broken down again.' He padded out of the room.

'Don't get up, Gladys,' said Madge.

'Yes, I will. I want to see you out.' Gladys Bellamy accompanied Madge to the front door, where Nigel was slipping into his boots. 'You must try to do something about Alison's car, Nigel,' she said. 'It's time she had a new one, I know, but . . .' The worried frown on her patient's face Agnes could well understand, having heard a little of the conversation between her and Sir Edmund and his demand for even more money.

'You're looking much better, Gladys,' Madge said.

'Isn't she, Mrs Hillier,' Carmichael chimed in quickly. 'She really doesn't need me now.'

'Don't say that, Agnes, please,' answered Lady Bellamy, clasping Agnes' arm as if she needed support, although only a moment before she had been walking well by herself with only her stick to help her.

Madge Hillier kissed her friend, went down the front steps and got into her car. She banged the door, then stuck her head out of the open car window. 'Anything else dropped off?' she asked, giving her cheerful grin. Nigel had followed her out and now stood looking critically at the car.

'We-e-ll, the back bumper is tied on with string at one end, but I can fix that for you.'

'Thanks. Backed into a hedge yesterday – Bernard wasn't too pleased, he tied it up. The garage won't have anything to do with this car now, they say it's too much of a wreck; but I love it, there'll never be another car as good as this old Daimler.'

Nigel waved to Madge, then strolled round to the back of the house to get the Land Rover.

'They're good friends, those two, Nigel and Madge,' said Lady Bellamy as Madge drove out, grinding her gears as she passed. She stalled and restarted at the drive gates, ready to turn into the road.

'That poor car,' said Lady Bellamy as the rough noise of its engine died away. Then she turned to Agnes. 'Now, Agnes dear,' she said, 'we've got a lot to talk about, haven't we? I want to tell you everything.'

'Upstairs or in the sitting-room?' Agnes asked, as she closed the front door.

Hetty walked through the hall to fetch the tea things and take them to the kitchen.

'Is Sir Edmund out, do you know, Hetty?' Gladys Bellamy asked.

'Yes, m'lady. Basil drove him out about three o'clock, I think, and they haven't come back yet, and Miss Alison's at the hairdresser's.' She disappeared into the sitting-room and quickly reappeared in the hall carrying the loaded tea tray.

Lady Bellamy looked at the hall clock. 'Twenty to six,' she said. 'We'll go into the sitting-room and talk in comfort – bring some ice, will you, Hetty?' The girl nodded and disappeared into the kitchen regions. 'I'll need a drink, Agnes, before I start telling you about Edmund and what he said.' She limped into the sitting-room and sat down, leaning rather heavily on Agnes' arm. 'Pleasant and unpleasant, I fear.'

She sat on the settee and this time Agnes sat down opposite

her. The fire crackled, otherwise there was silence for quite some seconds before she spoke to Agnes.

'Well, where shall we start, my dear?' she asked, leaning her stick against the end of the settee. 'Where shall we start?'

Hetty came in with the ice bucket and placed it on the trolley. 'Anything else, m'lady?' she asked.

'No, thank you, Hetty. Oh yes, tell Maud I'll have my meal in the dining-room with everyone else tonight.'

'Very well, m'lady.' Hetty took herself off, closing the sitting-room door behind her with a little bang.

'She'll never learn to do things quietly, that girl, always a clatter,' said Gladys Bellamy.

She opened her handbag, took out her cigarette case and lit a cigarette.

'Shall I get you a drink?' asked Agnes. She was well used to her patient's ways now.

'Yes, do, please – and join me, I hate drinking alone.'

When the drinks were mixed and she had sipped hers and Agnes had sat down again, Lady Bellamy still seemed unable to bring herself to start. Agnes waited, then, 'If you'd rather not say anything about Sir Edmund and your conversation with him, I shall quite understand.'

Lady Bellamy withdrew her gaze from the fire and looked up at Agnes. 'What? Oh, I was thinking of something else – Alison's wedding present. I wanted to give her a new car, but with Sir Edmund's demands I don't think I can.' She paused. 'Yes, of course, Agnes, I want to tell you, you're the only one I can confide in. I started to tell Edmund that a quiet wedding had been arranged; no reception, just a few friends, no fuss and no expense. That was a mistake, Agnes.'

She drained her glass and held it out to Agnes, who mixed a very small one this time. 'He said he was glad, because he had to have £5,000 immediately – some gambling debt. He had borrowed money to pay the bookmaker, now the loan firm were after him and interest was mounting.' She sipped her new drink, then put the glass on the small table beside her and lit another cigarette. Agnes noticed that the hand holding the lighter trembled slightly. Gladys Bellamy was not as composed as she was making out.

'I said I couldn't possibly manage more, no rent from the Top Farm and the Dower House needed a lot doing to it – he knew about Captain Forsyth, he'd been to his funeral. It made no difference. He said if I didn't let him have the money then he'd say something at the wedding. I really think he would – I think he'd sacrifice the £10,000 a year I promised him to get back at me and Alison.'

'How could he even contemplate such a thing – after all, Alison is his granddaughter!' Agnes' voice was incredulous.

'Yes, but he knows she's my heir. He would. You don't know Edmund as I do. Well, I've got to pay him off, I suppose; so that's that.' She paused for a few moments.

'Now the Dower House – do you really want it, Agnes?' For the first time since they had entered the sitting-room Lady Bellamy's face lit up; she became more animated and lost some of her anxiety.

Agnes got up and pulled the curtains on the darkness and then put two small logs on the fire. She did all this before she answered, partly to make a gap between the beastliness of Sir Edmund's behaviour and what was, after all, going to be the start of a new environment and a new life for her. Whether it was right or whether it was wrong she couldn't, at the moment, come to any conclusion about, but there seemed nothing else for her. The thought of London and the hostel was just too much. She watched the new log catch fire from the old one burning under it and she saw, for a moment in the flames, a house with a garden stretching down to a river, the willows dipping almost down to it and two french windows open, and Brian walking up the grass path towards her to ask her to be his wife. She heard again the ripple of the soft water against the river bank, then the log fell forward and the imagined sound disappeared.

'Yes, I do, Lady Bellamy, I really do – that is, if you would like me as a tenant.' Lady Bellamy was about to say something when Agnes continued. 'You really no longer need me as a nurse, you know that.'

'But as a friend I do, Agnes,' Lady Bellamy replied, 'as a friend I do.'

'Do you think I should mention the fact of the Dower House to Sir Edmund?' asked Agnes. What she really wanted was an excuse to talk to him; she felt that now was the time to face him with what she knew – with knowledge that might keep him permanently quiet.

181

'Yes, it would be a good idea. I suppose we ought not to leave him out of things to do with the estate,' Lady Bellamy agreed.

At that moment Alison and Nigel burst in, Alison to show off her new hair-do and the suit she had chosen for her wedding, so no more mention was made of Agnes' proposed chat with Sir Edmund. It was obvious that both she and Lady Bellamy agreed that Sir Edmund should be the next person to know about her tenancy of the Dower House.

'Knowledge is power.' Agnes was quite unaware that she had said this to herself very quietly.

'What did you say, Agnes?' asked Alison, scrunching up her hair with her fingers.

'I think it quite suits you, your hair.' She smiled as she said it.

'Doesn't it look sort of untidy?' asked Nigel.

Alison looked across at Agnes. 'Men!' she said. 'They've really no idea, have they?'

'None at all,' said Agnes. 'None at all.'

Lady Bellamy broke into the conversation. 'Agnes and I have come to the conclusion that I really don't need her any more as a nurse.' She cast rather a roguish look at Carmichael.

'Oh no, not before the wedding! Do stay.' Alison looked across at Agnes. 'She must, Gran.'

Nigel seemed genuinely concerned, too. 'Can you really manage without her? I don't think it's a good idea at all.'

Lady Bellamy shook her head. 'I've some good news. She won't be going away from us, but I can't tell you more, not until your grandfather knows, so don't ask me about it.'

'Great, whatever it is, as long as she stays.' Nigel took the ashtray from the little table by Gladys Bellamy and emptied the still smoking, crushed cigarette into the fire – he hated smoking.

'Yes, we have been talking about it very carefully most of the afternoon and Lady Bellamy has invited me to stay here until after the wedding.' The two women cast a conspiratorial glance at each other.

Carmichael was not quite as sanguine as Lady Bellamy as to what Sir Edmund's reaction would be to her proposed tenancy of the Dower House, but after all it didn't matter; she had, as it were, an ace in her hand. Tomorrow, she thought, Sir Edmund will have an appointment with me and maybe an appointment with retribution.

Things, however, did not turn out quite as Agnes Carmichael had expected.

'Are you trying to blackmail me?' Sir Edmund turned from the window of his office where he had stood listening to Agnes' recital of the events which had taken place during and after his disastrous, drunken drive home that fatal night when he had killed a man – hit him and left him to die. Sir Edmund's eyes were blazing, his tall figure turned to her menacingly, almost as if he were ready to strike her, but her reply was cool, her voice even.

'Yes, Sir Edmund, in a way I suppose I am,' she said.

'Is this how you get your money, finding out things about your patients or their relatives and then . . .' He did not finish the sentence.

Agnes waited a moment before she replied. Then, 'No, it's not.' Her voice was still calm. 'I will not let anyone know what you did if you agree, promise, to say nothing about Alison and Nigel's relationship.'

Edmund Bellamy came over to the desk, opened the box, took out a cigarette and lit it. Carmichael was glad to see that the hand which held the match shook.

'I could deny it, say you were lying – it's your word against mine.' He dropped the match as it burned his fingers; it fell into the ashtray, flickered for a moment and then went out. 'You were behind me, you say, picked the man up, took him to hospital. It's only your word against mine.'

Agnes looked at him steadily. 'Sir Edmund, you have two convictions for driving while under the influence of alcohol. The first time you were fined and warned, the second time you were fined and disqualified from driving for a year.'

'That's ages ago. Was it bloody Basil or Dwyer who told you?'

'No, it wasn't Basil and it wasn't Harry Dwyer,' Agnes interrupted him.

'I can't believe you. It must have been Harry Dwyer, that fat fool. Anyway, the man was jay-walking – probably had a few himself.'

'No, it wasn't like that and you know it, Sir Edmund.' Agnes

paused, but he didn't speak so she went on. 'As to blackmail –
isn't that exactly what you're doing to Lady Bellamy?'

'What happens between me and my wife is private and has
nothing to do with you at all. I need more money.'

'Which she can ill afford to give you, I believe. No, Sir
Edmund, that's got to stop, too, if you want me to be silent
about the drunken escapade and its terrible outcome – the man
had a wife and a baby.'

He stubbed the cigarette in a desk ashtray and the smoke
curled upwards in the very warm, centrally heated air.

'I'll do what I think best. I'll do what I think fit,' he said.
'After all, if you do tell them about it and I get fined or forbidden
to drive for five years that's going to cost my wife more. I can't
pay it, and anyway I've got Basil, it won't inconvenience me.'

'It might mean prison, Sir Edmund,' Carmichael said.

'Never. Rubbish. Not the way I'm known round here, not at
my age. You've only got to read the tabloids – a fine and your
licence suspended, that will cost Gladys far more than me. She'll
have to pay the damn fine and Basil extra for taking me around.'

Carmichael remained completely calm, but in the back of her
mind she had to admit that her trump card, her ace, had not
been quite as successful as she had hoped – although with this
man it was difficult to assess his real feelings.

Sir Edmund went to the corner cupboard and produced a
bottle of whisky and a glass and poured himself a generous
measure, watching her meanwhile. He took a gulp of the amber
liquid, then lit another cigarette. He touched both sides of his
moustache and looked at Carmichael, his red lips moist with
the whisky.

'You could be right, they might throw me in the clink – that's
what you hope, isn't it? But I doubt it.' Suddenly he laughed.
'You'll have to sweat it out, Sister Carmichael. You'll be at the
wedding. If I decide to stop the proceedings with a dramatic
disclosure, well, you can run off and inform the police of my
accident. But what will you do then?' He suddenly seemed
more sure of himself – he was mocking her.

Carmichael was not sure if he was bluffing, but then she
noticed, nurse-like, the vein in his neck beating rapidly. She
guessed his heart beat was about 120 a minute – much too fast –
and a little feeling of triumph gave her more confidence.

'If they arrest me it won't stop me telling the truth about

Alison and Nigel,' he said, but the pulse in his neck beat faster and gave him away.

'That would be unpleasant, wouldn't it, Sir Edmund?' Agnes' voice was now ice-cold. 'You would have such a lot to confess – an affair with your Italian servant, a man killed by you, drunken driving, an illegitimate son.'

This last seemed to get to him more.

'I'll do as I damn well like.' Sir Edmund drank the rest of his large, neat whisky. 'Get the hell out of here,' he shouted.

'Certainly, Sir Edmund.' Carmichael opened the office door. 'I'll leave you – after all, you've got a lot to think about.'

Sir Edmund raised the hand that held the glass. For a moment Carmichael thought he was going to throw it at her, but obviously he thought better of it. He lowered his arm and the glass and it landed with a thud on the desk.

Agnes shut the door softly behind her. She was not altogether satisfied, she was not sure of things and of how he would behave. But one thing she felt fairly sure of – nothing, nothing about the young ones' relationship would be told until the wedding – until he had got what money he could from his wife. Even then, maybe, the thought of an investigation into his drive home would keep him quite. What worried her most was his unpredictability. She thought again of Lady Bellamy's story of how he had forced his son-in-law and pregnant daughter out of the house, years ago, on that snowy, dangerous Christmas night.

The wedding would be a nightmare to Lady Bellamy, she thought, a nightmare, and he would play cat and mouse – taking more and more money in payment for his silence. Agnes thought again of the racing pulse beat showing in the side of his neck – there had been panic there in spite of his blustering attitude. She took heart from that as she walked away from the office, and managed a quick smile for Nigel as he clumped in his, luckily clean, wellingtons across the hall and rapped on Sir Edmund's office door.

At dinner that evening Sir Edmund's hostility towards Agnes was evident even to Nigel and Alison, as well as to Lady Bellamy. When at last he left the room after coffee Alison remarked, 'Grandfather seems to have it in for you this evening, Agnes. Didn't he like your idea of renting the Dower House?'

Agnes was startled for a moment. 'I haven't mentioned my

renting it, not to your grandfather, Alison. I thought . . .' She looked at Lady Bellamy, who answered tactfully.

'Yes, perhaps it's better if I told him, Agnes.' But she, too, was obviously a little curious at the coldness of her husband's attitude towards Agnes. He was never particularly amiable towards her, but that evening at the table he had once or twice been almost offensive.

That night Carmichael could not sleep. She felt in the middle of such eddies of malice and intrigue: the relationship of Alison and Nigel – blackmail – threatened exposure at the wedding – the part she had to play in safeguarding three people to whom she had become unusually attached. She turned, trying to banish everything from her mind, to make it a blank. Then she decided to concentrate on her decision to live in the Dower House. The thought of the two blue-eyed cats eventually drove other thoughts out of her mind. Animals – they were not complicated. She thought of Walt Whitman's poem of which she was very fond:

> I think I could turn and live with animals, they are so
>   placid and self-contained
> I stand and look at them long and long
> They do not sweat and whine about their condition
> They do not lie awake in the dark and weep for their sins
> They do not make me sick discussing their duty to God
> Not one is dissatisfied, not one is demented by the mania
>   of owning things
> Not one kneels to another, nor to his kind that lived
>   thousands of years ago.

That was all she could remember and, repeating it to herself, she eventually managed to feel calmer and fall asleep.

28

Some days later Agnes Carmichael was seated in the train to London. She had felt that she needed to get several things settled and tidied away.

First, she had persuaded Lady Bellamy to write to the Nursing Co-op saying that she no longer required Sister Carmichael's services. Then Agnes had decided that she would go to London to collect the few things she had in her flatlet at the Co-op hostel, contact the depository where her furniture from Cat's Cradle had been stored and tell them to send it to the Dower House in two weeks.

Finding decorators and double-glazers for the Dower House had been much easier than Carmichael had expected, for amongst the contractors who were handling the building of the bungalows on the field from the Bellamy estate were several men who would like to do some moonlighting. Carmichael had instructed that the walls should be all sharp white, as well as the paintwork. This would not only ensure a clean-looking finish, but also mean that she could easily change to any colour she would wish once the task was completed and her furniture installed. A wood sander and gardener from the village were already at work, the wood sander doing the floors. Already everyone, with the exception of Sir Edmund, had been helpful and enthusiastic. It was the Hilliers who had found the floor sander, and Nigel had interviewed the painters and decorators ready to do extra work in the evenings and at weekends. Agnes, used to doing things alone, felt she had never had more support, backed by real affection.

Today she felt relaxed and happy. It was some time since she had been in a train and she was soothed by the rhythm the wheels made – it almost made her feel sleepy. In her first-class compartment she nearly dozed, as she was not really interested in the countryside flashing by.

Miss Carmichael, The Dower House, Penny Stratton, Leicestershire. The wheels seemed to sing her new address – a new start in a new life. Would she go on with private nursing? What would she do? She had no idea, and that was pleasant.

She had needed to get away – to stand back from the problem of the Bellamys. Maybe, she thought, she had become too involved. Yet, to counteract that, if she hadn't become involved she wouldn't have gained these close friendships.

Agnes stirred and looked out of the window. At last they were nearing London. The backs of rows of terraced houses were flowing by, some with neat gardens ready for the spring, some with trodden-down patches of grass and earth – prams, children's go-carts. A white cat leapt on to a wall and was gone. Hundreds of people were living lives as complicated as those she had left behind, she supposed. No, surely not! Some, many, must be married to satisfactory husbands, have children who gave them no trouble, live lives of tranquillity and simplicity. She sighed suddenly and felt her complacent, relaxed feeling slip away from her. She shook out the *Times* she had bought in Leicester station and determinedly began to read it.

The London traffic was as horrendous as usual. She sat in the taxi outside the RAC Club noting the other drivers, watching them fume, beat softly on the steering wheel with their hands and some, occasionally, hoot. In spite of it being the first week in December, the sun felt quite warm on the taxi roof and the smell from the car exhausts almost made her cough. How can anyone live here, she thought. The taxi man, as if he had read her thoughts, turned round in his seat.

'Always like this, miss, round ten thirty in the morning,' he said.

'It's terrible, isn't it? I don't know how you stand it,' she answered.

'No, neither do I, miss. You come from the country, then?'

'Yes. Penny Stratton, Leicestershire.' She took pleasure in saying the name of the village.

'Well, you'd know that was country, wouldn't you – Penny Stratton.' He smiled, turned back and drove a few yards forward.

'Penny Stratton.' Carmichael said the words again to herself, quietly. She looked at the cars on each side of her and stretching away in front of her, the buildings, the bustle, people crossing between the cars from one pavement to the other. They looked tense, almost apprehensive, frightened the cars would suddenly move a few yards. Most of them looked tired. Was she exaggerating the highlights of the scene around her to justify her own resolutions? She'd done that before, but this time she didn't think so. A man in a red car peered into her taxi, his car directly beside them; their eyes met and he made a gesture with his hands as if to say 'What the hell can you do?' She shook her head at him and sank back into her seat out of sight.

The taxi rolled forward a little and Carmichael suddenly longed for her new home – longed to see it again in place of this chaos around her, the flat fields, the low hedges, even the strangled neglected garden, the blue-eyed cats, all waiting for her. She was staying one night in London and that, she thought, would be enough.

The traffic thinned a little and in about fifteen minutes she arrived at Beaumont Gardens and the London Co-op hostel.

She paid the taxi, picked up her empty suitcase and went into the lift. She met two people on the way up to her flatlet, but she knew neither and neither spoke. Out of the lift she unlocked the door and there it was, the home she had opted for after she had left hospital and was well enough to start out in the world again. Work. Nursing had seemed the only solution open to her. Now things were different. She went and unlocked the cupboard in the hall where the suitcases were kept and picked out her two, came back and packed the clothes and oddments she had left there – everything else was in store. She gazed round the impersonal room: built-in dressing table, small windowless bathroom, tiny kitchen. Well built, well thought out – whoever took it over would be glad; accommodation was not easy to find in London.

She pulled the door to behind her; the latch clicked. She went down in the lift again and parked her three suitcases outside the door marked 'Administration – Miss Haytor'. She knocked.

Miss Haytor was sitting behind her neat desk. For some reason she wore an equally neat nurse's uniform – strange, because she did not nurse. Carmichael could never understand why she was dressed like this, in navy spotted white, white cap with two dark blue lines round it, a navy belt with a silver buckle, a watch pinned on her dress.

'Ah, Miss Carmichael. You're back from your case.' She reached across, took a file from beside her right hand on the desk and opened it. 'A charming letter from Lady Bellamy. Your first case with us, wasn't it? You seem to have made a very good impression.' She smiled tightly.

It took Agnes some minutes to convince Miss Haytor that she was giving up working for the Nursing Co-op after only one case.

'Well, really, that's most unusual.' Miss Haytor looked quite put out. 'In any case you . . . we . . .' She drew to a lame halt.

Agnes did not know what to say. She placed the key of her flatlet on the desk. Miss Haytor gave up.

'Well, we must settle up then, if that's what you wish.'

Carmichael received the cheque. All she wanted to do was to get out of the place, leave it behind her, out of her life. She had not realized how much she had hated the hostel; perhaps her feelings had been dulled by all that had happened.

'Come back if you change your mind. We shall be pleased to . . .'

Agnes shook her head and beat a hasty retreat.

Outside the administration office were some pay phones and she was able to telephone Dunlop & Squires, where her furniture was stored, and make arrangements for it to be delivered in two weeks. As she put the telephone down she thought, By the time that furniture arrives Nigel and Alison will either be married or they will be exposed for what they are. It gave her a nasty little tug, a tug from Penny Stratton, she thought. Even here, in London, she was not able to get away from it – and indeed, did she really wish to?

She braved the traffic again. This time she got a taxi easily and received help from the cabby with her three suitcases. She went to Sloane Street, where she had booked a room in the Sloane Court Hotel for the night. As she checked in and was shown her room she felt unspeakably tired and rather hungry. After lunch she went out – looking in shop windows without interest – then returned to her hotel.

Tomorrow she would go to Harrods and find a suitable wedding present for Nigel and Alison. She had thought of a picture, a country scene, but she'd browse round and get a late afternoon train back to Leicester. She rang room service and asked for a brandy and ginger ale and when it came stretched out on the bed. Most of the unpleasant things had been done: packing up at the hostel, seeing the Administrator, giving her notice – those things were done. Ringing the repository, too, had been an ordeal. She wondered how she would feel about seeing her furniture again in different surroundings – but, for the moment, she would put that thought on one side.

She lay there sipping her drink and thinking. Most people, when something happened in their lives – something big, important – said, That is a chapter in my life that's over, but she felt that her life was a series of books, not chapters: long, long phases in which she shared many relationships but none of which had yet ended happily.

She changed and went down to dinner. She enjoyed the meal,

tipped liberally and suddenly she found she was looking forward to the next day.

As she left the dining-room she watched herself walking towards the long, pink mirrors, one flanking each side of the door. She was slim, her hair looked shiny and well cut. She saw herself in tweeds and brogues (something else she decided to look at tomorrow) – a country suit, shoes and perhaps a tweed hat.

'Good-night, miss.' The man at the reception desk smiled as he handed Agnes her key. Was there a touch of admiration there? Somehow, suddenly it was important that there was. She smiled back, a touch primly. 'Good-night,' she said. Another book was starting, she thought, or at least the first chapter of another book. How would this one end?

The bathroom adjoining her room was warm and well appointed, the bed comfortable. After a shower Carmichael was conscious of a lift in spirits again and a feeling of excitement, tinged with apprehension. She carefully cleansed her face before she got into bed, and before she fell asleep she thought that as well as a wedding present for Nigel and Alison, a tweed suit and country shoes for herself, she would buy a double washable cat bed for Ti-ming and Ti-sing. After all, they were part of the new chapter, part of the new book, part of her new family.

Agnes was in Harrods by ten o'clock, leaving her luggage at the hotel. After some thought she made for the china department and, with a great deal of care, she chose a Wedgwood dinner and tea service for Alison's and Nigel's present. She hoped, as she paid for it, that they would like the design.

Then to the pet department for the cat bed, feeding dishes, toys. Agnes really enjoyed herself there – the puppies, the iguanas and all the strange exotic pets.

'Madam has a very good figure.' The sales girl smoothed the lapel of the fawn houndstooth jacket. 'The skirt hangs beautifully on madam.'

Agnes had tried several suits, but this one she liked. In the long cheval mirror she looked at herself critically – a new 'you', she thought. She had put on her recently purchased country shoes in order to assess the length of her suit's skirt. '*Country Life*,' she said aloud and smiled widely at herself.

'Pardon?' the sales person said.

'Oh, nothing. Just talking to myself. Yes, I like it. I'll have this one.' She took off the shoes and put on the ones she had worn to London.

After making arrangements for the various items she had bought to be sent to Nettlestone Manor, she was ready for lunch. Her shopping had taken her less time than she had anticipated and she hoped to get an earlier train home than she had at first thought.

In the restaurant she was glad to sit down. She ordered lobster thermidor and a glass of white wine while she waited. As she sipped the wine she looked around her to try and place the various people at tables nearby – who was from the country, who from the suburbs? One woman two tables away with her back to Carmichael looked familiar and when she turned to speak to the waitress Agnes recognized her – Marcia de Curzon, Madge Hillier's daughter. Carmichael decided not to announce herself and idly picked up the large menu still on her table and started to read it. At that moment another waitress behind and to the left of Carmichael tripped and then dropped a silver-plated salver on to the floor. It made a resounding crash. Marcia de Curzon turned round, Agnes looked up and their eyes met. Marcia got up, spoke to the waitress at her table, pointed to Agnes' table and came over.

'Well, Agnes, isn't it? They say if you are in Harrods long enough you'll meet everyone you know. May I join you? I hate eating alone. What are you having?'

Just like her mother, Agnes thought as she greeted Marcia warmly. 'Yes, do. Lobster thermidor,' she answered.

'Great, that's what I'll have. I want to spend as much of my husband's money as I can while I'm here.' She lit a cigarette with a gold lighter. Two people at the next table showed their disapproval, which Marcia ignored.

They exchanged their reasons for being in London. Marcia's reason was rather more startling than Agnes'. 'I've left my husband. He's so *ennuyant*, thinks of nothing but medicine. He's a consultant, you know; brilliant, but *ennuyant*.' She again laughed her rather tinkling laugh. Anges looked at her. She talked and moved like a young woman, but she was betrayed by the lines under her eyes, the lift marks that Agnes' expert eyes did not miss, just in front of her ears, the slight scragginess of her neck.

She went on with her story. She had left her husband and was at the moment living in a flat lent her by a friend, in Hans Crescent. Asked if Madge Hillier knew, she said, 'Oh yes. Mummy's amazed it has lasted so long – she can't bear Raoul.' She laughed again. 'Mustn't eat too much,' she said when the lobster arrived. 'I'm dining out tonight with a new man. He's keen on me and at my age you mustn't be too choosy, must you?'

'Mustn't you?' Carmichael said. A little twist of amusement made her almost smile and she turned away her head so that Marcia would not see it.

It was pleasant lunching with Marcia. 'Do I mention we've met?' she asked as Marcia was leaving.

'Oh yes. Certainly, certainly, no point in trying to hide things.' Marcia finished pulling on her gloves, raised her hand, made her way to the cash desk to pay and was gone.

Agnes sat a little longer finishing her coffee. A new man – well, she thought, and remembered Harry Dwyer, the switched key, the dinner with him and his flirtatious manner. He wasn't young either, and why not, she thought, why not? Is he to be my new man? I don't think so.

She looked at her watch and decided to get the four o'clock train to Leicester. She felt that her visit to London had been very satisfactory, but she knew she would be glad to be going back to what she was beginning to call 'home'.

On the train the feeling persisted and she watched the houses and the tall office blocks of London give way gradually to small patches of green fields and large rolling meadows – Tudor stockbroker houses give way to old stone farmhouses – town to country. She watched until all remnants of London had disappeared.

29

'Drat it.' As Carmichael opened the kitchen door she heard Hetty.

'Be careful, we haven't got that many, no need to chuck them about.' Agnes went forward. 'Mind, Sister Carmichael, you'll tread on it.' Maud bent down and picked up a glacé cherry that Hetty had dropped. Hetty peered into the small plastic carton.

'Oh Lord, Maud, there aren't enough now. Have we got any more in the store cupboard?'

Maud shook her head and winked at Agnes. 'Put it on Sir Edmund's – about all he deserves today, I heard him shouting at Lady Bellamy.' She turned to Agnes. 'Have you had a good time in London?'

'Thank you, yes. I'll go and freshen up. I just came in to let you know I'm back.'

'Just taking these up.' Hetty picked up the tray of grapefruit and made for the door. 'I won't give you that one.' She inclined her head towards the contaminated cherry.

Carmichael was greeted most affectionately by Alison and Nigel and Lady Bellamy. She came into the dining-room on a remark made by Sir Edmund.

'Well, it's a damn nuisance. How long will he be in France, anyway?'

'Well, it is his brother, Grandpa.' Alison spoke reproachfully.

Lady Bellamy explained for Agnes' benefit. 'It's Basil, Agnes, he's had to go to France. Poor fellow, his brother has been killed, car accident, he's a chauffeur, too. He has no children and Basil has gone to help his poor wife.'

'Grapefruit? No thank you, I detest fruit, you know that.' It was obvious that Sir Edmund was in anything but a sunny mood. 'Races tomorrow and no one to drive me there, damn nuisance. I hate trying to park and I loathe trying to find the car afterwards. There was no need for him to go at all, in my opinion.'

'I'll drive you, sir,' said Nigel.

'That's one way of getting out of estate work.'

Nigel's white skin flushed pink.

'Grandpa, that's unfair,' Alison said.

Lady Bellamy switched the conversation. Agnes felt that she had had plenty of practice at this, battling with her husband's irritability during their long marriage.

Agnes described some of her two days' adventures, but omitted to mention her meeting with Marcia.

Dinner after that was a pretty silent affair and Sir Edmund did not join them in the sitting-room when it was over. This lightened the mood and Agnes was able to tell them more about her visit to London and her purchases. She left out her choice of wedding present, thinking it would be a nice surprise when it arrived. She could then safely talk about Marcia.

'Well, fancy Marcia. I wonder if Madge knows. I expect she does. I wonder if she'll be upset.' Lady Bellamy lit a cigarette. 'Somehow I don't think so, she's never shown any particular affection for her son-in-law.'

Alison laughed. 'That Frog, she always calls him. Well, three more days, Agnes, and I'll be Mrs Nigel Calvi.' She took Nigel's hand in hers. 'We want to ask you a favour, Agnes . . .' She looked appealingly across at Agnes.

'Yes?'

'Well, behind your back, as it were, we tried to make a sort of arrangement – you ask her, Nigel.'

Nigel laughed rather nervously. 'Well, the Hilliers are coming and they are bringing . . .' He hesitated. '. . . my future grand-mother-in-law to the church.' He stopped again and Gladys Bellamy smiled at him. He continued. 'Colin, my best man, will take me. Would you bring Alison in your lovely car?'

There was silence. Then, 'Of course, I would be delighted to bring the bride, but are you sure Sir Edmund . . .'

'We're not sure of anything as regards Sir Edmund, and that won't do, Agnes. He won't say whether he is coming or not, he won't say whether he'll give Alison away. In desperation I have asked Bernard and he's kindly taken on that role, so if Edmund won't do it we have a stand-in, as it were.'

'In that case, of course I'll be delighted.' Agnes felt genuinely pleased.

'A wash and brush-up for your car is also arranged, with your permission,' said Nigel. 'The bridegroom will do it, is that all right?'

'Of course. Honeymoon?' Agnes asked. Then, 'Don't tell me if it's a secret.'

'No, it's not a secret – Venice.' Alison turned and gave Nigel a swift kiss on his cheek.

After some more conversation and arrangements and talk about the wedding, Gladys Bellamy got up with some difficulty. Sitting for some time always made her stiff.

'Well, that's settled,' she said. Then, as Agnes also got to her feet and took Lady Bellamy's handbag and handed her her stick, 'Now, Agnes, you're not my nurse any more, you're my guest.'

Agnes Carmichael smiled as she offered her arm. 'Well,' she said, 'that's as maybe.'

Bidding good-night to Alison and Nigel, they made their way up to Gladys Bellamy's room.

'Sit down for a minute, Agnes.' Lady Bellamy herself sat down on the bed and Agnes made her way to the armchair. She felt tired; maybe it was the hustle of London, or perhaps the long day, the journey. She was conscious of the gap in her energy compared with the young ones downstairs. They were just starting out, their lives lay like a long road in front of them. She had travelled a long way along her road – half a century. She sighed suddenly.

'Is anything the matter, Agnes?' Lady Bellamy asked.

Agnes shook her head and straightened her back. 'No. No,' she said. She told Lady Bellamy about the china for the wedding present. Then the two women were silent and it was Lady Bellamy's turn to sigh.

'What will become of them, Agnes? What a sad little wedding. Edmund sulking, no knowing if he will let out this ghastly secret. It's only the money that's keeping him quiet, I'm well aware of that – and even then he might succumb if he drinks too much and the temptation to tell becomes too great.' She leaned back tiredly in her chair. 'I dread this wedding – dread it.'

Agnes got up and went over and sat next to her. 'No, I don't think Sir Edmund will tell. He might threaten, but I think he will be greatly influenced by your generous allowance. He won't want to lose that; he won't jeopardize that, I'm sure.'

'You're a great comfort, Agnes, you really are.' The conversation drifted into more pleasant topics. Wedding presents, the little bouquet she had ordered for Alison, Alison's wedding suit, the small reception afterwards. 'Champagne I am determined to have, and Maud is insisting on making the wedding cake herself. But how meagre it all is!'

Agnes shook her head. 'Nevertheless they love each other; they've got a home in a place they love, and friends. I think in some ways, in most ways, they're lucky young people.'

'They're half-brother and sister, Agnes, and he may let it out.' Lady Bellamy shivered in spite of the closeness of the room. 'As long as he lives, it will always be like a sword hanging over their lives. It will always be there.'

Lady Bellamy twisted her wedding ring round and round on her finger. 'I have always known he was weak and a liar, Agnes, but I've never hated him as much as I do now.'

Agnes did not, could not, answer – there was nothing to say. They sat a little longer, then she got up. Lady Bellamy would not be helped.

'No, Agnes, I can manage. You've had a long day, now have a good night's rest.'

As Agnes got ready for bed she tried to reorientate her position in the house. She was no longer Lady Bellamy's nurse, she was a guest. So much had changed since she had arrived here. She was no longer responsible for Lady Bellamy, nevertheless before she got into bed she crossed her room and opened the door and looked out. The door of the room next to hers was firmly shut, but the nurse in her would not let her close her own door. She left it open as she had done ever since that first night – she left it slightly ajar, just in case.

The next morning a large parcel arrived from Harrods. Carmichael took off the outer layer of green paper, revealing the wedding present wrapping paper she had requested in the store. Alison came into the hall as Agnes was folding up the green paper.

'Agnes, what a lovely parcel,' she said.

'It's your and Nigel's wedding present,' said Agnes.

'What?' Alison went over and attempted to lift the box. 'Agnes, what have you bought us?'

'Open it and see,' smiled Agnes.

'No.' Alison drew back. 'Not until Nigel's here.' She tapped the side of the box experimentally.

'It's china. I'd better tell you that much.'

At that moment there was the sound of a car drawing up at the door and in a few seconds a car door slammed. There was a loud rat-tat-tat on the door, sounding as if it was made by a heavy hand. Hetty appeared, but Alison had already opened the door.

'Yes, can I help you?'

On the steps stood a tall, burly man, his long black overcoat making him look even larger.

'I'd like to see Sir Edmund Bellamy,' he said. His voice was husky.

'Oh, you'd better come in. I'll see if my grandfather is in.'

The man crossed the threshold, removing his hat and undoing his overcoat buttons as he did so.

Alison went across, knocked on Sir Edmund's office door and opened it.

'What is it?' Sir Edmund's voice came through the door on a cloud of cigarette smoke.

'Someone to see you, Grandpa.' She opened the door a little wider and Edmund looked out. His face changed when he saw the man standing in the hall.

'You'd better come in,' he said.

The man crossed the hall and gave a slight bow in Alison's direction. She closed the front door behind him.

'Nice car,' she said. Agnes looked out of the hall window; a large black, rather funereal-looking car stood outside.

'What a beautiful parcel.' Lady Bellamy was coming slowly down the stairs.

'It's a wedding present from Agnes. I'm not going to open it till Nigel's here.'

'Of course.' Lady Bellamy's quiet voice was almost drowned by that of Sir Edmund shouting through the closed door of his office.

'I can't make it in a week. Tell Harris that.'

The husky voice answered, also raised, 'I'm afraid you've just got to, mate. Harris is choked about it all, wants his three thou now, not tomorrow, not next week – now.'

Lady Bellamy paused at the bottom of the stairs; her eyes met Agnes'. Alison looked from one face to the other.

'Grandpa in trouble again,' she said lightly.

Lady Bellamy did not answer her. She walked through to the kitchen, her stick making a tapping noise.

'I must go through the menus with Maud,' she said.

Suddenly the office door was thrown open by a furious Sir Edmund. 'Get out. Tell Harris what I've said.'

The man, taller than Sir Edmund, looked down at him. 'It's unwise, sir, that kind of message to him. I shouldn't.'

'Bloody well tell him.' Sir Edmund slammed the office door with all his might. The tall man stopped for a moment, looking at the door, then did up his overcoat and made the strange little bow, first to Alison then to Agnes. He, too, banged the front door behind him and they heard the car start up and drive away.

'Phew – lovely guy,' said Alison.

Unnoticed, Lady Bellamy had come out of the kitchen. She limped across the hall, leaning a little more heavily on her stick.

Alison ran up the stairs. She was going out and needed her coat, she said.

Gladys Bellamy came across and took Agnes' arm. 'I've asked Maud to bring us coffee in here,' she said.

In the sitting-room she sat down heavily. 'More trouble,' she said. 'I suppose he'll be asking me for even more money and I've ordered the car for Nigel and Alison's wedding present. I think I'll have to cancel it.' She put her hand to her eyes. Hetty came in with the tray of coffee.

'Thank you, Hetty.' In spite of her worries Gladys Bellamy smiled at her maid. As the door shut she turned again to Agnes. 'It will never stop. He will go on and on until I have nothing left, nothing even to leave Alison – maybe that's what he wants.'

Once again Agnes could not think of anything to say. What Lady Bellamy prophesied was, she suspected, right. Agnes had her secret which she could hold over him, and would. She still felt somehow that he wouldn't jeopardize his money, but when he had been drinking – what he would say then – nobody could tell.

30

After her talk with Lady Bellamy Agnes drove round to the Dower House. The cats came immediately at this time and no food yesterday had made them hungry. Agnes filled their new dishes twice before they were satisfied. She took them some way from the house, because the workmen were inside and in the tangled front garden a man was scything the dead brambles. This industry was very heartening to Agnes; she longed to get into her own home. She went into the house; the noise of the sander stopped as she entered.

'These floors are a bit of a mess, miss. They'll need a lot of oiling and polishing when I've done this – take a bit of time. Were you thinking of covering the floors with carpet?'

Agnes shook her head. 'No, just rugs scattered about,' she said.

'Oh well, glad to hear that. These are nice floors, shame to cover 'em. I've nearly finished this room – take me till about six o'clock time.'

Agnes coughed and the man smiled and pulled the mask up over his mouth and nose. 'Dusty work,' he said.

In another room a man was rubbing the flaking white paint off the window frames, ready for Agnes' 'sharp white'.

This time, without Lady Bellamy's safety to worry about, Carmichael decided to investigate further upstairs. The staircase was attractive; open oak banisters flanked the side – ten stairs, then a sudden turn and four more stairs led to the middle of the landing. To the left it opened into a space which was identical to the downstairs hall, with a bedroom opening on each side. Another ivy-obliterated window let in a small amount of the same green light as downstairs and at the other end of the landing there was another window. Agnes felt that when the ivy and virginia creeper had been cut back the Dower House would be a light, welcoming little place. She stood at the landing window and looked out across the field. Over the slight rise she had just a glimpse of Top Farm, which pleased her.

She went downstairs. The sound of the sander had stopped;

the man was no longer there. Agnes looked at her watch: twenty past twelve. Downstairs she heard a noise in one of the rooms and peeped in. One of the cats, Ti-ming or Ti-sing, she couldn't be sure, was there examining the sander. He looked up as he heard her footsteps but didn't, as she expected, run away. He straightened his tail and gave a little chirrup of recognition. She didn't venture near him and just quietly left, but she was gratified. When the central heating was working again she hoped they would come in.

The rest of the day passed peacefully at Nettlestone Manor. Nigel and Alison were up at Top Farm decorating. Sir Edmund had gone out in the Rolls and had not returned for lunch.

The late morning post had contained a letter from Herbert and Doris Bellamy saying they were unable to come to the wedding as Doris had a bad back. They enclosed a cheque as a wedding present.

'I can't say I'm sorry.' Lady Bellamy made a little face. 'Herbert upsets Edmund, they quarrel and it always encourages him to drink more than he should.'

There was a knock at the door – it was Maud. 'Would you care to come and see the cake, m'lady?' she said.

Gladys Bellamy struggled up. 'Of course. I think it's so sweet of you to make it for us.'

There, in the middle of the table, was 'the cake': square, with crisp white icing beautifully latticed, immaculate. There was a little house in the middle with 'Top Farm' written in piped chocolate. The whole thing was seated on a square of silver cardboard. Maud's face was flushed and beaming with pride and Lady Bellamy was obviously moved.

'Maud, how pretty – and the little house is like Top Farm.'

'I know, m'lady. I went to Leicester on my day off to look for it. It was hard to find.'

'I'm sure it was.' Lady Bellamy touched the little house gently with her fingertips. 'They will be so pleased,' she said.

Maud took a large cardboard carton and placed it over the cake. 'They're not to see it till the day after tomorrow, though,' she said firmly.

'Of course not.'

Lady Bellamy came out of the kitchen with Agnes. 'Such kindness,' she said. 'If only there were no complications, Agnes, no hidden problems.'

201

'Lady Bellamy, remember the only problem – if you can call it that – for Nigel and Alison is the baby. As far as they are concerned, there is no other problem.'

'Yes, that's true, but then . . . I hope they have a happy day, that's the least we can give them. Maud is really going to town with the buffet lunch – oh, I forgot to tell you, Marcia is coming.'

'Good, she's so decorative, isn't she,' Agnes said.

For the first time in what for her had been a rather worrying day, Lady Bellamy laughed. 'I'm glad you're here, Agnes. Please stop calling me Lady Bellamy, you're not my nurse now, you're a dear friend. Gladys, please.'

'Thank you, that will be nice. I'll try and remember.'

The conversation then turned to the Dower House and Agnes told Lady Bellamy how the work was progressing and how the cats had behaved to her. For the moment the spectre of Sir Edmund and of what he might or might not do receded a little.

He came home in time for dinner, morose and silent throughout the meal. After dinner he retired to his office. Lady Bellamy made one last effort before he left the dining-room.

'The Hilliers and Marcia will be at the church, Edmund. Colin, Nigel's best man, comes tomorrow. It would help, you know, if you would let us know if you wish to give Alison away.'

Her husband stood up, pushing his chair back roughly. 'No, I don't want to give her away . . . No, I won't give Alison away, and you know why, Gladys – you know why.'

Agnes held her breath. He was anything but sober, he might say anything. Nigel and Alison were looking at him curiously.

'Very well, Edmund.' Lady Bellamy's voice trembled slightly.

'I'll see what I'll do on the day – day after tomorrow – I'll see then.' Rather unsteadily he had left the room and they heard the office door bang shut.

Nigel and Alison looked at each other. Alison shrugged. 'Well, you thought Grandpa would act like that, didn't you, Gran – and we have prepared Bernard.' She went nearer to Nigel and they put their arms round each other. 'What does it matter as long as we're married?'

'Nothing matters as long as we are married.' Nigel's voice was gentle; no bitterness, no reproach.

'Indeed,' said Gladys Bellamy and her voice was just as gentle. 'What does it matter?'

When they all retired Carmichael had the feeling that no one, with the exception, perhaps, of Sir Edmund, would have a good night. She, herself, could not sleep. Feelings of apprehension, feelings of excitement about the day after tomorrow, feelings about the Dower House, kept her awake and she was sure Gladys Bellamy wouldn't sleep. Neither would Alison and Nigel; but their night would be filled only with pleasant anticipation.

Next day Nigel's friend and best man, Colin, arrived during the afternoon. He was a pleasant young man, round-faced and earnest in manner. At dinner that evening he was obviously a little scared of Sir Edmund and Lady Bellamy. She tried to put him at ease, but the same could not be said of Sir Edmund. He questioned the young man as to his knowledge of farming, cut him short before he could reply, and was as disagreeable as possible, as was becoming his habit now. He left the dining table before anyone else and after a few minutes they heard the front door bang shut, and as Lady Bellamy led them across the hall to the sitting-room for coffee they heard the Rolls crunching on the gravel drive and out into the road. The car wing had, Agnes noticed, been beautifully repaired.

Lady Bellamy tried to make Colin Drayton forget the rudeness of her husband by being extremely nice to him. Alison was charming and Agnes was glad to see that after about half an hour the mood lightened and the three young people started chatting animatedly and ribbing each other. Colin had recently become engaged to a girl in Northampton and his parents were apparently not best pleased that he was spending his weekends with her and not with them.

'Well, parents are something we don't have to worry about, do we, Nigel?' Alison said, then, realizing the implication of her remark to her grandmother, she went across to her. 'Sorry, Gran, I didn't think,' she said.

Gladys Bellamy smiled, though rather ruefully. 'That's all right, my love, be happy,' she said. She decided to retire early. 'Busy day tomorrow, darlings,' she said, embracing both Alison and Nigel. 'Final preparations before the wedding.'

'I think I'll come with you.' Agnes, too, rose.

'You going too, Agnes? It's early yet,' said Alison.

'Yes, lots to do tomorrow.' She kissed Alison lightly on the cheek.

As they walked upstairs Agnes was silent. She felt a strange apprehension, a feeling she recognized. The wedding – what had Sir Edmund really decided to do? He must have made up his mind by now. Would he turn up tomorrow and behave as if he had always intended to do nothing, or would he attend the wedding only to expose the relationship of the two young people at the appropriate dramatic moment in the wedding service? She wondered. The wedding was at midday, plenty of time for him to get loose-tongued enough to say anything or do anything.

After she had said good-night to Lady Bellamy, Agnes went to her own room. She felt restless and anxious, afraid for Gladys Bellamy, of whom she had become very fond. She was anxious, too, about the effect such a scene would have on her should it occur. She still in her heart thought of Lady Bellamy as her patient.

After a hot bath she felt slightly more relaxed. She got into bed and lay there, looking frequently at the slow-moving hands of the luminous bedside clock. She could not get Sir Edmund's face out of her mind. He seemed there, in the dark, to become larger, more evil, more menacing. She had not heard his return – where was he?

She sat up suddenly, alerted by the sound in the still night of a car coming down the road. She glanced at the clock, ten past two, an unusual time for a car to be heard. An owl hooted, then there was a scraping noise, as if the car had misjudged the entrance and had struck the brick gatepost. The engine stalled, then started again and crunched across the gravel. She heard it going towards the stables. She lay back on the pillows. Minutes went by – a quarter of an hour – there was no sound of anyone entering the house. What had happened?

Carmichael got out of bed, slipped on her coat and outdoor shoes and picked up a hand torch from the bedside table. The night was cold and starry. What was she going to do? She had no idea.

Agnes Carmichael crept down the stairs and out of the front door, then as she reached the bottom of the steps, a dog barked and another answered it. The still fields brooded round her. She looked up at the sky then, guided by her torch, made her way towards the garages.

As Agnes approached one of the horses in the stables stirred, whinnied, bumping against the wooden door. It made her jump.

The Rolls was in the garage. She drew nearer and switched on her torch again, keeping the beam low. Had he come into the house without her hearing him? She drew nearer still. Then she heard it – heavy stertorous breathing. She drew nearer still, into the garage, and she saw its source.

Sir Edmund Bellamy was slumped over his steering wheel, his left arm curled round it. The torchlight glinted on the signet ring on his finger, his head rested on his arm, his eyes were closed. His mouth was half open and saliva was trickling down from his mouth and running down into his beard. Agnes was nauseated by his appearance. The window of the car was wound down, the keys dangled in the ignition.

Agnes stood quite still, her eyes were fixed on the keys, then she raised them to his face. She knew exactly what she had to do. Her hand reached out, almost automatically, through the window. She switched on the ignition. The engine started with a soft purr, hardly disturbing the night's silence. She did not draw away at once, but stood and looked without pity at the man who could, if he so chose, ruin the lives of three people, one yet unborn.

She backed slowly out of the garage. The piece of wood supporting the unrepaired garage door was heavier and more difficult to push away than she had anticipated, but it eventually fell sideways with a wooden clatter. She caught hold of the descending door with both hands and lowered it gently shut, though noise hardly mattered – if anyone in the house heard it they would think it was Sir Edmund just come home. The door fitted well, the converted stable was windowless – stoutly built, low-roofed. She hoped that what she had done was enough.

She walked back slowly, almost casually, up the steps, closed the front door behind her and went up the stairs to her room. When she got there, however, the full impact of her action hit her. She felt numb with cold and could not stop the shaking of her whole body. She got into bed and switched on the electric blanket.

The clock on her bedside table gleamed ten to three; so much done in so little time. Slowly, as the warmth of the blanket stole through her, the shaking stopped and she began to experience a comforting sense of achievement.

31

The blue van marked 'Leicester Laundry' drew up at the gates of the Manor. Basil got out, lugged out two suitcases and then looked up at the driver.

'Thanks, mate,' he said.

The man nodded at him. 'Any time, Bas,' he said, and turned the van expertly, using the drive entrance in his half-circle.

Basil stood for a moment. He was glad to be back. He picked up the suitcases and started forward. He looked at the unknown Ford Metro standing at the front of the Manor, Miss Carmichael's Carrera Porsche behind it. The other rather battered car behind that he recognized as the Hilliers'. Then he remembered.

'The wedding! Of course!' He had completely forgotten it.

At that moment the front door opened and Miss Alison and Nigel came out on to the top step, a group of people behind them. He could see Lady Bellamy leaning on her stick. He put down the suitcases again and went towards them.

'Oh Basil, you're back.' Miss Alison came down the steps towards him. 'Oh Basil, I wish you'd been here,' she said.

'I do, too, miss. I'd like to have driven you to the church in the Rolls. Anyway, I'm back in time to wish you all the best.'

'Thank you, Basil.' Nigel and Alison spoke in unison.

'You've had a sad time, I'm sure, Basil, while we've been having a happy one.' Lady Bellamy had limped down the steps, aided by Agnes.

The young people got into the back of the Ford Metro and a young man Basil did not recognize slipped into the driver's seat. There were kisses, goodbyes, hand-waving, and Basil stood there as the Metro drove out of the gate, everyone calling, 'Goodbye, have a lovely honeymoon,' and 'Goodbye, Colin.' The car swept into the road and away.

Basil turned to go to his own quarters.

'Basil, do please come in and drink their health.'

'All right, m'lady, thank you. I'll just take these round.'

Lady Bellamy nodded and they all went back into the house and closed the door behind them.

Basil's hands burned with the weight of the suitcases. Lady Bellamy was right, he'd had an awful time as well as a sad one; he felt exhausted. His brother's wife had, as he put it to himself, taken it out of him. Her hysterical reaction had lasted for days; she had insisted that he take some of his brother's clothes back with him. His suitcase and the extra one she had given him weighed a ton. He hadn't wanted the clothes, but she had persisted. Shoes, too – dead man's shoes, he thought.

He approached the garage. Funny, it was shut. Sir Edmund must have got the cable repaired – not like him. The wooden stake that had held the door open was lying on the ground. He drew nearer. Good God, what was that? He slowed down, drew closer still – unmistakably he heard the sweet, soft sound of the Rolls engine. He dropped the cases, bent down, forced his fingers under the bottom of the metal door and heaved, then let it go down again – he must have the prop. He lifted it again, this time with the wood in his other hand. At last, sweating, he managed to get the stake in place and the door open. As he had opened it a rush of heat had come out of the garage. He lurched forward, and looked into the car. 'Sweet Christ,' he said and turned round and raced towards the house.

He flung open the back door; the kitchen was empty. As he crossed the hall he could hear Maud and Hetty in the dining-room, and the clinking of china. They were giggling.

He crossed the hall. The sitting-room door was closed and he paused for a moment, trying to get his breath – then he burst the door open, almost falling into the room.

Four pairs of rather startled eyes looked at him. Madge Hillier was sitting on the settee – her husband was just handing her an wine-filled glass. Marcia was seated in the Sheraton chair, her slender legs crossed, sipping her champagne. Lady Bellamy was standing with her back to him, one hand gripping the mantel-shelf, the other clutching her stick. Sister Carmichael was standing in front of her.

Lady Bellamy turned rather awkwardly. 'Oh, do come in, Basil,' she said, 'and have a drink with us.' Then she saw his face more clearly. 'Whatever is the matter, Basil?' she said.

'M'lady, I've got terrible news for you – Sir Edmund is dead.'

Everyone in the room said something, their voices distorted by incredulity.

'What?'

'How?'

'It's impossible!'

'Dead!'

The only person who said nothing was Agnes Carmichael.